RETURN BY LAND

TRACEY JERALD

xoxo,
Tracey Jerald

RETURN BY LAND

Copyright © 2020 by Tracey Jerald

ISBN: 978-1-7330861-8-9 (eBook)

ISBN: 978-1-7358128-0-9 (Paperback)

Editor: One Love Editing (http://oneloveediting.com)

Proof Edits: Holly Malgieri (https://www.facebook.com/HollysRedHotReviews/)

Cover Design by Tugboat Design (https://www.tugboatdesign.net/)

To my Jen.
I'm sorry they wouldn't let me bring an actual lumberjack back from Alaska with me. But cruise ships and airlines are persnickety about things like body counts.
I hope this makes up for it.
Hold tight. You know where the magic is.
I love you. Always.

PROLOGUE

Meadow - Seventeen years ago from present day

"I suppose congratulations are in order?" Kody's voice washes over me.

I stepped away from the barbecue the Smiths were throwing because I need to get my bearings. My sister, Rainey, and her boyfriend, Brad, begged me to come and celebrate Jed and his friends being up from Ketchikan even though Mitch couldn't join me. And tonight, it was the last thing I wanted to do. To be truthful, he wasn't overly thrilled to be picking me up here when his shift ended. He wanted me waiting at my parents'.

But when I explained it would be just as easy for him to pick me up from the Smiths' as it would be from my parents' to leave for our honeymoon, he relented. "Of course, sweetheart. Go. Celebrate with your friends. After all, you may not have much time after tonight," he teased before he hung up.

After all, everything changed from yesterday to today. I wasn't Meadow Jones any longer. I'm now Meadow Borneman.

The cool, green grass beneath my toes feels more real than the fact I'm married or the fact Kody's talking about it with me. So it's no surprise when my voice sounds like it's asking a question. "I guess?"

Even though I don't look at him, I can feel the warmth of his body as he steps up next to me. "Is this what you want, Meadow?" Between us lies the unasked question of "Is he who you want?"

And therein lies the reason I fought coming tonight. I'm still fighting a war inside myself because there's what I want and what I have. And only I know they're two entirely different things.

What I want is to sink down to the green grass with the man next to me and forget about yesterday and tomorrow. I didn't put much stock into when I caught Kody sizing me up year after year as we'd sit under the midnight sun talking for hours.

Over the years, he's told me about what it's like to have sisters who range from a year older than me to his mother's pregnancy with the youngest. I told him about my dream of working in hospitality, of getting to know people from all over the world. It's incredible how on so many different levels we connect: friends, family, our desire to raise large families. And yet, we're so different. He's meant to change the landscape of the world while I'm meant to live in my piece of it.

Hell, we've even talked about our past relationships. He knew—he *knew*—I was dating Juneau patrolman Mitchell Borneman for the last six months. Which is why anger spikes as I whirl around to face him. "You don't get to do this."

"Do what?" His hair matches the sunset that's finally starting to lower behind us.

"Question me about whether Mitch is the one when…"

"When what, Meadow?" His voice is rough. "What did I have to do to make you realize I was interested in you beyond friendship?"

"Maybe tell me? Maybe ask me out?" I yell.

He shakes his head. "I couldn't do that."

"Why not?"

"Because the one thing we agreed upon when we talked all those nights, lying right fucking here, was that we both abhor cheating. And if I finally worked up the nerve, what would you have thought I was asking you to do?" I feel the blood drain away as his words penetrate. "That's right, Meadow. I couldn't do a damn thing. Not unless you did."

God. I turn away, pressing the heels of my hands to my eyes.

"Is he who you want?" Kody's question comes at me again.

"He's who I married."

I feel his hand on my shoulder, warm and strong. It's not a sexual caress, but my body doesn't understand that as his simple touch sends fire through every nerve ending. A shudder races through me. His fingers tighten down in response.

Turning, I meet his glorious eyes. I want to apologize for being so blind, for not understanding. I open my mouth, but he just lays the finger of his other hand on top of it.

Then he destroys me.

"I have to tell you once while we're standing in the place where it happened that I fell in love with you, Meadow Jones. I only hope that today, tomorrow, twenty years from now, he appreciates the heart he won. Just know I'm going to be in love with you long beyond that."

Tears stream down my face as Kody leans down and brushes a kiss on either side of my face. Lingering for just a moment, he whispers, "Be happy, Flower," before he steps back.

Just as he does, I reach out and capture his hand. "Kody, wait. I..."

But as if he can read my mind, knowing I'm about to offer the unthinkable less than twenty-four hours after promising to love, honor, and cherish another man, Kody whispers, "You can't. You'd hate yourself. And eventually, you'd hate me for encouraging it."

Dropping my hand, he turns and walks away, each step slow and measured. I fall to the earth and let the grass absorb my tears. After all, the earth below me listened to so many of my dreams, maybe they'll use the water from these to eventually grow them into something.

When Mitch finds me hours later, ready to drive off for a few days for a quick honeymoon, I'm just lying on my back. "Meadow? What are you doing, honey?"

"I'm just wishing on the stars," I tell him honestly. I don't mention that every wish I've made since I've calmed down is for Kody.

"Well, it's time to go grab our stuff if we're going to catch the early ferry. Hop to it." He reaches his hands down to pull me to my feet.

"Give me just a moment," I beg. Finding the last star in Ursa Major I haven't wished on, I wish that Kody Laurence finds the right woman to love. After all, a man who has a heart as big as the land I'm standing on needs to move on.

He needs to forget about me and find happiness.

That's all I want for him.

KODY

"Will someone turn down that fucking music?" I bellow out as I step into the great room of the estate my crew should be finishing the punch list on. I'm left with a headache as I try to figure out how we're going to deliver this home on time. The pounding baseline of Linkin Park abruptly dies as I step carefully over extension cords and cables leading to air compressors. "Everyone stop what you're doing and go home until you receive a call to get your sorry asses back here."

Bravely, my site foreman Shane says, "Kody, man, calm down."

I shoot him a fulminating glare. "It's not your money that's going to be tied up in court if we don't have this house ready to deliver. Meanwhile, what the fuck is happening here? If the city came by and saw what I just did, we'd lose our permits."

Hands up, he backs away. "Point taken. You know I just got here myself."

As he drove over with me from one of the other builds on-site, I let out an aggrieved sigh. "It's the only reason I'm not firing you when I threw the subs off the job." I point out the window at the van carrying three subcontractors, who were caught using as Shane and I pulled up, peeling away. "Now, I need to check everything they were responsible for. Do you want to have that on your conscience?"

"No, but wouldn't it be quicker to keep a small crew of us here to run through their list?" Shane's calm logic in the face of my fury irritates me because I'm not this guy. I'm the person my crew relies upon for everything from picking out gifts for family members to helping them inspect homes they want to buy. I'm the nice guy who always has a smile on his face.

Just not today.

"Fine. Keep the crew here. I need a few minutes." Without another word, I storm out the open triple slider and stand on the intricate paver patio. Knotting my fingers behind my head, I tip my head back and let out a frustrated growl.

"Why can't people do what I want them to do?" My face is misted with cool rain that reminds me of the tears I've shed in private so many times this past year ever since I learned one of my "brothers" died suddenly in a tragic car accident. Jedidiah Smith slipped away from us way too early. And my mood is probably not helped by the fact that today would have been his fortieth birthday.

"Goddamnit, Jed. We should be somewhere celebrating. I shouldn't be here fixing yet another fucked-up mess. I should be giving you a raft of shit for being old. Instead, there's no explanation for your tomorrows being gone." My voice cracks at the end of my whispered tribute.

When the reminder popped up on my phone this morning with a crazy as hell photo of Jed grinning at me, the world stopped moving. My heart stopped beating before pounding so hard, I thought it was going to burst from inside my chest. The agony of loss was so intense, it was just like that moment I received the letter from the lawyer in Juneau a little over ten months ago notifying me Jed was gone.

Losing Jed was sheer devastation. He was the only person who understood what it was like for me to walk away from the woman I loved without a fight. Our lives have bumped against one another occasionally over the years, making me feel at peace knowing the dreams she shared with me have come true.

After I pulled myself together, I immediately reached out to Brad, Jennings, and Nick—my other "brothers." I didn't say a word, merely sent a screenshot of Jed's face and the reminder proclaiming, "Happy Birthday, you crazy bastard!" Jennings replied with a picture of his wife and son standing at the beach near their home in Florida, wrapped tightly in each other's arms. Brad texted, "I feel like we need to see each other soon. It's been too long." After quickly agreeing, I waited to see if Nick would respond. After a few hours of nothing, I stopped checking my phone every few minutes. I'm not surprised, and to be honest, Jed wouldn't be either—not from the infamous former MMA fighter Nicholas Cain. Nick holds every emotion too close to the chest, including how Jed's death affected him. It's only when we're together that he lets that control slip, as if it's safe for him to do so.

The mist of the rain mingles with my tears. "What I wouldn't give for one more day, a chance to say goodbye." I scrub my hands roughly up and down my face before I head back into the house.

Shane is frowning, never a good sign. And the lack of noise almost makes it eerie. "Why don't I like the expression on your face?" I approach warily.

"We passed inspection on the wiring, right?"

"Yes. Why?" Suddenly a churning begins in my gut I can't suppress.

He flicks open a switchblade and bends down from his great height to unscrew an expensive wood outlet cover. I wince as his knife makes scratches, but that's forgotten as he pulls a twisted mess of wires out when he yanks out the wires behind the outlet themselves. Crouching next to him, I hiss, "Are you kidding me?"

"No. And I've looked at three in this room alone. We're going to have to check every damn outlet. In fact, we need to close off the breaker. Now."

"Right." The fact is, we're operating as a fire hazard. "Do you want to shut down operations until we check everything?" I trust Shane's judgment.

He nods. "I don't want to do any more finish work before we check to see if we need to take any wallboard down, Kody. It might be those assholes just took what they could reach because of the fact the split bolts and screws were copper, but still."

"Still," I agree. "Who do you trust to stay?"

"You, me, Lenny, Bob, Jimbo," he declares immediately. I'm not surprised by his choices as the five of us have worked together as long as I've owned Laurence Construction.

Using a closed toolbox to stand on, I let out a piercing whistle. "Everyone is getting off but Lenny, Bob, and Jimbo. You will receive a call as soon as we know you'll be able to come back on-site. I can assure you that you will all be paid," I address the immediate question I know will be asked as there's a buzz forming in the room. "But before you leave, I need you to go through every room and make certain all equipment is unplugged.

The men and women who had congregated in the great room immediately scurry. Stepping down from the toolbox, I tell Shane, "Let me go out to the truck and get the blueprints."

He scoffs. "Kody, we know this house like the back of our hand."

Raising my brow at the mess of wires he's holding, I say softly, "Do you want to be responsible for us missing a single outlet and it torching because of that?"

"Damnit, no."

"I'll be right back."

"THOSE MOTHERFUCKERS TOOK the copper floor-plate covers." Shane is still astounded.

I swallow another drink of my beer to wash away the bitterness of the day. Well, I wanted something to distract me from Jed's birthday. "Be careful what you wish for."

"Why do you say that?"

"It started out being a shitty day and just got worse. So, the grand total was we checked 280 boxes and found they stripped ten from the great room," I conclude.

"Including the copper floor-plate covers."

I bark out a laugh. "I swear I'm going to get you some engraved for Christmas, the way you're acting."

"You do that, I'm going to make you eat them," he grumbles before finishing the rest of his beer. "So, tomorrow's Sunday."

"Back on for Monday," I confirm. My phone buzzes against my hip.

Pulling it off the clip, I'm shocked to find it's Nick. "I have to take this."

Shane stands and holds out his hand. I clap mine into it as I stand. "Thanks for everything."

"You never have to ask, Kody." He shoots me a low wave as I press Connect.

"This is a surprise," I start to taunt Nick, but I'm floored when he begins to sing.

"Happy Birthday, to Jed. Happy Birthday, to Jed, Happy Birthday, that-crazy-fucking-bastard-we-miss-every-day, Happy Birthday, to him." His voice is slurred.

"Jesus, Nick. Where the hell are you?" I drop back into my seat and reach for the water. No way am I drinking more tonight.

"At s'haunted house."

"Huh?"

"My house," he enunciates clearly.

"Why did you say it's haunted?"

"He's everywhere. If it's not him, it's *her*. I can't escape them." Just then my waitress comes back with a flirtatious smile and points to my beer.

"No. Check, please."

Her eyes wander up and down me before she sashays off. Christ, she's barely older than I was when I met the drunk man on my phone. I roll my eyes before focusing on Nick. "Have you talked with..."

"Talk to Jed every night, man. What about you?"

I was going to ask if he had spoken with Maris, Jed's younger sister. Maris not only is a knockout, but she's also been in love with Nick since that first summer we visited Jed's family home in Juneau when we were a part of the Great Alaskan Lumberjack Show. When things got uncomfortable for Nick, he swore he'd never go back to Alaska. And Maris has only one thing left of her family—the bar and home she inherited. Instead of clarifying my question, I answer, "On occasion, yeah."

"Can't forget, won't forget. Best of all of us."

"I agree with you, Nick. That's never been in—"

"I almost lost his cross." His confession freezes me in place.

"What?" The single word comes out as more of a hiss than anything.

"Something happened to the clasp. It fell off during training. I didn't realize it until one of the punks picked it up and taunted me with it. Almost killed him." I almost wonder if he said the last part or he breathed it into my mind, but either way I heard him.

And I don't fucking blame him.

"What did he want it for?" I barely acknowledge the tray with the check in front of me.

"Said he was going to melt it down to cap his tooth."

Pulling out my wallet, I frown down at the bulge beneath the check. My brow raises to my hairline when I see my waitress has left me her phone number on top of a sealed condom. "Which tooth?"

"His front, of course."

"How long did it take for you to knock it out of his mouth?" I ask conversationally.

"Five minutes, but that's because I wanted his shit to bleed first. Damn, Kody," Nick laughs. "I should have called you weeks ago to feel better instead of going to bed with a bottle."

"Jed would have wanted you to reach out, whether you'd lost the cross he left you or not," I remind him.

"And that's the truth. So, you're heading home?"

"Yeah. Hey, have you ever had a woman leave you her number with a condom."

"Yep. You're actually interested?" His voice holds disbelief.

"Not even close." I think back to the few women I've enjoyed a relationship with over the last seventeen years. While it's been some time since I've been intimate with one, I've never been the kind of guy who jumps into bed just because of my glands. I've always been particular when it's come to the women. Probably because deep down I knew it wouldn't go any further. *I guess that comes from leaving the pieces of my heart in the past along with the best summers I ever had.*

Nick's voice jolts me back to my current predicament. "Then the way I see it, you have two choices. You can be the gentleman and ignore it."

I quickly scribble in a tip and scrawl my name. "Or?"

"Or you can use that pen to poke a hole in the condom. Bet she knows better the next time."

It takes me a second before I'm cursing Nick six ways from Sunday. "God, you are such a dick," I conclude.

"Yeah, but I'm just lucky you assholes love me anyway." And just like every time we've spoken since Jed's death, I hear the true appreciation for our friendship in that statement.

Sliding out of the booth, condom untouched, I ignore my waitress as I make my way to the front. "You're right. We do."

I push open the squeaky bar door before Nick asks, "You left the condom intact, didn't you?"

"Fuck you, Nick."

He tsks me, and I laugh on a day when I never thought I would because I can predict his next words. "No, Kody. It's 'Fuck me, Nick.' How many times do I have to remind you of that?"

And as I make my way back to my truck, the longest day in ten months ends with me trading jokes with one of my best friends.

I can feel Jed's approval.

MEADOW

"It's a celebration!" Maris exclaims.

"How can you say that?" Rainey demands, before I can get a word in edgewise. Her hand slaps down on one of the two folders I placed on the bar when I slid onto the stool.

Maris snickers. "Easily. Mitch was a goddamn fool."

Then a voice from the iPad jumps in. "I think today is whatever Meadow wants it to be. Emotions of this magnitude are never categorized so simply," Kara interjects.

"Again, proving this is why you're the smartest of all of us," I declare. My cheeks warm as the attention of the three women returns to me. I try to sum up the swirl of emotions coursing through my system. "Do I regret the fact my marriage has been ended by nothing more than a notarized document? No. The problems I'm facing are enormous. I still have to convince the kids the reasons are just because Mom and Dad didn't work out and what's happening to *their* lives will be the best thing for them when I don't entirely believe it myself."

At my words, a shot of tequila appears by magic in front of me. Shoving it right back toward Maris, I laugh for the first time since I opened the mailbox. "Getting drunk won't help."

"Will it keep you from crying?" she asks sagely.

Before I can answer, Rainey does. "Yes, it will. And I want one too." Twisting on her stool, she's already whipping out her phone.

"What are you doing?" I demand.

"Texting Brad to come pick us up so you'll relax."

"See? This is why I would cry." I pick up the papers holding the copy of my final divorce decree and wave them in the air. "I'm being forced to move my family from the only life they've ever known, the only security they've ever had. Because of these—the judge's agreement to everything Mitch and I amicably discussed with the attorneys." Then I drop the papers and do the shot, welcoming the burn in my stomach to counteract the memory of the brief hearing where I was the epitome of polite and sweet to a man who didn't deserve it. But I just wanted out.

"That sounds awful. What did you have to agree to?" Kara asks curiously.

"As part of our settlement, Mitch agreed to certain financial stipulations. The largest is that he can't leave the pension he earned here to anyone other than our children in the event of his death. Also, he agreed to pay his share of their monthly college fund payment. Considering the imbalance of our long-term incomes, I felt backed into a corner to accept his demands regarding his job," I admit to my closest friends.

Friends. A year ago, I never would have believed I had more than my sister to rely on, but the death of Maris's brother, Jed, forced a reunion almost twenty years in the making where Rainey and I reconnected with Maris and Kara.

And, God, were there so many secrets exposed when that happened.

In the background at Kara's, she's mostly ignoring the sounds of her family preparing dinner. But the serene look on her face makes me envious. At a time of my life when I thought I'd be making plans to enjoy the best years of my marriage as my children began to grow and develop their own personalities and interests, I'm about to leave the only home I've ever known to start over in a whole new place with no one but myself to rely on.

It's terrifying, exhausting, and, I secretly admit, maybe a little exhilarating. Looking back to last summer, I can't believe so much has changed. I quit working for Donna's—the waitressing job that morphed into my becoming an assistant manager over the years. I put my two-year degree to use and took on managing Brad's office, freeing up time for me to go back to school and finish what I started so long ago because I never thought I would need to start over at the age of thirty-eight years old.

I've forced myself to stop relying on other people, to actively watch and learn from the guys down at the dock. I'm no longer the woman who can't hang a picture on her own, or who waits for her husband to take out the trash; those days are long gone.

Now, I'm a doer. And I've forced myself to admit that little by little, my marriage had disintegrated into shades of fiction long before the final act that destroyed it. But the betrayal of our vows still stings. My husband was still my friend, my confidant, and my lover. I could have lived for the rest of my life without having that spark if I had trust and respect. When Mitch violated both so blatantly, ignorance was something I could no longer hide behind. And since I've never told Elise and MJ the truth of what happened between me and their father, it's something I'm bearing the brunt of. And Mitch doesn't just know it, he actively encourages it.

God forbid he doesn't appear to be perfect, I think as bitterness washes over me again.

Through the antique glass window of Smith's Brewhouse, the sun glimmers in the waning springtime sun. It casts an almost ethereal glow onto the polished floors. It brings back memories of a man with hair as bright as the midnight sun—a sun that will soon encapsulate the land my heart is entrenched in. He was laughing in front of that very window, making it hard to breathe in a room filled full of people on a rare night we didn't spend in Maris's backyard.

Kody Laurence teased more smiles out of me during our summer interludes than Mitch did in our marriage. Even the last time I saw him, when the world was just beginning to crumble beneath me, he still managed to elicit one. My lips curve in remembrance.

"See? She's well rid of that prick." Maris slides another shot in front of me. Without thinking, I toss it back.

"Maris..." Rainey starts to protest, but I interrupt.

"No, Rainey, Maris is right." A groan escapes from Kara at my words, but I plow on. "I'm not brooding the end of my marriage."

"Then what is it?" my sister demands.

"The loss of all of this." I wave my hand to encompass the interior of the bar, but I mean the budding lushness beyond the walls, the majestic beauty that only someone who has spent time in Alaska can comprehend. For all the ways she punishes us year after year with winters that would terrify the heartiest of outdoorsmen, she blesses our land by illuminating it longer during the summer. The sounds of birds seem brighter, the green of the trees more majestic, and our sunsets are a gift streaking across the sky.

It's not a land for the weak of soul. It's meant to celebrate the survivors. "Every time I remember Mitch is forcing me to uproot our children to accommodate his new job to accommodate their financial needs, I get infuriated all over again. They're already so confused, so angry."

Maris mutters something vile. Rainey looks troubled, but Kara offers comfort. "I never thought I'd be forgiven for the secrets I kept, Meadow. Time together is what you all need to establish your new normal."

I recognize the truth in her words. But still— "I wish I had more of it before I had to leave."

"Tell us about your new job," Maris encourages.

"I really owe it all to Brad," I start, once again crediting my brother-in-law for finding me the perfect position.

"No," Rainey counters. "Brad may have found out about the opportunity, but you earned that position, Meadow. Brad says his office has never been as efficient as it is right now. He's already mourning your loss."

"Come on, Rainey. It's just us girls. Admit you blew the man's mind as a thank-you," Maris drawls.

My sister flushes to the roots of her hair. "Moving on." She picks up her wine and takes a large glug.

I stare at it pointedly. "You're certain Brad's picking us up?"

"Already arranged, sister, so relax and enjoy yourself," she says smoothly.

"I can't remember the last time I did that," I admit.

Kara's voice precedes her lifting her own glass. "And that's something I can commiserate with."

We all laugh. Maris leans her elbows on the bar top. "So, how much longer do we have you?"

"Another month. I wish I could stay longer, but I have to be down there before the season begins. I'm just grateful Rainey agreed to keep the kids until the end of school." I sneer slightly. "Fortunately, even Mitch thought that was a good idea—not to uproot the kids before the end of the year."

"We'd do anything for you—for them," Rainey says immediately.

"Crap, that reminds me, I have the papers to give you for medical treatment and whatnot." I begin to dig into my bag, but Rainey lays a hand on mine.

"Later. We have a month to sort that out. Finish telling everyone about the new job," she encourages.

Right. "Well, the owner of the rental company said he wished his employee would be there to transition the role to me, but he's moving to Arizona."

"You're going to begin a whole new chapter to your life," Maris declares.

I nod before tacking on, "Kara, can you tell Jennings thank you again for all his help? I'm really not certain how I would have afforded to transport our belongings otherwise."

Kara's elegant head tips back as she communicates my message. A deep male voice can be heard faintly. When her head rights, there's a happy curve to her lips. "He said, 'Stop thanking him. You're family, Meadow.' And he's right."

A warmth steals through me as Rainey squeezes my hand. In the last year, I've come to realize some of the strongest family isn't just through blood. It's through friendship. And it's more binding than the vows I exchanged as I stood in front of a judge seventeen years ago.

Lifting my shot glass, which Maris surreptitiously refilled, I announce, "I know what we're celebrating."

My sister and friends wait with bated breath before I continue. "To our family. To those here who are deeply loved every day and to those who are gone. We hope you know you will always be cherished."

And with that, we drink, giving our thanks as always to the foresight of Maris's brother for loving the brothers of his heart beyond the grave so much he inadvertently reunited the women connected to them.

"Mom," my daughter snaps the minute I step through the door two hours later, "Dad's called like a million times to talk to you."

Unperturbed by her proclamation, I hold up my cell phone. "He didn't call my cell."

She scoffs.

I chuck it in her general direction. "Have at it, kid. You know the password. Don't believe me? Call Aunt Rainey. I was with her." I drop my oversized purse on the foyer floor before surveying the mess I have thirty days to resolve.

And not just the packing.

For just a moment, Elise appears remorseful. "I'm sorry, Mom. It's just Dad—"

"What, Lise? Tried to..." I snap my mouth shut before I say something I shouldn't that would irreparably damage my children's relationship with their father.

"Anyway, he asked for you to call," my daughter finishes awkwardly.

"Later." Mitch lost all rights to demand anything unless it pertains to the health and well-being of our children the minute I found out he was regularly sinking his cock inside his partner on the force. A wash of bitterness and shame wash over me as I make my way past my daughter. How much did I teach her to look for a man just like her daddy? I despair. Frantically, I think back to what my mother taught me and Rainey. "Look for a man who will put his family above everything and anyone," her words echo in my ear as if she said them yesterday instead of my teens.

I passed that along to Elise. Now, look at where we are? My foot hits the top of the landing, and I survey the boxes packed. Like it or not, we're poised to take steps into an uncertain future in a brand-new place.

"Mom?" Elise comes up behind me holding—thank God—just the white envelope containing my degree. "What's this? I didn't think I was old enough to be looking at schools yet." Her confusion is evident.

"You aren't." Elise really needs to enjoy her childhood despite the last year maturing her emotionally well past her precarious age of twelve. Thirteen, in just a few short months.

God, what a year it's been.

"Then why do you have..."

"It's mine." Taking a deep breath, I announce, "Surprise. Your mom's a college graduate."

"What?" Confusion mars her brow.

"Between the downtime I had working at Uncle Brad's and after you and MJ would head to bed at night, that's what I was working on. After consulting with the professors about my professional and past work school experience, I only had a few classes left. Last semester was it. I finally did it. I earned my degree, baby." I wait for her reaction.

And my heart shatters when she stomps up to me, shoves the now crumpled envelope in my hand, and hisses, "Dad was right. You do keep secrets," before storming off in the direction of her room.

Deflated, I fall to my knees right where I stand. I smooth out the wrinkles to my degree I'd finally worked my way around to feeling proud of earlier. I whisper, "I wish I could hate you, but I can't. If it wasn't for you, I wouldn't have Elise and MJ. But damn you, Mitch. You don't get to do what you did and leave me to put their hearts back together without consequences."

Staggering to my feet, I walk over to the boxes marked with green tape. Those will come with me on the flight Jennings arranged. Slipping my degree inside, I head into the kitchen to begin making dinner.

Later, I'll deal with my now ex-husband.

KODY

"You're starting to become as hard to get a hold of as Nick," my best friend, John Jennings, complains good-naturedly.

"Well, hello to you too," I grumble, scrubbing my hands over my face. "Do I want to know what time it is?"

"Noon."

"Whose time zone?"

Damn bastard laughs in my ear. "Does it really matter? Normally you're up and about on a Saturday, Kody. What happened? Did I interrupt something?" Like Nick the other night, he sounds surprised.

"Not hardly. I've been putting in a ridiculous amount of overtime on the latest phase of the builds because we had two contractors screw up on their delivery for parts of the homes."

"Jesus, man. No wonder you sound exhausted."

I yawn in his ear, punctuating his point. "Uh-huh."

"Want me to let you get some more sleep?"

"Nah, I can sleep when I'm..." My voice trails off before I mutter, "Fuck. Is the pain of losing Jed ever going to ease up?"

"Truth?"

"Always," I reply, shoving aside the covers and making my way to the kitchen with my cell on speaker. A quick check out the floor-to-ceiling windows in my unit confirms the weather is as bleak as my mood. Instead of being able to view Mount Hood in the distance, I see nothing but low-lying clouds. "Perfect, just perfect."

"What's that?"

"It's raining," I declare.

"You say that like it's a surprise, brother." Jennings is amused.

Popping a pod into my coffee maker, I press Start and prop my hip against my concrete countertop. "I don't know what it is," I finally admit. "Ever since I got back from Jed's funeral, I feel so out of sorts. Like I'm waiting for the other shoe to drop." Fortunately, my coffee maker informs me it's ready. Taking a scalding sip, I welcome the burn and caffeine while I wait for Jennings to question my sanity.

Who knew I'd welcome the nosy interference of brothers when I grew up with six sisters who felt it was their life's mission to poke their nose into my business. Instead, I embraced the brotherhood I found when I worked between my summers at college at the Great Alaskan Lumberjack Show in Ketchikan, Alaska.

At first, I went to Alaska all those years ago desperate for a way to help my father, the sole family provider of our enormous family, who was working two jobs to pay for the portion of my tuition to MIT that wasn't covered by scholarships. I wasn't there to make waves or to cause trouble. I volunteered to work any shift someone bailed on, and I didn't care how ridiculous I had to act while throwing an axe or wielding a chainsaw for the audiences. The money I was able to sock away that first summer was more than enough to help my parents with my room and board.

When I returned, I came out richer not because of the money but as a result of the friendships that have spanned almost two decades.

Only now, Jed's gone. And there's this hole in my heart that just doesn't work the same way. I've only felt like this one other time. And she was just that special, I don't know that I'll ever be able to fit anyone else into that place carved out of my heart that was made just for her.

If only I hadn't waited so damned long...

"What do you think Jed would say if he heard you right now?" Jennings muses.

I bark out a laugh. "He'd tell me to get off my ass and do something for someone." I rub my hand against my chest. The pain of having lost Jed and his husband to a freak car wreck hasn't abated much in the last ten months. Then again, does the pain of losing someone you love ever end? "Likely telling me I need to take a vacation to Florida," I can't help but mock as Jed did that on more than one occasion to Jennings.

Jennings chuckles. "His hair would be in every which direction too. Don't forget how he'd act when we wouldn't listen to him."

"How could I forget? Apparently, it was so legendary, it spanned two coasts," I retort.

Jennings makes a sound of assent while a mental image of Jed comes to mind. Born and raised in Alaska, Jed Smith was the glue that held a bunch of young men from diverse backgrounds who descended on his state together through more than acting like fools on stage. He was plagued with getting caught up in our shenanigans, acted as the steady voice of reason on more than one occasion, and when things went to the crapper as they inevitably did, he provided a shoulder to lean on.

He was that friend for all of us, and every day since we got that call, the chasm of dissatisfaction inside me keeps growing.

"Maybe you do need a vacation," Jennings suggests. "Take a few weeks and come see the house in Florida. You know Kara and Kevin would love to have you here."

I frown before I take another drink of coffee. "That idea isn't completely ridiculous," I acknowledge.

"Dick." There's a soft voice. Jennings covers the mic before responding. "Apparently, I'm supposed to curb my language now that I'm a male role model, so try to not be the reason I curse, okay?"

I shake my head before remembering Jennings can't see it. "You're on your own, buddy."

"No, I'm not," he returns smugly.

No, he isn't. And knowing that makes my heart a little lighter. "I'll give some thought to what you said. I probably do need a vacation after this clusterfuck."

"If you're here, maybe we can install some crown molding. You wouldn't believe what an asshole the builder was. He wanted to charge me an arm and a leg to install that crap. I told Kara I'd give him a piece of my mind and have it installed after we closed on the mortgage. So, how about coming down for a workman's holiday?" I can hear him smirk through the phone.

Knowing exactly how much of a surcharge my company adds for niceties like the upgraded crown molding Kara fell in love with, I can't help but grin before saying, "Say goodbye, Jennings. We'll talk about installing the crown molding your bride wants another time."

"Goodbye, Jennings." Right before the smart-ass disconnects the call.

I toss my cell on the counter and contemplate the bleakness outside.

Maybe a few days away is what I need when this job is done.

"How is this possible?" I groan. "I swear to God, this house is possessed."

My immediately younger sister of the six my parents saw fit to torment me with, and lead project manager of Laurence Construction, Greta, scratches her head before walking over to the cooler, snagging two beers, and tossing me one. "You'll get no arguments from me."

"First the factory delivered the wrong wall framing. Then the wiring got stripped by those shits who decided smoking weed at lunch was a good idea. We'd have lit the place up the minute we turned on the breakers." I twist off my cap and salute her with it. "Excellent toss. Who taught you how to throw?"

She tips hers back at me, silently allowing me to rant. "This guy I know. Pain in my ass for most of my life. Wouldn't let me go on a decent date until I escaped from him when I moved out and went to college. Still tried to grill me over Christmas dinner though."

I chuckle at her retort because it's true. Candy and Vicki, my two older sisters, escaped my big-brother routine. But Greta, Alissa, Amelia, and Sandra—Jesus, especially Sandra—have had me riding them about every little thing since the day they were born. Especially boys. I shudder. "Do you remember the last time I went out with you and your friends?" And all night long I was subjected to the way they talked about men. It was hell. Pure unadulterated hell.

And—my smile widens just a little—Jed laughed so hard when I told him about it, he cried.

Greta rolls her eyes. "Yeah, let's never do that ever again. Okay?"

Ignoring her, I return to the reason we're even together in the first place on a Saturday afternoon. "We finally pass inspection—a month behind schedule—and the insulation delivered is the wrong R grade. More fucking delays."

"That one's on Shane," she bites out.

I ignore the arctic sting to her voice when she talks about my lead foreman. I really don't want to know what's happened between those two. "At this point I almost don't care who it's on. We've had wrong fixtures, appliances, and all I wanted to do today after cleaning up the mess at the other two houses was see this place ready for the walk-through Monday. Instead, you're holding a punch list and"—my fury wars with an insane desire to laugh—"they hung the chair rail where the crown molding is supposed to go and vice versa."

"So, what do you want to do about it, Kody? Push back the closing? Again?"

"Not a chance in hell. These buyers are already requesting reimbursement for their moving costs and an additional month's rent between the screwups we couldn't control and the ones we damn well should have. I'm not delaying them moving into this house another month."

"Then what?" Greta excels at her job because she sees the faults from the carefully laid plans before her, but what she doesn't see are the possibilities.

That's where my imagination takes over.

I reach down into my backpack, and my fingers graze over one of the many worn sketchbooks Jed left me. More and more as of late when I've needed to clear my mind, I've pulled one out and just stared at his crude drawings. It's made me feel closer to the crazy bastard with a heart so enormous the gap in my heart from his loss may never close.

Sitting down on the floor, I flip through Jed's nautical designs while Greta uses the time to call every member of the subcontractor for tomorrow, growling, "If you'd done the job right the first time, maybe you would be getting double time."

But my eye is caught by one of Jed's rough drawings of his boat he purchased in Florida. "There's something about the stripes," I murmur, before I drop the cloth-covered sketchbook and flip over a sheet of paper on my clipboard. Giving the hot mess near the ceiling a quick once-over, I begin drawing.

By the time I'm done, there's a custom-designed molding around the room inspired by the sea views and by the boat Jed loved. Without saying a word, I shove the paper into Greta's hand as she berates the subcontractor we hired.

Her jaw drops before she snaps out, "Hold on," to the person on the other end of the line. Holding the phone to her chest, she says, "This is genius, Kody. You incorporated their mistake and made it something better for the client."

"We have to get the supplies and they have to execute it in a 600-square-foot space by 9:00 a.m. Monday."

"There won't be any mistakes," Greta vows.

"Trust me, I know."

Cocking her head to the side, she raises a brow before asking, "How?"

"Because with the state of affairs, I'm not letting them hang a damn piece of quarter round without approving it first," I say grimly. "Now, get the lumber ordered. I want everyone here in the next two hours to start."

"On it." And after disconnecting the call without another word, Greta pulls up the website of our wood supplier to arrange a delivery. Another unaccounted-for expense. I cringe when she calls out the amount.

Then my phone rings in my pocket. The number for Vielbig Wood-working pops up. No, the expense for this isn't going to be mine at all. I put the call on speaker before greeting him coldly. "Skip."

"What the hell gives you the right to call my people in to work on a weekend without paying them right, you cheap son of a..."

"Maybe if they hadn't fucked up the job, I wouldn't have had to," I say calmly.

"Bullshit. I guarantee that the work is perfect."

"What are you willing to bet on it?"

"Try me," he snarls.

"My carrying costs are a little over 13k for this house if I miss my delivery date, Skip. Your people made it so I don't have time to rip out their mistake in the great room." He sputters. "Fortunately for you, I came up with an idea how to fix it. Not only will you pay for the lumber, you're going to cover the overtime so I don't get hassled by your people when they start arriving in..." I look at Greta.

She calls out loud enough for both of us to hear, "An hour and fifty-two minutes."

"Fine," he spits out.

Nodding at Greta, I inform him, "The email with the proof is incoming. Honor our agreement and not only will I consider this a mistake, I won't sue you for obviously not having someone halfway competent come out and approve this project because there's no way you were the one who did. I've worked with you too long for you to make this kind of error." I hear the ping on the other end of the line. "Do we have a deal?"

There's a long silence before Skip's bewildered voice says, "Kody, how does a crew of professionals with a hundred years' combined experience royally screw up a job that badly? And how does my son assume you're not going to recognize it in point six seconds flat."

"I wouldn't call your crew back for nothing, Skip." The tension in my shoulders eases slightly.

"No, and you have my apologies for that. Buddy called me just before you did honked off because... well, the reason doesn't matter. Let's just say he and his crew will have an additional incentive to finish tomorrow."

I crook a brow at Greta. "Oh?"

"I'm not so old I can't swing a hammer," he declares. "And it's still me paying the bills."

Not the least surprised, I let my head fall back on my shoulders. "Still prefer sugar raised donuts from Voodoo?" I name the insanely popular donut shop in downtown Portland not far from my condo.

He barks out a laugh. "Yeah. Still can't believe you remember that."

"This guy I worked for once told me it would behoove me to pay attention to the details."

"That guy's getting old." There's regret in Skip's voice.

"Nah. He's just annoyed he hasn't caught a decent fish yet this season. I keep telling you, you should take a vacation."

"Look what happens when I take a day. And besides pot, stop talking to the kettle like it's made out of something different," he returns.

I grin. "Cover the labor cost and I'll pick up the wood. Then we'll call it even, my friend. This design..." My voice trails off as I picture the new picture rail in place.

"You got it. See you in a few, Kody."

Greta's remained silent throughout the entire exchange. But a heartbeat after she's sure the calls ended, she asks, "Why didn't you take over Skip's company?"

"There's a number of reasons," I reply vaguely.

"That tells me absolutely nothing."

With a quick grin, I shake her hand and ignore the question. "You have everything covered for the next few hours? I'm going to check in with the other crews to see if we want to add that"—I nod at the new chair rail design—"to the new homes before it becomes apparent it was a mistake."

"Sure thing, brother. At a surcharge?"

I hand her the sketch of the drawing and frown. "No. As a gesture of goodwill if the homeowners want it. We're behind according to your schedule. And I'd like not to push our bad luck any further. Besides, none of us expected... I mean, there was no way to expect—" I can't finish the sentence.

Greta clears her throat. "Right. Fortunately, I always factor in additional time."

Swiping up my backpack, I swing it over my shoulder before flatly stating, "There's not enough time you could have allotted in the schedule to have accounted for my emotional state after Jed died, Greta. And I pray there's never a day you understand." Without another word, I walk out of the room and begin the mile-long trek to the next house in the middle of the rain, needing my skin to wash away the emotions living inside me until my body is as numb as my mind.

KODY

Ten exhausting hours later, I'm ending the day much the way I started it with a cup of coffee in hand, on FaceTime with a family member. This time it's with a member of my blood family, not just one I adopted due to the bonds of brotherhood. The youngest of my six sisters, Sandra, is begging me for a favor as usual.

"It's ridiculous for you to consider Nick is going to escort you to your junior prom."

Sandra tosses her long reddish-gold hair that perfectly matches mine in color. "It's a total win/win, Kody. You won't have to worry about my date pawing me, and I can rub Cait's face in the fact she asked the guy I liked first."

I can't laugh, I remind myself. "Honey, I'm not sure Nick would want to..."

"But you'll ask him," she says with all of the confidence of a beautiful sixteen-year-old who has never been told no in her life.

I take another drink of coffee to hide the smile at imagining what Nick is going to say when I proposition him on behalf of my insane but lovable family. Likely, since he's dealt with this craziness from all but my oldest sister, who was happily married when I introduced him to all of them, he'll do what he normally does which is bitch at me like

I somehow slipped the suggestion in Sandra's mind. Then he'll set up a video chat with her, making her the envy of everyone in her high school. Hell, the entire county. Which, although she would by no means say no to Nick escorting her, is really all Sandra wants anyway. "So, who are you really going to ask?"

"Oh, you'd love him." But something in the way she says it puts all my overprotective brother senses on high alert.

"I sincerely doubt it."

She scowls before launching into a long diatribe about this new guy she's going with who's "just like Jennings."

"Fuck no!" I bellow. "What are Mom and Dad thinking setting you loose on the world?"

"Jennings is your best friend. What could possibly be wrong with dating a guy who reminds me of him?" Sandra tries for an air of innocence, but a twitch at the corner of her lips gives her away.

My baby sister was born to make my life sheer torture. When we were last together in Montana at a reunion, I said something similar to Jed, and he roared with laughter before saying, "Welcome to the club. I've said that since the moment Maris was put into my arms, and I'm only two years older—not twenty-two."

I'm pulled back from the aching memory by Sandra's barely suppressed laughter. "Remember, I know every single thing that went through Jennings's head from the time he was eighteen. How old is this boy?"

Sandra blatantly ignores me, instead trying to distract me with a description of her dress. It doesn't work, instead firing me up more when I realize her bathing suit might cover more than her formal gown. "Sandra Marie, answer the damn question."

"You need to find yourself a woman and settle down, Kody. You're sounding too much like the 'rents."

"Don't make me call them," I threaten.

She huffs. "If you must know, Tatum is nineteen. Okay?"

"No, not okay! Not if he reminds you of Jennings!" I'm flat out yelling now, and I don't care. Out of view of the camera, I rub my hand over my chest, certain I'm having a heart attack. Remembering the promise Brad, Jennings, Nick, and I made when we arrived last spring in Alaska for Jed's funeral by agreeing we would not be in a position anytime soon to be gathered together for such a ghastly reason, I'm suddenly terrified I might end up breaking it by croaking on the spot. "Not a chance in hell, Sandra. No college guys."

She rolls her eyes, causing the blood to pump harder through the overworked organ she's constantly taxing.

"Is this the crap you give to Mom and Dad? No wonder why they stopped having kids after you."

"I broke the mold, Kody. Not a damn thing wrong with that."

"Watch your mouth."

"Watch yours," she snaps right back.

"I'm having a coronary! Cut me some fucking slack!" I shout.

Of course, right then is when my mother decides to intervene. It doesn't matter to her she has seven children ranging from forty-two to sixteen, she's raised us all the same way: to love and respect each other. "Kody Jacques, Sandra Marie, what is wrong with both of you?" Uh-oh. I might be thirty-eight, but I still cringe every time my mother whips out my full name. "You're both yelling so loudly your father can't even enjoy the show he's watching on the History channel. Now what in sweet blazes is the problem?"

Immediately, Sandra takes the offensive. "Mom, Kody's treating me like I'm three. I'm almost a grown woman."

Before I can formulate a reply, my mother demonstrates the no-nonsense approach that allowed her to raise seven relatively normal children. "Then stop provoking him. You know darn good and well he's feeling overprotective of you these days with good reason, young lady."

Sandra's "Yes, Mom" is sullen but heartfelt. But before I can relax, my mother turns on me. Coloring the same as mine and Sandra's, and hair a faded gray that illustrates what my own will look like in twenty more years frames one of the most beloved faces in the world. "And Kody, you should know better," she scolds.

"Mom, the kid's nineteen," I growl, as much because she used my full name than anything else.

"He's lovely. He's Miss Dora's great-nephew. I do believe you remember him, darling, as you helped him..."

I glare at my smug-faced sister over my mother's shoulder. "... get an introduction to Nick?" After Nick retired from the Extreme MMA Championship about ten years ago, he began traveling all over the world recruiting new talent for the sport. "Shouldn't Tatum"—my voice twists his name—"be getting his ass kicked or learning how to get out of a submission?"

"I'd like to submit him," Sandra drawls. "That would be..."

"Enough!" my mother and I both shout simultaneously. I pinch the bridge of my nose before demanding, "Now, do you understand why I was yelling, Mom?"

She chuckles. "I wouldn't worry too much, son. Despite what your sister is alluding—"

"Tormenting me with," I finish her sentence.

She continues on as if I haven't spoken. "—to, I doubt the cracked ribs and broken arm Tatum's recovering from will permit him to be anything but the perfect gentleman. And if not, well, your father could probably take him in his current state," she concludes.

Somewhat mollified, I still make a mental note to call Nick—and not just because my princess of a sister wants me to. "Okay. Fine."

"Now that the two of you have ceased this useless bickering, Sandra, give me a moment to speak with your brother alone." Before my sister can object, my mother tacks on sternly, "Now."

With another flick of her long hair like she's practicing for a shampoo commercial, Sandra calls, "Bye, Kody! Maybe Tatum's lips will be healed by prom," before she disappears from view.

"Was it your mission in life to have her to pay me back for sins I hadn't committed yet?" I ask my mother when my sister is out of earshot.

"Darling, that's just an added perk. How are you feeling?"

"Physically or mentally?"

"Well, judging by the fact you're normally much swifter to pick up on any of your sister's machinations, I'd say you're exhausted, my sweet boy. Need an ear?"

So, I give my mom a rundown of my mental state of affairs: how the business is going, my continued anguish over missing Jed, and the frustration inside myself to do something more since I received his bequest to me. "It's my name on the company, Mom. I should feel something more than frustration every time I walk onto a new job site," I conclude. She hums, processing all of the information I dumped on her. Of the five of us who met and became brothers deep within our souls, Jed, Brad, and I had the most conventional upbringings. Though, I think not without a touch of amusement, having six sisters is not by any means normal.

"Maybe it's time for you to grieve, Kody." Mom's voice tunes me back in. "You came back from Jed's funeral last year and buried yourself into work."

"I put all my focus in moving past the pain. Work was a focus for me to do that."

"No, Kody. Work became your foundation to protect yourself against the heartache you weren't ready to accept. The problem is foundations can only accept so much strain before they start to crack. You're a smart boy; you know that."

Putting my now empty cup aside, I run my fingers through my overlong hair. It's been so long since I've done anything for just me, I can't even remember the last time I had it cut. "You're right," I admit.

"Now, promise me you won't let the force of these emotions explode on some poor soul while you sort yourself out, Kody," she chides.

"What? I'm a nice guy, Mom."

She laughs at me in the way only a mother can. "True, darling. But you're a force of nature."

"That doesn't sound so bad."

"Most days, it isn't. You're as warm and glowing as the sun. You're like a calm breeze. But Lord help us all when the clouds start gathering."

"Come on, Mom. I think you're watching too many nature shows. Either that or *Bewitched*."

Her eye appears full screen again. It rolls creepily. "Kody, I'm not saying you're a witch, I'm saying your personality is very elemental. Most of the time, you're all sunny days, but when your frustration ignites, it's a thunderstorm, fast and furious to be sure."

I start to scoff before I think back to that last night with Meadow —a regret I've paid long and hard for. Anytime I've seen her since, I've never had the chance to apologize for it. Damn, it's not her fault I waited too long. "Mothers are always right, aren't they?"

"Most of the time. Just remember that Sandra's very much like you, and the rest of us are mere mortals who have to deal with the cleanup after your redhead tempers clash. Okay? You are supposed to be the adult here."

Chastised appropriately, I nod in assent. "Yes, ma'am."

"Keep saying that, Kody, and any woman you meet will think your mother did a fine job raising you."

I laugh, and the sound comes out rusty. Following it, I can't prevent the tear that slides down my cheek.

And being my mom, of course, she notices. "Why don't you come home for a few days?"

I smile crookedly. "Can I time it to be there when Sandra goes to prom?"

She glances to the side before leaning so close to my sister's phone all I can see is her nostril and half an eyeball. "If you do, I won't tell your sister. It will be a very fitting punishment for her behavior tonight. Don't you think?"

My shoulders shake as I acquiesce. "Send me the dates. I'll come home for a few days no matter what I have going on."

Mom pulls back so I can see the rest of her face. "Perfect. Now, are you going to call Nick?"

"Did you have a doubt?" I ask wryly.

"Wonderful."

"Why?"

"Because your father would like you to ask a few questions about this Tatum boy, but he doesn't want to irk your sister." I get the nostril again as she leans forward to whisper, "I do say, Kody, I think your father's a little scared of her. Why, after raising six of you before her, I don't know."

And I bark out a laugh before answering truthfully, "Probably because she has him wrapped around her finger."

"True. She certainly was a surprise for all of us. Now"—Mom's voice gets businesslike—"when you talk with Nick, your father would like to find out for certain his cast will still be on by the time of prom."

My shoulders shake. "And if it won't be?"

"Well, we know Nick's a good boy."

"I'll be sure to tell him you said that." I'm already imagining the lazy humor on my friend's face when I tell him my mother's comments. "Would you like for Nick to fight him to seal his fate?" I tease her.

"Dear me, no. But he is awfully handsome and does look a great deal like Jennings did..."

I just groan hearing that. My mother goes on. "But it would be cruel to hurt him." She chews her lip. "Maybe a stern warning from Nick?"

"Maybe we'll both come home for this thing," I think aloud.

"Oh, that's a brilliant solution, Kody," my mother exclaims. "Let me get you the information and you can contact Nick. Now, is there anything else going on?"

Grabbing my mug, I make a new cup of coffee before heading over to the couch to settle in for a long-overdue talk with my mom. It isn't until Sandra storms back in infuriated we finally stop talking which gives me an opportunity to call Nick.

He answers my FaceTime call half-naked and sweating. I don't question whether he was working out or engaging in extracurricular activities. Before he can take my head off either way, I drawl, "Did you know your boy Tatum is taking my baby sister to her junior prom?"

His darkly handsome face flushes red. "The fuck he is! He's supposed to be healing and recuperating."

"Yeah, well, apparently he found another way to do that."

"What the hell is the age of consent in your damn state?"

"Sixteen." The night my baby sister became legal, making all the bozos who hit on her no longer eligible to be sentenced for crimes against juveniles, I got rip-roaring drunk and called Jed looking for someone to commiserate with. It was a week before he died. Since he was away on a vacation with his husband that precipitated the accident that led to his death, I know why I never heard from him after I left him a rambling, drunk voicemail detailing my agony.

I didn't know what agony was.

I rub my hand over my chest again, feeling a different ache.

Damnit, I know this one won't go away with a few words from my mom. "Besides, she's almost seventeen anyway."

"Fuck us all," Nick moans.

"That's the point. I don't want her doing that anyway. Especially with one of your fighters," I point out.

"What do your parents think about this?"

"Well, Mom was asking if you thought the doctors might be able to keep him in his cast longer," I begin before I'm cut off by something I so rarely hear—Nick roaring with laughter.

"I swear, Kody, I'd do just about anything for your mom," he wheezes, giving me the perfect opening.

"Well, I'm glad to hear that because she asked if we wouldn't mind making a trip to go see her."

"Oh? When?"

"The night of prom." I let that sink in for just a moment.

Much to my surprise, Nick's smile widens even further. "Do you think Brad and Jennings are too busy to join us in the middle of nowhere, Iowa? We can rent tuxes and everything for the photos?"

Now, I'm the one howling with laughter. "It sounds like something Jed would cook up."

"Yeah, which is exactly why I think we should do it. When is it?"

Right then, a text pops up. "In just under a month," I tell him.

"Let's do it. We'll even spring for a limo to get them there. Wait, before we make any more plans, let's get the guys on the line."

Seeing the time, I groan. "Jennings is going to kill us. It's almost eleven in Florida."

Nick shrugs. "So what? Kara's a mother. Think she doesn't worry about this stuff? Hold on."

A moment later, our call has all four of us on it. Jennings demands instantly, "What's wrong? It's a work night."

"We need you, Jennings. One of my fighters is hitting on Kody's sister," Nick declares without preamble.

Jennings immediately says, "Hell to the no," as Brad sucks in an enormous breath.

"Let me set the record straight." I catch them all up, including our impromptu plan. "So, what do you think?"

Brad's already yelling to his wife, "Honey, I'm flying to Iowa to keep one of Nick's fighters from jumping Kody's baby sister." There's a muffled question. "No, it works out perfectly with that in case I'm needed." After a pause, he announces, "I'm in. I think we should all wear crazy-colored cummerbunds in honor of Jed."

"God, that's perfect. And Kara just confirmed it's the week before Kevin's prom, so I'm good to go," Jennings confirms.

We spend the next hour laughing and plotting ways to alleviate the worry from my mother's eyes. But I can't help but flinch a bit every time Jed's name comes up in conversation.

MEADOW

"I think that's all she'll hold," I tell Rainey as I slam the lid closed on my last suitcase. She sits on it while I zipper it shut. Together, we heave it off the bed, which is being sold with the house.

When I accepted the job being the day-to-day supervisor over several rental properties on Flathead Lake in Bigfork, Montana, I was relieved when they said I would be living rent-free on one of the larger properties in what used to be the guest house. "Since the owners decided to list it for rent, they appreciate having someone from the management company on-site to ensure nothing happens to the property," my new boss, Russell Covington, confided. "Once you arrive, I think you'll understand why."

"Of course, Mr. Covington," I replied, but inside I was dancing over being able to save the money from the sale of Mitch's and my home for unforeseen emergencies.

"I have to say, I'm glad you're not driving." Rainey pulls me out of my thoughts. "I remember when Jennings and Kody used to make that trek back and forth each summer. It took them almost four days from Iowa, and that was only because Kody's mother would beg them to stop and sleep."

"I remember. They drove from Kody's family home. But if it wasn't for Jennings, there's no way I could have afforded to have shipped all of this." I wave my arm to encompass the boxes and bags piled up, ready to be loaded into one of the Northern Star Flights planes. "One good thing about giving them this time with all of you before they come down is getting all of this sorted and put away. Then the kids will have the time to personalize their rooms and spend the summer getting to know the area before school starts in the fall. Besides, I think I need this time for just me. When was the last time I had that?"

Rainey slings an arm around my shoulder. "Maybe when you were nineteen and you hadn't started dating Mitch yet?"

"I have to let out of some of this anger, Rainey."

"And you will," she assures me. "But you need to remember you're not alone in feeling it."

I rest my head on her shoulder. "I'm going to miss you so much. And God, Rainey, I'm..."

"What?"

"I'm so scared I'm going to fail. I mean, now I have this degree in hospitality, but what do I really know about it? Slinging plates of food at people qualifies me to do what?" Hearing Mitch's words come out of my mouth taints the clean happiness that followed Mr. Covington's call two months ago telling me I had the job.

Rainey turns to face me. "You know more about managing than anyone I know. Between the work you did for Donna's and then at Brad's, you're going to knock them dead."

Doubt creeps in like it does every night before I go to sleep. "I know Brad is friendly with the owner because he and the rest of the Jacks rented one of the properties. Maybe it's because of him—them— that I got the position." I use the shorthand Maris and Kara taught Rainey and me when talking about Brad, Jennings, Nick, and Kody. And, tragically, it used to include Jed.

"It's a variation of playing for higher stakes," Maris explained breezily one night.

"I'm kinda pissed you two never told me that before now," Rainey grumbled good-naturedly.

"You weren't in the game. You'd already won your jackpot," Kara informed her.

We'd all laughed, but it was the truth. Rainey and Brad have been together since high school.

Rainey startles me by mumbling something about kicking my ex's ass. As much as I'm sure her anger might let her do some damage, I feel it prudent to remind her, "He's a federal agent now, remember? I think beating the shit out of him—as much as I agree he deserves it— might land you in the clink for a while."

"Damn. I don't think I can live without Brad's cock for that long." We both laugh before she sobers. "All Brad did was make a phone call, Meadow. You know as well as I do that only puts your resume to the top of a pile. You're still the one who went through the interview process, and that's before you fought Mitch about your custody agreement."

"It originally said we'd live no more than fifteen minutes apart," I remind her.

"Which would have left you living in Idaho working at a job that may or may not have accommodated the fact you still have young children living at home. Now, your children will be essentially on-site with you."

"True."

"And you did this by pointing out the fact they'll be in a wonderful school district and will finish growing up in a safer environment because they're going to see their father a guaranteed once a month due to the nature of his new job." Rainey turns to face me. Taking my hand, she gives it a hard squeeze. "I'm not surprised you may have nerves; I would too. But the woman who was able to swallow her pride and then find her strength will find this is the best thing that happened to her. You have a chance to start over and be happy."

"Maybe one day, I'll believe that." Like when my kids stop blaming me for their father leaving.

"I hope you do."

IN MY BED later that night, I lie alone as angry, frightened tears release. Every day, every hour, I've been suppressing all the anguish so no one sees the terror I'm truly feeling about making this enormous step in my life. And like a bad movie, I keep hearing the words hurled at me by Mitch's lover.

"No wonder he fell in love with me. What's so special about you?"

And through those early months, when I tried to repair my marriage instead of ending it, I never questioned that. What was so special about me? I was a waitress, a high school graduate, a relatively pretty woman who had married her high school sweetheart. I was a mom, albeit a damn good one.

And here was this smart, tough woman willing to put her body between herself and my husband without a thought, in more ways than one.

What answers did I have as those accusations were hurled at me? Memories of how still I stood in my own living room as Sheila lashed out at me play out like a bad movie in the dark recess of my mind.

My right finger dances over the indentation of where the rings I wore for sixteen years used to rest. Breaking my revolving thought process, I frown. Of all the things I've dealt with over the last ten months, I can't seem to fix this—removing the final brand of Mitch Borneman from my skin. How long until I'm finally rid of him except in the capacity of our children's welfare?

Flopping over onto my back, I struggle to put my future into perspective as I have so many nights since Mitch reneged on our custody agreement. "So much suffering, for what?" I whisper aloud in the empty darkness. But I've asked that question so many times, I know I could fall down a rabbit hole trying to figure it out. And all the hurt and lies will just carry me backward and not where I need to be.

Moving toward the future. Stronger. And ready to handle what Elise and MJ need.

My hands smooth over my stomach where I had my C-section with MJ. I dance my fingers along the faint scar there.

I have to figure out a way to harness this fear and pain into something positive. I have to embrace our move as a chance to step away from the negativity that surrounds my thoughts, my decision making. This is a chance to forge a new life away from the daily deception I've shouldered.

But how? A wave of terror washes over me. Pressing my hands hard against my abdomen, I begin to rock as tears fall, burning a path down my cheek.

I was so young when I married Mitch, I don't know if I ever had a chance to meet Meadow Jones before I became Meadow Borneman. And I'm slowly discovering, she's not quite who I thought she was.

I'm not the quiet docile woman I thought I was. I have a temper and well of untapped strength. But what about control? Rolling onto my stomach, I catch my forehead into my hands. What if I drive the people I love away from me because the Meadow I'm becoming isn't the person I've been for the last thirty-nine years?

My lips curve reluctantly as images of Rainey, Brad, Maris, and Kara flash through my mind. God, I don't have to worry about them, at least. Between the four of them, I'm not certain who's leading the charge to shore me up more. But I do know one thing: I'll never really be without them, no matter where I am.

But what will happen to me if I go?

As my eyes drift shut, my breath starts to even out. Yes, losing the comfort of my life—our lives—will be devastating, but maybe we'll find something to salvage if we walk away now on our own terms.

By leaving, we'll avoid turning as dark as the Alaskan nights. If we go, there's hope of breaking through the dirt covering us and finding the sun again.

My lungs seize before they let out a long sigh as I fall face-first onto the pillow, exhaustion winning out finally. Tomorrow's another day to look for the sun.

DAYS LATER, I'm driving in my rental along the two-lane highway in Montana after departing Alaska midday. The road to the guest house is dark, but I'm not surprised. It just adds to the comforting solitude I've been enveloped in since I left Jennings's pilot, Jasper, at the airport an hour ago. He assured me he'll be over tomorrow with the rest of my things.

I just want tonight alone with the bag of Arby's I snagged before leaving Kalispell and heading along the north side of Flathead Lake. I turn off Montana Highway 35 and follow Covington's directions to get me to the gate. After punching in the code, the gate swings open.

"Well, Meadow. You managed to keep your shit together long enough to get here. That's one accomplishment down," I congratulate myself as I pull through the gate. About a hundred yards ahead, I press the brakes and watch in the rearview mirror for the gates to close behind me. "Now, the turnoff for the guest house should be right about...here it is." I let out a relieved sigh.

The three-bedroom guest cottage has what Covington described as an "obstructed lake view, Ms. Borneman. But I do believe it will be quite lovely for you and your children even if there are renters in the main residence. Yes, there's a path leading to the main house, but it's hidden very well unless you know where it is. More often than not, it will be easier to drive over."

I groan aloud remembering another thing I have to do. "I need to buy a car before these rental charges kill me." Then as a particularly nasty bump in the lane jars me, I gasp, "Or this road does. Whoa. Definitely need to get another SUV here. Otherwise that would be hell on a...oh, my." I slam on the brakes as my first view of the cottage comes into view. Entranced, I fold my arms over the steering wheel, and for the first time since I left Rainey sobbing in Juneau, a smile breaks out across my face.

Jamming the car into park, I scramble for my phone. I pull up my notes and read, "'Much like the main house, the cottage is framed by natural log pillars. You'll enter into the living area which has a glass overlook into an expansive tree line instead of Flathead Lake. I believe you'll find plenty of privacy and happiness here, Meadow. It is an exquisite property—even if it is only the guest cottage.' Well, Mr. Covington, I think you may be the master of understatement." Tossing the phone onto the seat, I drive forward into the circular drive and park.

Having already memorized the code, I quickly turn off the car and climb out. Deciding I'll come back for my bag, I want to make certain the utilities are on. I dash through the cool night air to the numeric keypad—making a mental note to change the code—and quickly enter. The alarm sounds, and I turn that off as well.

Then I flip the lights and realize dreams can come true.

Quickly, I lift my phone to check my signal. Grateful I listened and switched carriers before I moved, I call Rainey. Before the first ring ends, she answers. "You made it. Is it wonderful?"

Voice warbling, I answer, "It's absolutely beautiful." Then because I haven't cried since I left Rainey a few hours ago at Juneau International Airport, I christen my new home by sitting down in the foyer and do so while I babble to my sister about everything I can see. A while later, I tell her, "I guess it's time to go get my bags and my dinner."

"You haven't eaten?" she screeches.

I shake my head when I remember she can't see me. Yet. Cable is supposed to be connected tomorrow morning, and then I can take her on a virtual tour. "We've been talking for so long, my phone is getting angry with me."

"It's a good thing Brad's not here, or he'd be angry too."

"Oh? Why's that?"

"Because I haven't let you talk with him. He's worried about you as well, Meadow."

Looking around, I let out a happy sound. "I think you both can stop worrying."

And maybe, for just a moment, I can too. Spinning in a small circle, I try to take in everything in one glorious whirl. Even though I'm all alone, I feel like I'm being embraced in a long-overdue hug by the log cabin and earthy decor.

It's a perfect omen.

MEADOW

I swear there's something to be said for being organized.

Yesterday, I awoke early, disconcerted due to the different view out my window. It wasn't a bad one with spruce-fir trees interspersed with low-lying clouds. For a while, I lay in my new bed staring out the picture window as the clouds raced over snow-tipped mountains.

Then the cable company called letting me know of their impending arrival. Quickly getting dressed, I made coffee from the pods available in the little stand next to the Keurig, when Brad called to talk about the certified pre-owned SUV dealership I planned on visiting later that day. We were interrupted twice by the doorbell ringing—first Jasper with my boxes that he flatly refused to let me carry in, and second, the cable guy.

After a quick lunch in Kalispell, I asked Jasper to drop me off at the car dealership. "Are you sure you don't want company, Meadow?" he asks doubtfully as we pull up.

Spying my electric-blue RAV4 parked in front, I grin. "There's no need for you to stay. That is unless you want to learn something about buying a car?"

"I've got a lifetime of getting screwed over all stocked up, but thanks for the offer," he drawls.

We both laugh. Impulsively, I lean over and give Jennings's hotshot pilot a quick hug. "Thank you for everything."

"It was nothing." He smiles. And when he does, I can see one day, he's going to turn some woman's world upside down. Thank God, I'm immune to the Y chromosome right now.

With a quick wave, I slide out of the rental and head for the front entrance to be greeted by several people at once. I ignore them until I spy a man dressed in a long-sleeved flannel shirt and khakis. "Mr. Wesson?"

"Yes?"

"I'm Meadow Borneman. I believe that's my RAV4 you're holding out front."

He holds out a hand that reminds me of the paws of a Kodiak back home. Capturing my hand, he pumps it up and down. "So we did. Would you like to take a test drive?"

"I would. And while we're driving, let's see what kind of deal you'll be willing to cut me if I pay cash."

Without losing my gaze, he drops my hand. "How about I ask..."

"No, sir. Just you and me. After all, this was just a goodwill down payment and—" I purse my lips. "—you're not the only dealer in the area. However, if you're not interested...?" I let the unspoken question dangle between us

He sputters. "Now, that's just ridiculous. Why don't we go for that ride and talk some numbers?"

I suppress the out-and-out grin that wants to break out across my face. After all, it's too soon to celebrate. I'll do that once I decide this really is the car I want to be driving and I take it off the lot. But once his back is turned, my lips do curve a bit. The devil's in knowing the details before you face your adversary.

Boy, did I learn that lesson this past year.

TODAY, I've been familiarizing myself with the area after making an early morning grocery run. I'm driving the gently used RAV4 up to the gate when the hands-free rings. The display shows Covington's

number. "Mr. Covington, sir. What can I do for you?" My voice is filled with exuberance and excitement.

"Ms. Borneman, I need you to come to the main house immediately. Something terrible has happened."

Instead of taking the first turn to head down the bumpy lane toward my cottage, I keep straight on the path. "I'm on the main road now."

"I know. Your code came up when you came through the gates. Oh, thank goodness. The police just pulled up to the gates; I have to open them."

"What?" I can hardly breathe as I slowly navigate my new car along the road.

"Just come in through the front door. You'll understand soon enough." Before I can ask what happened, he disconnects the call.

I check my rearview mirror, and sure enough, there's an official vehicle closing in on me fast, lights flashing. With nowhere to pull off on the tree-lined lane, I roll my window down and wave to the officer and receive acknowledgment when he passes me by.

In less than a minute, we're both pulling into a wider part of the road. I pull to the side to either let him pass me or park behind me. And the pit in my stomach grows as he races past.

What on earth could have happened?

Then I slam on my brakes in shock as I get my first impressions of the cabin. "Oh, God. It's breathtaking."

I've seen pictures, of course, but they don't do justice to the two-story waterfront mansion on the Flathead Lake shoreline. As I move at a crawl, my head is at an almost unnatural angle as I try to capture both the magnificence of the home that seems to sprout up from the natural surroundings organically as if woodland fairies designed it instead of one hell of a talented architect. Multiple arched rooflines give way to sections of glass overlooking the driveway, allowing for easy views of the mountains. A tingle runs through me as I anticipate what I'll see outside the backside of the house, knowing the owners own almost two miles of the coveted shoreline.

Pressing down the accelerator, I pull up behind another heart-stopping shock since I turned the bend a few moments ago. Sliding out of my car, I approach the vehicle warily, afraid if I breathe on it too hard, it's going to disappear. "Oh, God. Is that a Shelby? It can't be real."

A distinguished man in his late fifties holding an iPad comes down the steps. "It was a gift from my father, Ms. Borneman." He holds out his hand.

"Mr. Covington. A pleasure to meet you in person, though I was looking forward to it being under better circumstances." I take his firmly and shake it. "What happened? Why are the police here?"

Russell Covington always appeared more youthful in our online interviews. Now it appears stress is adding years to his impeccable bone structure. He's visibly shaken. "Mr. Covington?" I prompt him again.

"Meadow—if I may?" After I give a quick nod, he continues. "Please call me Russell. After you see what I'm about to show you, I think you'll understand we're about to get to know each other very quickly in a very short time."

"Did something happen?" I ask as we ascend the stone steps.

He doesn't reply. Instead, he pushes open a ten-foot door that is a grander version of my own. I almost gag at the stench that emanates. "What on earth is that smell?" My voice comes out nasally as I've reached up to pinch my nostrils closed.

Russell covers his face with a handkerchief he whipped out of his pocket. The police are milling around taking photos. "The entire place has been vandalized. We're just not certain by whom. The last time I have an entry on my log for someone entering the property was the cleaning service."

"And they're reputable?" I question.

"Extremely. In the fifteen years I've been running the company, there have never been any issues with them." He rattles off a few of their other customers including a nearby four-star resort Russell advised me to recommend for some of our potential guests who might want to book with us in the future but, "are unable to due to our properties being already reserved."

"I agree. It seems highly unlikely they'd do something like... Oh, is that tile inlaid?" Instinctively, I move closer to get a closer look, but

Russell holds me back. "Oops. Sorry. I'm a former cop's wife. I know better. That kind of work is a labor of love though."

"The owner certainly agrees with you." With a heaving sigh, he admits, "This was Mr. Wilde's fear about using his family's retreat in the first place. We're not talking about broken dishes, Meadow. This is a desecration of his family's sanctuary that he rented to very select individuals."

"Yes, it is." No matter how much graffiti decorates the walls and cabinets in the kitchen, it still can't hide the woodland beauty of what was. "Has Mr. Wilde been notified?"

"Just before I called you. He's demanding a copy of the police report be sent to the man who coordinates his personal security—a man named Calhoun Sullivan." My face must show my confusion, and Russell continues. "I don't know the man, but Mr. Wilde trusts him implicitly."

I whip my phone out of my pocket and begin to take notes. "Of course. Do you have this Mr. Sullivan's contact information available?"

"Mr. Wilde said he'll make it available once the police have finished. Then, we have a limited time to restore the house, Meadow. I need that to be your focus since you live on property."

"Of course," I respond without hesitation.

"No, Meadow." Something in his voice catches my attention. "I need this to become your sole project. I will continue on managing the other properties, but I can't do that and be managing a restoration of this magnitude. And frankly, I don't quite know where to start. During your interview, you said you'd supervised some remodels including some areas of your home. You also indicated you helped restore the diner's interior in the off-season."

"By hiring people, Russell," I stammer. "Nothing of this magnitude."

"Then hire who you need to. The police are doing everything they can. You'll have a corporate card and access to a special corporate account for this with an equivalent to what the insurance funds will be by the end of the week. What else do you need?"

Spinning in a circle, I know I could make a million and one arguments about why I can't do this, but there's really one answer why I have to.

It's now my job to.

Facing Russell, I find the determination deep down and give him the reassurance he needs. "I need a list of general contractors you trust. I'm too new to the area to make that kind of decision alone."

"You'll have it by the time we're done here. Also, I'm having your computer and a tablet delivered to your home. Anything you need to buy, save the receipts."

I open my mouth to reply, but we're interrupted by one of the officers. "Mr. Covington, I think you should come with us."

"Officer Rome, this is Meadow Borneman. She's the assistant manager of Glacier Executive Leasing."

The officer sizes me up before holding out his hand. I shake it firmly without saying anything. "Mr. Wilde just got back to us with the codes," he explains.

"Codes?" I ask, confused.

"Mr. Wilde has the entire house monitored," Russell explains. He places a hand in the small of my back to help guide me around the trash even as Officer Rome trudges through it. "There's a room behind the wine cellar downstairs that holds all the recording equipment."

"And it hadn't been breached," Rome explains. "We think we know who the perp was. Perpetrator," he automatically translates.

"I was married to a cop," I explain for the second time in less than an hour. "You really don't need to give me a lesson on jargon."

We carefully make our way down a set of steps that are slick with puddles of glass and red stains. It doesn't take magical powers to guess that wine bottles were shattered over them as they match the path we follow down the hallway. I speak my thoughts aloud. "This seems more than just a prank."

Rome stops in the cool hallway to face me. "Are you sure you want to work for him?" He jerks his thumb at Russell. "We've got an opening in the department."

"Thanks, but no."

"Pity. Watch out for stray glass we've tracked in," he warns.

Grateful I decided to wear my boots today, I step into an electronics haven. "Pull up the video, Dan," Rome orders the young man sitting at the desk.

Silently we all watch a video where the housekeeper uses her code to enter. At first sight, she stumbles backward. "She must have been terrified," I murmur.

"She may have, but still, look at the timestamp," Rome urges.

I lean to get a closer look and swear under my breath. "Almost a month ago."

"I missed that the first time I saw it too," Rome assures me.

"Why didn't Margaret just tell me?" There's painful confusion in Russell's voice.

"We'll find out." Inside I cringe. Poor woman. I wouldn't want to be her when Officer Rome and his team get through with her. He barks out, "Dan, pull up the other video."

Soon, we're looking at a man who appears to have the fury of ten ripping wine bottles off the racks right outside this very room. He's flinging them to the wall, the floor. But all we can see is his back. "Great, so we know what date he was here and his back," Russell bites out.

"Just wait," Rome warns.

A moment later, the man reaches up high for the few remaining bottles on the rack he was set on desecrating, and Dan hits Pause. Russell sucks in a breath through his nose. "No, it can't be."

"Who is it?" I ask tentatively.

"Meadow, all of the Wilde family close to Mr. Wilde have special codes to reserve the property. Under normal circumstances, we'd have gone over this in the office. They have permission to visit the property simply by letting us know at a moment's notice. That's one of the main reasons he wanted someone on-site—because there could be someone here at any time."

"So, you're saying this man is a relative of Mr. Wilde's?" I demand.

He shakes his head, and I relax marginally. But his words make me almost choke on the saliva in my mouth. "Not just any relative—his brother, James. I'd have to go back and look at the media reports, but I'm almost certain this corresponds with him finding out his accountant swindled most of his money."

"And here's his brother, Kristoffer, making hand over fist in the music industry, representing acts like Brendan Blake," Rome concludes grimly.

"Is this going to make it better or worse?" I wonder aloud.

Russell's uncertainty doesn't answer my question.

"So, we have a positive ID of the perp. For the case file, I'd like to validate his access code was used. Based on the fact his name wasn't mentioned earlier, I'm presuming your codes don't go back that far?" Rome asks, all business.

"Not in the app version of the program." Russell holds up his tablet. "I'd have to pull an audit from the software, and at this point I'd feel more comfortable with either Mr. Wilde's approval or a warrant."

"Russell, why don't you let me call him to pave the way for the officer's request?" I'm shocked to hear my own voice. All three men turn and look at me with varying levels of disbelief. "If I'm going to have to deal with him for the renovations, he needs to know I can handle him." Also, my boss needs to know I can handle what's about to be thrown at me.

Russell unlocks his phone and hands it to me. "Just hit Redial. And Meadow? Good luck. He's behaving like a wounded bear."

I don't bother responding to my boss. I'm too busy dealing with the roar of "What the fuck do you know, Russell?" in my ear.

Calmly, I reply, "This is Meadow Borneman, Mr. Wilde. I'm Mr. Covington's new assistant manager for Glacier Executive Leasing. Officer Rome and his cyber forensic team are with me. We need your authorization to provide data beyond what Mr. Covington has available on-site. I need written authorization to be faxed to..." Rome quickly rattles off a fax number, which I repeat into the phone.

"Ms. Borneman, first, how the hell do I know you are who you say you are?" he demands.

"Sir, I'm calling from Mr. Covington's phone number. And even if I wasn't, I strongly suspect you're having a dossier made on me by your associate, Mr. Sullivan."

"Russell told you about Cal?" I wince as Wilde's booming voice takes out my hearing temporarily.

"To identify the individuals I would be working with over the next few weeks, yes."

"Well, okay then." I'm startled by his quick capitulation but don't remark on my good fortune. He continues. "What information did they find?"

"That's something you'll need to discuss with Officer Rome," I reply pertly.

"Ms. Borneman, forgive me for asking, but are you related to a lawyer named Caris? She was a pain in my ass at the worst of times too."

"Just for that, I'm redecorating your great room in hot pink with streaks of orange and lime," I inform him, not entirely joking.

There's silence for a heartbeat before Kristoffer Wilde bursts into laughter. "I needed that, Meadow—can I call you Meadow?"

"Yes, of course, sir."

"Thank you for stepping up during a difficult time. Please let Officer Rome know the fax is en route right now." His voice turns grim. "I hope the cottage wasn't found in the same condition."

"Not at all, sir," I assure him.

"Small blessings."

"We take them where we can." The next thing I know, the phone is being plucked out of my hands by Officer Rome. He steps outside of the room to the vestibule of broken glass and wine to talk to Mr. Wilde.

Russell gives my shoulder a squeeze. "You were terrific, Meadow. You're going to be amazing at this job."

God, I hope so. But as I scan the destruction on the cameras in the public areas of the home the Wilde family built, a knot forms in my stomach.

I just hope there's a contractor out there with enough skills to bring it back to its glory in a short amount of time.

MEADOW

Three physically and emotionally exhausting days later, I'm impatiently waiting for the insurance adjuster to finish his appraisal so I can do more than conduct a courtesy outreach to one of the contractors from the list Russell provided to me. All of the men I've spoken with want to get their hands on Nature's Song, the home Kristoffer Wilde built for his family, but they have no idea of the dumpster fire they're about to walk into.

Meanwhile, every time I've tried to connect with my family to speak with Elise and MJ, Elise has refused to come over to FaceTime with me. MJ, on the other hand, seems anxious—something I immediately brought up to Rainey.

"I noticed it too, Meadow. Have you spoken with Mitch?"

"No, why?" I asked as I paced the living room of our new home.

"Because he came by and took the kids out last night. They came home upset."

"What the hell was he doing there?"

"He claims the dates he was flying down to Idaho were mixed up." Her words send my senses tingling.

After wrapping up my call with my sister where I learned that

Maris was taking some major steps to change the landscape of her future—finally—I immediately called my ex.

Mitch answered before the end of the first ring. "Meadow. It's good to hear from you. How are you settling in?"

"What happened with the kids?" I didn't bother with any niceties. If this man wanted them, he should have divorced me before shoving his cock inside another woman. As it is, I'm bearing the brunt of his crimes with our offspring who don't know Daddy couldn't keep it zipped up while he was under a vow to love, honor, and cherish me.

"What do you mean?" he hedges.

"I don't have time for this crap, Mitch. I'm working and trying to prepare our new home for when Elise and MJ get here. Just tell me what you said to them last night so I can fix whatever the hell you did this time."

"I don't know why it's such a big deal," he huffed out.

"Everything to them is a big deal these days. It could be the wrong kind of chicken patties and it causes an avalanche of emotions. You're just not around to see it."

"Well, maybe if you didn't race for the divorce lawyer, I would be," he fired back.

I stop pacing and rub my free hand across my forehead. "So, what? I could be your home life while you had your side piece too? I don't think so. Why don't you just tell me what happened now so I can figure out how to clean up your latest mess."

That's when Mitch told me he was going to be away training for his new role for the next twelve weeks. "You have got to be fucking kidding me. And you told them over a damn Happy Meal?" I screeched.

"No, I took them to Subway. They love Subway," he defended himself.

"Your kids love pizza. They love Donna's. They adore getting crab downtown and the Italian place that was on *Diners, Drive-Ins, and Dives*. The only time they like getting Subway was when we'd be going bowling," I howled.

"Oh." There was a lengthy pause. "I can't get out of this, Meadow. It's a requirement of my job."

"I'm not saying you should, Mitch. What I am saying is, this is the kind of crap that as co-parent to your children I'd appreciate a heads-up on so I could help—gee, I don't know—navigate our children through with some assistance." *Especially since I'm the one who has to figure out what to do that's best for them in light of what's happening down here in Montana*, I added to myself silently.

"You're right. I'm sorry." But the damage was already done. And once again, Mitchell Borneman narrowly escapes dealing with the full measure of his consequences.

"I'm not the ones I hope you said that to," I bit out, before I pressed End to the call. "God, I hope one of these days, all of this penetrates both his big and little brains!"

Now, as I wait for the adjuster, I debate what to do about the kids. While the cottage is in perfect condition, having dedicated time to devote to getting Nature's Song back to the showpiece it used to be is awfully tempting. But I can't ask Rainey for more than I already have.

Can I?

As I have an internal war with myself, the adjuster comes out. He whips the mask off his head. "I've never seen anything quite like it. I need an hour to process some information for the policy. Do you want to meet at your office to go over the estimate?"

"Let me make certain Mr. Covington can join us, but I don't see that as a problem."

"Excellent. I'll see you both there." He holds out his hand. I hesitate, not out of rudeness, but because he's still wearing a work glove covered in God only knows what. With a quiet chuckle, he whips it off before offering his hand again. "Let's try that again, shall we?"

"Much better," I agree.

"Until then." He offers a smile before heading to his truck.

After we're all gathered around the conference room table at Glacier Executive Leasing, some of the tension that's been building inside of me starts to ease. The number the insurance adjuster pronounces staggers me. I've never heard of such a figure being paid out by an insurance company, but much to my shock, it causes a completely different reaction in Russell.

"Half a million dollars isn't going to scratch the surface of what was lost in that house." His voice is cold.

"True," the portly man allows. "But the problem, Mr. Covington, is that certain items are not covered under the policy under sections..." He begins to drone on while I take quick notes.

I almost go cross-eyed, and my hand cramps by the time he's finished.

"So, what you're saying is that because Mr. Wilde didn't have his wine collection covered, nor his furnishings—though they were hand-crafted by the same individual who hand carved most of the woodwork in his home—they can't be claimed against the policy."

"I'm sorry." And he seems to be. "I've never seen such personal tragedy outside of a natural disaster. And for it to have sat for so long made the damage worse."

Russell pushes to his feet. "Meadow, can I speak with you outside for a moment?"

"Certainly. Excuse us." I follow Russell out of the room.

When we're safely ensconced in his office, he bites out, "This just keeps getting worse by the minute."

"I don't understand." And I really don't. The insurance adjuster appears to be giving a generous settlement to cover the ruined structure and items that have been covered.

Flipping his monitor around, Russell gives me an education. "Some of the rugs in the living room were antiques, Meadow. They're not covered by policy. If we—and by we, I mean you—can't find someone to restore them back to their original condition, then they're a loss. And I'm fairly certain the adjuster knows that."

It finally dawns on me why he's so concerned about the number. "You don't think Mr. Wilde declared any of those items."

"The man has the Midas touch. Why would he? It would simply drive up his premiums. But at a time like this, that policy is every-thing." He pins me with his hawklike gaze that intimidated me during our interview sessions. "The other problem is the fact that while I believe in the quality of the work of the contractors you're going to interview, undoubtedly they're going to increase their bid once they get a look at Nature's Song."

I sputter, "But that's just wrong!"

"That happens all the time. It's like the difference between a party and a wedding. Amazing if you price the same two for the exact same weekend, one is ridiculously higher than the other. So, that five hundred thousand is going to go just like that." Russell snaps his fingers to accent his point.

I stand. "I have an interview with the first contractor in an hour. Let's see what we get back. Then we can make some decisions."

He nods sharply. "If I haven't mentioned it yet, I appreciate the cool head you're maintaining, Meadow. I know Mr. Wilde does as well."

I'm just grateful neither of them is telepathic because my mind is reminiscent of the infamous Edvard Munch painting. And not just because of the catastrophe we're facing at the house.

AT THE END of the day, I'm debating whether or not to call this day a win or a loss while I talk with Rainey.

"The police have released the home as a crime scene since they've collected all the necessary evidence. And while the adjuster's estimate is much lower than anticipated, I've hit upon a few major wins such as the specialized antique carpet cleaning company in Billings."

"Why would someone even do that?" Rainey's shock is evident.

"The brother had apparently just lost all of his money. And I guess deep-seated resentment against his big brother came pouring out. From what I understand from Russell—"

"Who's Russell?" Rainey interrupts.

"Mr. Covington. Trust me, after you've sloshed your way through a 250-bottle wine cellar in what used to be your best boots with someone, you get past formality with your new boss."

"Ouch. I don't know what I feel worse about, your boots or the wine."

Lifting my glass in salute, I silently agree before going on. "As part of making restitution, the cleaning service Russell contracts with will partner with a restoration service to waive their normal fees for the next two years to clean the house once we've restored it. But they're not hazardous cleaning experts which is what's listed on every single bid. I don't know why though. I mean, most of it is broken glass and rotten food. I need to clean as much of the mess out of the house as I can so I don't get another bid for the work that's closer to seven figures than mid-six figures."

"To repair what? What the hell did this guy do?"

After taking a slug of wine, I rattle off, "Left out rotting food on all of the custom woodwork, including milk which smells like ass after a month. He took a sledgehammer to tile and granite—and I'm only certain of that because he left it right next to the kitchen where he did the most damage. I don't even want to know what's smeared on the walls in the upstairs rooms." I shudder as I recall the unidentifiable brownish substance. "That's not to mention the fact he smashed out all of the lake-view windows and doors. So, we have to rip up carpets, potentially replace windows and doors if the panes themselves can't be replaced. Every backsplash in all the wet areas were destroyed. Oh! And I didn't mention the shower tile." I close my eyes in agony. After the classes I took at the local hardware store to learn how to tile, I think that might have caused me the most distress.

"This guy sounds like a lunatic. Are you sure you're safe there?"

"Yes. Of that I'm certain." I don't mention to her my very interesting call with Calhoun Sullivan, who assured me people who work for him at Hudson Investigations have already picked up James Wilde and presented him with two options, jail or therapy. He chose option two for an indefinite period of time. I also recall the rest of our intriguing phone call with a little trepidation.

"Don't worry about yourself, or your children, once they arrive on the property, Ms. Borneman. Mr. Wilde is insisting I send out Sam to install some additional security at the cottage," Calhoun advised me.

"Umm, who's Sam?"

"Sorry. Sam Akin. He's a computer wizard who works with us at Hudson. He'll fly out in the next few days. If you provide me your email, I'll send you a picture so you know who he is."

"I'll need to give him the codes..."

I was interrupted by Calhoun's laughter. "No, Meadow. You really won't." The amusement in his voice both terrified and comforted me.

Wondering when I'm going to meet yet another new stranger in this place I've barely settled into, I bring myself back to the conversation at hand. I hold the cool glass to the side before telling my sister, "Right now, all I want is to talk with the kids. Where are they?"

The intrigued look on Rainey's face falls. "They're not home, Meadow. They're out at a movie with the Stones."

"Isn't it a...damn. Tomorrow's a teacher workday, isn't it?" I curse myself for not calling earlier. Of course my kids would be making plans with their friends while they can.

"It is. But I don't know if they would have come to the phone, hon. Mitch did one hell of a number on them."

I bite my lip. "I spoke to him earlier as well."

"And that's not what you started this with? What did Tiny Douchebag have to say?"

I bark out a laugh. "That's brilliant. Have you shared it with the others?" Meaning Maris and Kara.

"No, I had to see how his new nickname fit for you."

"More like it didn't always fit. Why do you think I still owned a vibrator despite being married for sixteen years?"

The two of us are doubled over laughing. Dabbing tears from my eyes, I warn her, "Brace yourself for this, Rainey." I then tell her what Mitch told me earlier about not being around for the next three months.

"I'd ask if you were kidding me, but I'm not really surprised by anything he says or does anymore."

"I know. The problem is, they were expecting to spend time with their father once they get here. Now, they're going to move here, school's not going to be in session, and hey, guess what? Mom's now going to be up to her elbows with restoring a house at least twelve hours a day. I don't know what to do." I drain the rest of the wine in my glass. Frowning, I look over to the counter where I left the rest of the bottle. "I knew I should have brought the bottle over."

Rainey chuckles before saying, "So, let them stay here for a few more months." My head whirls around, and I gape at her. She just shrugs as if having two more people in her house isn't a big deal.

"Are you kidding me? No, I can't ask that of you."

"Please." She snorts. "You know they'll love being around for all the end-of-school events, barbecues with their friends, and to be honest Elise and MJ have been a big help around the house."

"I remember when they were around mine," I whisper painfully.

"Meadow…"

"Right now, I feel like this is a desperately needed reprieve for all of us. And what kind of parent does that make me?"

"Human? Stop beating yourself up so much. If they knew the reason for the divorce, maybe they'd understand the choices you made."

"And what would that do to their relationship with their father?" I snap.

"It would knock him from being a damn hero to being human. I'm not saying to tar and feather him, but Meadow…"

"I know." I pinch the bridge of my nose. "Let me see what I can do about flying up to see them. If I can swing that, then I'm probably going to take you up on your offer. I'm not comfortable with the idea of them moving here and then being trapped at the cottage while I'm over at the main property so much. When they get here, there's so much I want to show them."

"Like what?" Rainey asks.

For the rest of our call, I tell her about the general area around Flathead Lake that I've seen as I've driven back and forth between the Glacier Executive Leasing and Nature's Song. I try to put words to the beauty that reminds me of home so much my heart aches.

And I try to push aside the fact it feels like I'm holding up the weight of the world on my shoulders while my hands are sinking deeper into the earth beneath my hands.

KODY

"I'm certain if it wasn't for the fact Nick is posing for pictures with all of her high school friends, Sandra would use those lethal heels she's wearing to stab me dead on the spot." I grin at Brad and Jennings as we wait for the group photo before we accompany my baby sister and her friends to the entrance of their prom being held at my old high school gymnasium.

"Without a doubt, brother." Brad claps a hand down on my shoulder. Jerking his chin over at Jennings, he practically pleads, "Can we do this next week to Kevin?"

"No," Jennings responds firmly. "That kid has it completely together. He's already gone over every detail of what his plans are with me almost down to the minute. I know this sense of responsibility didn't come from me." A quick flash of pain crosses his face that morphs into an expression of pure devilment. "The one thing I'll get to torment him with is this though: he has no idea that since he's nominated to be prom king, Kara and I will actually be at the dance. Maybe I'll FaceTime you guys." Brushing an imaginary piece of lint off his tux jacket, he continues. "I imagine the look of horror on his face is going to be priceless."

"If you can't, make sure you get that shit on camera," I urge as I snap another picture of my sister's mutinous face.

"Like that was in doubt. Kara's going to be too busy tearing up over our baby boy growing up."

"Like you're not going to be struggling with that yourself?" Before Jennings can try to deny the claim, Brad plows on. "Trust me, I know what I'm saying. Mine do well at a spelling bee and I'm hooting and hollering from the back row."

"In other words, you're making an ass out of yourself," Jennings deadpans.

We grin at each other before focusing on the spectacle occurring in front of us as Tatum and Nick pose—without my sister, I note with delight—for a few photos. "Well, that's royally going to jerk her chain."

"Did you two always clash like this?" Jennings asks.

Frowning, I give his question some serious consideration. "It's not so much that we clash. I love her more than anything. Truthfully, she's the baby and I have an overprotective streak. Why?"

"If Kara and I have another child, I'm trying to prepare myself for what Kevin's reactions are going to be since the age gap won't be so different between them. Then again, I imagine that will depend on if we have a boy or a girl."

I choke on my own breath so hard, I garner the attention of a few people, including my sister. Her frown of annoyance transforms to one of concern. "I'm...fine. Swallowed...bug." Jennings begins whacking me on the back to lend credence to my lie. Brad, the asshole, has turned his camera on the two of us.

I can't wait to get these pictures in email at some random moment to remember the hilarity.

Sandra starts to laugh, sending her curtain of red-gold curls dancing. "Don't die on me, big brother," she calls out teasing, before turning her attention back to the antics wrapping up in front of her. Nick performs a courtly bow, causing her to flush to the roots of her hair, before escorting her back to Tatum, who holds out an arm to receive her. She turns up a beaming face at him.

I growl at the sight while the two schmucks next to me laugh.

Nick joins us, a wide smile on his normally taciturn face. "Trust me, Kody?"

"Of course. Always." We're missing something vital in our tight circle on my parents' front lawn, but nothing will break the bond between us. Over the course of four summers working in the Great Alaskan Lumberjack Show, these men became my brothers in every sense but blood. We worked and bunked together. Whenever we had days off, we spent time exploring Alaska together. And when the time came for each of us to continue on the paths life had already established for us to live out our dreams, we never lost what we had.

There's a part of me that knows if it wasn't for Jed, maybe it wouldn't have happened that way. Maybe we would have drifted apart and wouldn't have been the first ones Jennings called when he purchased Northern Star Flights. Or received invitations to Brad and Rainey's wedding—even if Nick didn't come. We sure as hell wouldn't have carved out time in our busy schedules for a reunion year after year until Jed fell in love with his husband and time became scarcer—at least that's what he told us.

Last year, we mourned together when we learned of Jed's death after he and his husband were killed in a pileup on an expressway. And the secrets Jed had been hiding for the last few years finally began to shake free.

Nick's voice pulls me from my memories into the present. "Then let your sister and her friends go on with their original plans." Leaning forward so he can't be overheard, Nick confides, "Tatum isn't stupid. Maybe in a few years you'd have something to worry about. Not tonight."

Casting a glance over my shoulder, I catch the joy and eager anticipation on Sandra's face and the tender amusement on the young man standing next to her. "No, I guess I don't have to worry tonight. Instead I'll just have to pick up the pieces tomorrow."

Jennings declares, "Is there any way if I have a second child to ensure it's a boy? Because right now, I'm glad I have a son."

Brad snickers. "Do you think their sex makes a difference? They're your kids, Jennings. If they're hurting, you're hurting." Suddenly, the phone in Brad's hand rings. "It's Rainey. Hold on a second." He steps away to take the call while the rest of us watch the flurry of activity as kids climb into limos and parents blind them with pictures like they're secretly paparazzi out for a million-dollar shot. Just as the last door closes, Brad's voice gets louder. "Wait, what happened? Tell Meadow to calm down." A pause. "No, it's not her fault she arrived and the place looked like that before she ever took over. Covington can't hold that against her." His eyes bug out. "Holy hell, it was *that* property? Christ, Rainey. No, I'm not worried about her, I'm worried about who she'll be able to get to fix it." A longer pause before he sneers. "Of course they jacked the bids. I'm glad you called, sweetheart. Let me see what I can think of. I'll call you back."

Before I can open my mouth, Jennings asks, "What's wrong with Meadow? Is there something wrong with the Montana job?"

"Wait? What's she doing in Montana?" I demand.

"That's just what I was going to ask." Nick folds his arms across his chest.

Brad and Jennings exchange confused glances. "How do you not know? It's all Kara's been talking about for the last couple of months," Jennings asks, truly confused.

Grasping for patience to tamp down a rising anger, I remind Jennings, "I don't have the direct connection into the goings-on now that Jed died, you dick. Remember? He's the one who used to talk about everyone."

"Except Kara," Jennings tacks on grimly.

"Well...yeah," I agree helplessly, not going into why. Jennings's relationship with his now wife first began when we were all in Alaska together seventeen years ago. After Jed's funeral, they worked through the barriers keeping them apart and are now blissfully happy together in Florida.

"Back to the topic at hand, I get your point, Kody." Brad passes his phone from one hand to another. "With Rainey filling that spot for me..."

"And Kara for me," Jennings jumps in.

"I never noticed the void in hearing about what was happening in lives of all the other people we knew," Brad concludes.

"Like Meadow," I deduce.

"Or Maris." Nick's jovial expression is gone, replaced with something so ferocious, we all take an instinctive step back.

"Right." Brad clears his throat. "Well, Meadow is living and working in Montana. There's been a problem on the jobsite..."

I cut him off. "Why? What happened to Mitch's job on the force in Juneau?"

Brad and Jennings exchange another unreadable look. "I swear to God, if someone doesn't tell me what the hell is going on..."

Jennings clears his throat. "Kody, this isn't the place to go into why, but..."

"But what?"

He takes a deep breath. "Meadow and Mitch are divorced. It became final about two months ago..." His words trail off when I shove him. Jennings falls back a few steps with the force of the move. Fortunately, our antics aren't noticed by my parents or the parents of my sister's friends.

Jennings narrows his eyes. "Carrying a torch much?"

"Are you kidding me?" I shout. "That's what you have to say?"

"No. I just didn't think you still harbored these kinds of feelings for Meadow after all these years," Jennings retorts.

I remember the way Meadow tried to ignore me at Brad's house when we saw each other after Jed's funeral. It took about two minutes of being in the same room as her again for me to realize I'll never feel this way about anyone else. Ever. And neither did I give a damn she wore another man's ring on her finger. All I saw was Meadow. If she had asked me to walk out the door with her, I would have. I'd have chucked years' worth of morality away without looking back. I'd have said to hell with my business and anything else standing in my way. That's what this woman means to my heart.

All I say is "I would have wanted to know."

Jennings studies me for a moment before nodding. "Fair enough. But honestly, Kody, until you said something it slipped my mind that it was Jed..."

Fiercely, I remind all of them, "We promised in the back of the car before we walked into Jed's wake we'd never leave him behind because to do so is to forget everything about the crazy bastard we loved. We're doing that by forgetting everything he did for us."

Nick comes up and throws an arm around my shoulder in support before suggesting, "Why don't we get out of these monkey suits and get caught up? Then Brad—" He pins our friend with a stare. "—you can tell us what kind of trouble Meadow's in and how we can help."

Thoughtfully, Brad's rubbing his thumb back and forth across his lips. "Actually, I think it's all going to work out just fine because the only person who can help her is Kody." With that ambiguous statement, he turns and heads for my parents' front door to get changed. Jennings isn't that far behind him.

Nick sums it up beautifully when he says, "And you were worried about your sister? I think you might have bigger problems coming your way, brother," before he heads in the same direction, leaving me gaping after all of them in a tux in the rural Iowa sunshine.

KODY

I splutter my beer down the front of my shirt at what I hear Mitch did to Meadow. Mopping it up, I threaten, "I don't care if he's now a federal agent. I swear if I see him, he's a dead man."

"Calm down, Kody," Brad warns me. "I didn't tell you all of this to—"

"He *cheated* on her!" I bellow.

"We know." Jennings tries to calm me down.

"Well, I'm so glad that some of you knew and didn't bother to share with the rest of us. Is there anything else you forgot to mention? Like is Maris pregnant or something?" I bite out acidly.

Nick spits his beer everywhere at my off-the-cuff commentary. I'm pleased to see the majority of it lands right in Brad's and Jennings's faces. Serves him right for trying to hold himself back from a good woman who wants nothing more than to love him, I think. Out loud, all I say is "So, let's do a little post-game catch-up. From the beginning, what the hell happened?"

"Meadow didn't say anything until after Jed's funeral," Brad hastens to tell me.

"I figured as much." Or I likely would be throwing another punch.

With a heaving sigh, he takes a long swig of his beer before admitting, "Meadow told Rainey not long before a barbecue we had when Kara and Kevin were visiting. It was tearing her apart."

"How did she figure it out?" I demand.

"She went into his work bag to dig out his dirty work laundry, T-shirts, socks, crap like that, because the lazy son of a bitch didn't do it. Motherfucker had used condoms thrown in there—likely forgot to throw them out." Brad's voice is filled with disgust.

I surge to my feet after putting my bottle down on the nearby end table. My mother won't appreciate if I hurl it in a fit of temper. "You've got to be kidding me." I begin to pace back and forth.

"No."

"What did Meadow do?" Nick asks.

I pause and wait for an answer.

Jennings's smile is nothing short of evil. "Well, let's say that Meadow's been all over the stages of grief. But that morning she shot straight to anger. From what Kara told me, she also found a box of unused condoms. She proceeded to cut open all the unused ones with scissors. Then she gathered them as well as the used ones up before waking Prince Charming up by setting off the alarm to the house."

"What was she thinking? He's a damn cop!" I bellow.

"Oh, Meadow had a rule for Mitch," Brad reassures me, taking my anger down a notch. "All of his weapons had to be locked up the minute he hit the house. He had a biometric safe where his service weapon was stored on the nightstand as a compromise. But Meadow's one sharp woman; she had already moved that."

"In other words, she was fucking with him..." I begin.

"The same way he fucked her over. Damn straight. So, after she set off the alarm, he comes flying down the stairs dressed in just his briefs," Brad continues.

"And finds his wife with the safe and his work duffle at his feet. And a box of cut-up condoms between them and the alarm panel," Jennings concludes. "And while he's begging, pleading it was a onetime thing, guess who breaks in the door to answer the call from the alarm company?" He nods as he sees me putting all the pieces together.

"The other woman was a cop?" I ask, even though I know the answer.

"Someone he'd go out on patrol with. We'd consider them partners, I guess," Jennings confirms.

Nick begins to chuckle. I whirl on him. "What the fuck about this is funny?"

"The fact that Meadow so nicely did an offensive strike and then double takedown without ever using her fists. All she had to use was her fucking brain. Maybe I should hire her to come teach a course on tactics to my recruits," Nick says admiringly.

My mouth opens and closes like a fish. No words come out. Ignoring Nick for the moment, I point at Brad. "What happened next?"

Brad stops grinning at Nick's assessment of Meadow. He swallows hard. "Well, now that everything was out in the open, the woman started spewing a bunch of shit Mitch said about Meadow."

My gut tightens. "What did Meadow do?"

"Not a damn thing. She still hadn't turned off the alarm. So, they sent out a second unit," Jennings says grimly.

"Christ." I drop back onto the sofa. "And?"

"And that's when his sergeant storms the house with a few other officers. All armed. And since the answering officer in question had engaged her radio unit before approaching the house, they heard every single word," Brad concludes. "Meadow didn't say a thing while both Mitch and the female officer were being verbally eviscerated in front of her. What she did find out is this wasn't the 'first time' crap Mitch had been trying to shove at her."

Every word Brad says is tearing me apart. "So, she filed for divorce?"

Brad shakes his head. "Not right away. Remember, she's Meadow. She puts everyone and everything ahead of herself. She always has. But with Elise and MJ, she had no choice."

"What did she do?"

"She tried to be fair." Before I can start ranting at the injustice of it, Brad holds up a hand. "I get it, Kody. There's no one who wanted to go after him more than I did."

Not true, but I don't give voice to the fact I've been in love with Meadow Jones Borneman since the first night we lay on the grass together talking all night until the first signs of the setting Alaskan summer sun began. If there's ever a chance in this lifetime I ever get to say those words, it's going to be to her.

I'm grateful when Nick asks, "So what happened?"

"I went with her to a public place to meet with Mitch. Meadow wanted the easiest of transitions for the kids, and for a while it appeared that's what Mitch wanted to. It took hours—going through every debt, visitation schedules, tears, apologies." Brad scrubs his hands over his face. "Next to the day I found out Jed died, it was singularly the worst day of my life."

We're all quiet as we recall the emotional shock we all endured when we found out about Jed's death. First came denial, then a pain so swift and debilitating it brought me to my knees right where I stood. For Brad to liken Meadow's interaction with her ex-husband to that, I wonder aloud, "How did you manage to not kill him?"

"It was difficult despite the promise I made in advance to Rainey," he admits.

I snort. "You're a better man than I am. I wouldn't have been able to hold back."

"Just wait. I'm not done," he warns. My body tenses upon hearing those words. "They had everything written down. Meadow was going to use Isler to file based on 'incompatibility of temperament' when..."

"Why that?" I hiss. "She could have taken him to the cleaners with what she had."

"Because she wanted out, Kody. If she filed for reasons of infidelity, she would have had to have produced witnesses," Jennings explains. And a lightbulb goes off in my head.

"And she wasn't sure if they'd stand behind her or Mitch," I conclude grimly.

"That about sums it up." Brad nods. "But at the eleventh hour, Mitch did something none of us were expecting."

"What's that?" I ask.

"He got a new job here in the lower 48. So, he reneged on the entire custody agreement. Then he tries to say my presence at the meeting caused 'intimidation' and he never would have agreed to Meadow's requests otherwise."

Nick jerks up from his deceptively careless position. "Shut. The. Fuck. Up."

"No. So, what should have been a simple dissolution of their marriage ended up escalating into arbitration. It took months. And all through this, Daddy Dearest was telling the kids Meadow was hiding things. The kids are still treating her like she's some kind of pariah," Brad concludes.

I announce to no one in particular, "My number for my lawyer is in my cell phone. Last name, Roberson. Because I truly am going to kill him."

Nick slaps my shoulder in support. We wait for the rest expectantly.

Brad doesn't hold out long. Chest heaving, he admits, "Meadow and her attorney met with Mitch and his. He wanted—no, demanded—Meadow live in the same city so he could still see the children at his convenience. Meadow's team asked questions about his new position and asked to come back to arbitration in a few days. She conceded to moving to the lower 48, but she claimed based on the work she could get, she would argue the two of them living in the same town. Even the same state was hardly pertinent based on the amount of time he'd be able to spend with his children." Brad's face turns cunning. "Her attorney pulled out his timesheets from his job in Juneau, including overtime. Using that information, and with the statements he made under oath that he'd have—perhaps—every other weekend to see his children, why should their lives be disrupted beyond what he was already doing to them?"

"God, I wish I had a camera in the room to see the asshole's face," I announce.

"I said almost the exact same thing," Jennings agrees. "He had no leg to stand on. None. Especially since the reason he claimed he wanted Meadow so close was so he could see his children as much as possible due to overtime. So, the final agreement is they each can't live more than three hours apart from the other until both children are eighteen. They each have to be able to drive ninety minutes to meet the other."

"Where did he want her to live?" I ask out of curiosity.

"Bonners Ferry, Idaho. What kind of life would Meadow have had in a small town like that with Mitch lurking over her shoulder?" Jennings demands.

"None," I say flatly.

"Exactly. So, I made a call to Russell Covington." Brad names the head of the exclusive rental company we've used in the past for our annual retreats.

Immediately, Brad's words from outside begin to filter through my brain, and the puzzle pieces start fitting together. "She's in Bigfork? Doing what?"

"She's the new assistant manager for Covington and running the operations for all of the Flathead Lake properties. As part of her wages, she gets to live in the Nature's Song cabin guest house free of charge. But there's a problem."

The cabin. Suddenly, the words from Jed's last wishes flash through my mind. *"To Kody Laurence, I leave my travel journals, sketch books, and drawing kit. There's also an open-ended monthlong trip paid for at the retreat we went to in Montana. Inside one of the journals, you'll find a drawing of a tree house I thought would be perfect there. Make that happen, will you? Sorry, Kody, the sketches suck. My skills were never up to yours. If I could wish anything for you, it's to see there's more than houses that needs your magic touch."*

"For how long?" I choke out.

"For good. Or until something else happens, I guess," Brad sighs.

"You said there was a problem?"

Brad tips his beer back and finishes it. "Yeah. An enormous one." He explains what Meadow walked into when she inspected the property upon arrival. By the time he's done, I'm on my feet heading for the doorway.

"Where are you going?" Nick calls out.

"I need my computer. I need to see who I can switch off jobs to get a crew ready to head to Montana."

I'm partway to the stairs when I hear Jennings say to Brad, "Well, that didn't take much for you to convince him, did it?"

"No. Now, someone just needs to convince Meadow." Brad's voice holds a note of worry.

Pausing on the stairs, I call out, "Don't worry about Meadow. I'll let her know what's going on the moment I get to Montana." The way I should have spoken up and dropped the masquerade about what I was feeling almost seventeen years ago in Alaska.

Maybe then none of us would be in this mess now.

KODY

The moment my flight touches down on the tarmac in Portland, I'm whipping my phone out of my pocket and dialing Greta's number. "I need the projected schedules for the crew's availability for the next three months starting next week."

A moment later, I wince as her screech is loud enough to likely reach the passengers in coach. "No, I'm not testing you. There's a job in Montana we're going after...yes. You heard me correctly." Harvesting what little patience I have left because I can't afford to have Greta decide to take her ridiculous project management skills somewhere else when I need her the most, I whack my head on the overhead compartment and curse. Rubbing the spot, I bite out, "I'll give you more answers when I get to the office."

"How long is that going to be, Kody?" she snaps.

"I'd say a couple of hours. We literally just touched down."

"And you couldn't, I don't know, have maybe called me on a Sunday instead of giving me this ludicrous deadline?" she demands.

I admire the efficiency of the airport personnel as they bring the gate closer to the jet. As the passenger I sat next to moves out the way, I reach up for my weekender. "I needed the time to determine if going after the work was feasible. I think it is. Yell at me later after you get me the data I need to confirm it." Without another word, and knowing I'll deal with her wrath soon enough, I disconnect the call. I step back to allow the person across the aisle to precede me off the plane.

What I told Greta was no lie. While all of my protective instincts rose to the surface after Brad and Jennings explained the situation Meadow was facing, I've been struggling trying to decide how much I should intervene.

On one hand, there are few people in the world who know the structure of that property the way I do. But on the other, I'd be working in close contact with the woman who claimed my heart seventeen years ago. Despite time and distance, and even though she never knew it, there's no sign my heart intends on moving on.

I honestly don't have the answer on how I'll survive this intact. The only thing I keep circling back to is Meadow needs help. Besides, in a roundabout way, we're family—her to Rainey, me to the guys. And there isn't anything you don't do for your family.

"I can give her the head start she needs as she begins her new life," I tell myself as I slide into my waiting truck.

With that in mind, I drive to my condo to pack enough clothes for a few weeks. After throwing my bag and my personal toolbox in the back of my truck, I head back upstairs to shut off my utilities. Just as I'm about to head out to my office to find out how many of my crew I can spare for a long-distance restoration, a framed photo on the wall catches my eye.

Almost twenty years old, Brad's then girlfriend, now wife, Rainey, snapped a picture of the five of us in the Smiths' backyard. Brad has an arm hooked around Nick's neck to keep him in the photo—scowl or not. Jennings had a huge smile on his face, likely at the woman who changed his world. I was leaning against Jennings's shoulder to keep myself upright, and I was laughing. "God, Jed. No one made me laugh like you did." My fingers graze the edge of the frame as I stare at the wild-haired man who had just strutted out of the house wearing... "What was it I said? Did you pay money for that 1920s fetish wear?" I bark out a laugh that's riddled with pain.

Jedidiah Smith, you are irreplaceable. No, I correct myself. Jed Malone. The most spectacular thing about the brother of my heart was his capacity to love. And I'm just grateful that for whatever duration they had together, he and his husband, Dean, found it together.

Too impatient to wait for the elevator, I jog down the three flights of stairs and push open the door. Leaping into the cab, I head downtown. The anticipation I've been trying to tamp down begins to worm its way through me as the one insidious thought I've refused to allow myself breaks free from the chokehold I've maintained since Brad broke the news.

Meadow's no longer married. God, she's free after seventeen fucking years.

"What would you do, Jed?" I murmur aloud as I navigate my truck around a bunch of fuel-efficient vehicles with an ease born of long practice.

And a memory of Jed and me drinking and throwing axes one night after work, shooting the shit, comes to mind. I was hoping for a definitive answer to whether or not I should shove a wedge between Meadow and Mitch when Jed, looking like a lunatic in oversized overalls, imparted words on me I've never forgotten.

"You love her for exactly the things you're asking her to betray. In the end, where does that land the two of you? Anywhere good?"

While I was still reeling from the one-two punch to my heart, Jed hurled his axe dead center into the bull's-eye before walking off the open set the Great Alaskan Lumberjack Show took place on.

Pulling into the garage beneath the building that houses my office and the design studio, I realize none of those initial barriers stand between us. "Instead, there's only the last seventeen years to rise above."

Slamming out of my truck, I may be insane, but my decision's made. Even if it's only to put the past to rest once and for all so I can move forward, I'm going to Montana.

But I can't prevent a stray thought from trickling through my head as I push open the door to my office and confronting one seriously pissed-off Greta. This could be the moment I've waited my entire life for. Shoving it aside, I focus on helping Meadow adjust to her new life. After all, what kind of man would I be if I didn't do everything in my power to help the woman who's always owned the pieces of my heart find her way?

An asshole, just like her ex.

"Do you want to explain what on earth is going on?" Greta demands the moment I push through the doors. She has a handful of papers in her hand.

I hold my hand out for them. "I'm taking a crew to go help a friend."

Her lips part in shock. "Are you insane? We had plans, Kody. We were finishing the estates from hell, and we just put an offer in on—"

"I know what our plans are." An exclusive piece of property came up for sale just north of the Portland—acres and acres of farmland begging for Laurence Construction to build on it. "You can take lead on that if it happens," I decide on the spot.

Greta's shocked. Then her eyes narrow. "Who is she?"

Uncomfortable, I shift my attention to the paperwork in my hands. Frowning, I question, "Lenny isn't on this list?"

"He won't finish the millwork on the estates for another two weeks." Her voice is filled with barely restrained patience, much like when we were kids and she was trying to explain why I'd irritated Victoria so badly. "If you need him added—"

"I do."

"Fine." She snatches the papers out of my hand. "Now, start talking."

Avoiding the real question, I make my way to my barely used office to gather up the equipment I'll need. My laptop and iPad are in my bag from the weekend, but I also need a portable drafting table and the kit holding my drawing, measurement, and cutting tools. "I heard about an opportunity over the weekend when I was home." Gee, that's the understatement of the century. "I thought I'd check it out."

I pray Greta doesn't associate my blatant attempt at obfuscating the truth with my inability to meet her eyes. If I'm lucky she'll associate it with the way I'm rushing around.

But my sister is just too damn astute. "So, that's it? You're dropping everything for a chance?"

I finally hold her gaze when I say words from the depth of my heart. "I've waited a lifetime for a shot at this."

"For a crack at the house or the woman who lives in it?" The only benefit to the sharply drawn breath I make is I know I haven't expired from shock. "What, do you think I'm an idiot? Do you think I don't see the fact you won't commit to anyone when—damnit, I hate saying this because you're my brother—you're what every woman is looking for?"

I'm about to protest when she begins ticking off my attributes as if they're a punch list on a job. "You're good-hearted, funny, and gorgeous to boot. It always amazes me out of all the women you dated, not one was capable of capturing your heart."

Probably because the one who's owned it has it for seventeen years, I think to myself. I let out a breath, and with it unload the burden I've kept inside except with the brothers of my heart.

Quickly, I bring my sister up to speed on the situation at Nature's Song, including my history with the house, the damage done, and the fact I personally know the property manager. "All of that aside, apparently she's been trying to get bids to have the work done locally, but the contractors are adding an unnecessary surcharge based on the prime location of the real estate," I growl in frustration.

Greta's lashes dip downward. I can't tell what she's thinking. Then again, she's always been the hardest of my sisters to read on a good day. When she finally raises her eyes, I'm shocked by the fact they're diamond bright. Forgetting about the fact I was trying to get on the road as quickly as I could, I step forward and grip her arm. "Greta?"

"She's the one," she whispers fiercely. "The one you lost your heart to all those years ago in Alaska."

Whoa. Dropping her arm, I step back in shock. My sister is one of the most astute people in the world, but— "What makes you thinks that?"

Shooting me a filthy look filled with disbelief, she proceeds to blow me away by saying, "You met the one, and she filled your soul. Then between one day and the next, you changed. All the life drained from you. Everyone attributed it to you leaving your friends."

"Maybe it was," I challenge, uncomfortable by my sister's armchair analysis.

Greta rolls her eyes. "Nobody who knows you can say you haven't had a full life, but it's been missing the kind of fulfillment that comes from having met that one person you were meant to connect with."

I stay silent because the problem isn't that I haven't met the one. It's that I couldn't be with her. Well, now I finally have a shot at changing that. Then again, that depends on what I find when I get there.

If I ever get a chance to leave.

"Then you came home from Jed's funeral, and I honestly thought you were going to go mad." A lone tear falls down her cheek.

"I miss him. I never realized how much I could." Especially right now when I could use his wisdom more than ever.

Stepping forward, Greta pushes a lock of hair off my face. "I know you do. The only thing I give you credit for is you didn't try to ruin some other poor woman's life by shoving her in someone else's place."

"Give me a little more credit than that," I mutter, unintentionally confirming everything she's insinuated while in my office.

"So, what's your plan? You're going to ride in on your big black truck with your cavalry of workers and save the day? To what end, Kody?"

"To the same end I've always had—to help make her happy. And in the end, if it means giving her that and walking away, I will," I respond simply.

Greta's lips part, but no words come out. After a few moments where nothing but the outside hum of the office can be heard, she finally asks, "How are you sure it's real?"

I pause, not out of uncertainty of how I feel about Meadow, but because I'm trying to remember exactly what I said to Jed at the house we rented a few years ago. The home Meadow now manages, in a twist of fate so unexpected, I'm still reeling from it. I think back to the night Jed and I sat on the deck overlooking Flathead Lake and pull the words from deep within my memory. "Because even after all this time, it didn't matter that she didn't choose me as long as she's happy. I could live the rest of my life content with glimpses of her so long as I know that."

"Kody..." Greta begins, but I plow on.

"On the rare occasions when I saw her, my heart forgot she didn't choose me that night."

"Why?"

"Because one smile from her and I was transported back to a time when we'd lie together talking with the earth at our back." I take a deep breath and finish. "If I could have that memory every night for the rest of my life, I'd never want for anything more."

"Or anybody else?"

I shake my head, suppressing a smile over the irony of my sister's question. It's the same one Jed asked me that night. "The heart loves who it loves. I don't believe it's a choice we make but something destined between two souls."

"Then why didn't you do something back then?" Leave it to my sister to ask the question I've been tormenting myself with for seventeen long years.

"Because back then, I was a young man who foolishly thought destiny would step in to bring two souls together. Then I became a man who recognized love isn't always about being together. It's about wanting what's best for the other person." I lean down and press a kiss to her forehead. "Now there are repercussions to deal with as a result of that."

"What do you mean?"

"I mean that in the process of being Mr. Altruistic, I essentially walked away from someone who was one of my closest friends to protect myself. And as a result, I only found out about what's happening in Montana the night of Sandra's prom. Now do you under-stand—umph!"

Knowing my sister, I should have expected the jab to the stomach. "What was that for?" I wheeze out.

"For years, you taught me, Candy, Victoria, Alissa, Amelia, and Sandra to not put up with a man who would treat us any differently than our brother or father would." She narrows her eyes. "And yet, what have you done?"

I can't find the words to respond, but I can't find them because my sister's right. I let Meadow go because it hurt too much to keep her close, expecting others to keep me informed of her.

What kind of reception am I about to walk into?

Greta reaches up and cups my chin. "It's going to get complicated, Kody. You just have to keep in mind that once you commit to her for the job, you can't storm off if the personal stuff gets to be too intense. This time, you have to see it through to the end."

Having such a large family has driven me crazy on more than one occasion, but right now, I'm grateful to my younger sister's words of wisdom. "Thanks, G." I tug her forward and wrap her in a hug.

"I've got your back, but you still can't have Lenny for two more weeks." Her words are muffled against my chest.

"We'll see," I croon against the top of her head.

She whacks my back with her perfectly organized schedules over and over. When I let her pull back, she asks, "What can I do to help you get ready?"

I don't know whether I'm praying to God or Jed, but if either are listening, let there be a day where I can introduce Meadow to my family. Because if the young woman who haunts my memories is anything like the woman I'm about to confront, she'll fit in perfectly with the Laurence clan.

Letting Greta go, I circle my desk and hold out my hand for the papers. "Let's go through these and come up with a rough bid that I can upload and adjust on-site." I'm calmer now. And with Greta's help, taking the time now will save me hours in Montana.

Which is where I'm going to need them with Meadow.

MEADOW

It's a dark day even though the sun is shining brightly outside.

I should be grateful for the weather as I lug another box of salvageable items out of Nature's Song down to the portable storage I rented. The unusual lack of snow and rain have kept me from having to bring in the contractors before I was ready to make a decision on one of the bad choices I'm being presented with.

Russell was shocked when he came by the other day. "If you asked me what was going on, I'd say the homeowners were in the middle of a flip, not that they had any kind of vandalism. I can't believe you did all of this on your own, Meadow."

I nodded toward the bids on the bar. "With each and every one of those, this should knock off the 20K they line-itemed for 'Unknown Trash Removal.' Despite the police report, the contractors still wouldn't remove that, so I took it into my own hands."

Russell gaped at me like I had two heads. "Meadow, your job description doesn't involve disposing of all of this." He waved an arm to encompass the waste of food and rotted hardwood on the first floor.

"You tasked me with getting a job done, correct?"

"Well, yes."

"And I'm doing just that." Russell started to protest, but I held up a gloved hand. "Take a look at the bids on the counter before you say anything else."

Turning, he picked up the bids I laid out to remind myself why I was going through this disgusting exercise. There, circled in bright red, was the trash removal charge from each of the general contractors. I snapped open another bag to prepare it for another shovel full of rotted food I knocked off the shelves earlier. I'm utterly infuriated by the bids we've received over the last few days. "Tens of thousands of dollars to remove trash? I'll have this place cleaned out in a few days. Then maybe the stench won't be as apparent and influencing the numbers I see on those pages. I mean, it's not like he cut every wire in the damn house or blew off a wing!" I shouted.

He became thoughtful. "I agree. And I'll agree you can clean up enough to get those rugs out, but that's it." The smile that began to form on my face quickly died. "We need to get the professionals in soon, Meadow."

Rolling my head on my aching shoulders, I knew he was right. But with so much spinning out of control in my life, I needed just a few moments where I felt like I had all the power. "I know."

With a quirk of his lips, he declared, "I'm impressed, Meadow. It's been a week and you're well on your way to earning your first bonus."

A thrill ran through me at his words. "I don't want you to ever think you made a mistake in hiring me, Russell."

He barked out a laugh. "I can assure you, I don't. And don't be surprised to find something waiting on your doorstep. Also, Anne and I would love to have you over for dinner this weekend."

After I made it to the cottage, I found a gift certificate for a day of pampering at the Lodge at Whitefish Lake with a note stating, "My wife assures me you deserve this. There will also be an adjustment to your salary. Upward. — RC." Tears pricked my eyes at the simple gratitude. "I guess I can do this job after all," I whispered, clutching the note to my chest, Russell's words meaning much more than anything, including the money.

Back at work, I discovered buried treasure in each of the closets I found to be locked. Russell hurried over with a key. Other than smearing them with the unknown substance, Mr. Wilde's brother didn't include them in his rampage. "It seems so small in comparison to the rest of the damage, but it's something," I exclaimed to Russell.

"I agree. There's an excellent cleaner who handles fire and water damage. I can't handle the physical work you're doing, but I can handle this."

Even as Russell gathered the family's clothes to be brought to the cleaners to be cleaned and put into storage boxes, I've hauled loads of linens to my own cottage to be washed and folded before doing the same.

Finally, two weeks after finding Nature's Song in the condition I first saw it in, the most I can say for it is that it's clean from the rot and rubbish James Wilde left it mired in. "I'm looking forward to seeing you the way you once were in your full glory," I say out loud. It's about the only thing I'm looking forward to these days.

Especially after the FaceTime call I had last night.

"I think she'll be different. The one thing I've learned about Nature's Song is she evolves as if she truly is a part of nature and the people who stay in her. A piece of timber they find on the slopes, a rock from the top of the glacier, her visitors always leave a part of themselves here."

I jump at the sound of Russell's voice. "Where did you come from?" I laugh.

"Sorry about that. You did such an amazing job getting everything cleaned out, there's no more glass outside to announce my presence."

Laughing, I walk over to the cooler I now feel comfortable bringing inside with me from the cottage filled with water and pull out two. He shakes his head. Dropping one back in, I twist the top off and take a long drink. Wiping my mouth, I answer, "What's going on?"

"I received a call from a potential contractor from out of state. Very exclusive. Word is getting out about the house needing repairs." His face is worried.

Even though my heart is thumping inside of my chest, I say calmly, "Well, at least we haven't been wringing our hands together and saying woe is me."

He barks out a laugh. "That's because you haven't, Meadow. You're a strong, determined woman. I might have curled into a ball."

And just like that, the wounds from Elise's shrieks over FaceTime begin to mend just a little. "Thank you. But I have to say, I'm not entirely certain I would have been that person before my separation a year ago."

He opens his mouth, I'm sure to ask me more, but the reason for dropping by pulls him back. "The contractor says he'll be here in a few hours and will check into his hotel before dropping by. I'd say that gives you at least two in order to get cleaned up."

"That's an excellent idea. And maybe I should burn these clothes while I'm at it." We both laugh.

"Would you like me here with you?" Russell asks as he helps me pack up and carry the packing materials out to my SUV.

"If you'd like." I slam the tailgate down. The sound echoes in the quiet. "I'm so glad the worst of the dumpsters were picked up yesterday," I murmur to myself before turning to my boss for his decision.

He opens his mouth and then closes it. "I think you'll do fine on your own. But if you need assistance, any kind at all, I'm only a phone call away." He starts to move back toward his Shelby with an economy of motion.

Just as he's about to slide in, I call out, "Russell?"

He pauses and looks back over his shoulder.

"I'm glad that since I had to move anywhere, it ended up being to a place where someone feels concerned about me. How lucky am I that person is my new boss?" Leaving that hanging in the air between us, I walk to the driver's side of my SUV and slide into the seats I've covered in garbage bags.

Russell still hasn't moved when I drive by and wave as I head back to the cottage to shower and change.

I have a contractor to negotiate with.

STANDING under the sharp needles of the shower spray, I can't prevent my mind from drifting back to the conversation between me and Elise last night.

"What do you think about Aunt Rainey's idea?" I asked as I laid out the idea of her and MJ staying in Alaska a little longer than expected.

"It's fine. Whatever." Elise's hair fell in front of her face as she ducked her head.

"It would give you longer to spend time with your friends, do all the fun things you—"

"What do you care?" She lifted her head up, her desolate eyes blazing. "All you care about is you and what's best for you. So, it has a side benefit for me and MJ. So what?"

My breathing was so shallow, I was surprised I didn't pass out. "Honey, all you have to say is you want to come to Montana like we arranged and nothing changes."

She laughed bitterly—a sound I've heard so often over the last year, but still haven't gotten used to. "What difference does that make to you, Mom? You're just going to move on with your life as if there's been no changes in ours."

"What? No, sweetheart. That's not true," I protested.

"Then tell me why we have to move away from everything we know," she demanded.

But just like all the other times she's asked since I kicked Mitch out, I held steadfast and refused to respond. Elise and her father have a special bond, and I refuse to be the one to shatter it. That might cause more damage to a child who's already feeling so much than I can help her through.

"Yeah, it's just like I thought. More secrets. Just like Dad said."

"No, Lise. It's not like that."

"Is it a guy?"

"What? No!" I exclaimed. "Honey, your father and I barely made things—"

"Save it, Mom. I'll be glad to stay here for a while longer. Does that make you happy?" Before I could answer that no, what would make me happy is having my daughter back, she ended the call.

I couldn't even pick up when I saw Rainey try to call me back.

As the sting of the shower mingles with the pricks forming behind my eyes, I realize as bad as last night was, it still wasn't the worst.

No, that was shortly after our family friend Jed Smith died. I had taken Rainey's kids home with me right after his funeral. Mitch came home from his overnight shift, dropped his gear bag on the laundry room floor, and gave me a kiss on my lips in that order. And then everything erupted.

After returning Rainey's kids to her house, that night we told the kids that Mitch and I would be separating, Elise hurled at me, "I wish you'd died instead of Uncle Jed," right before she ran out of the room. MJ didn't say a word, but he followed his sister.

Mitch opened his mouth, but I just held up a hand and hissed, "Go. Haven't you made enough of a mess of our lives?"

And without saying another word, he did.

I've been paying for his crimes ever since.

Stepping from the shower, I deliberately pull myself from the head-space I could so easily drown in. And I pause in the act of slipping on a pair of panties and a bra, because inadvertently I do owe my ex-husband a thank-you. If I were still living in Juneau, I'd be constantly hovered over by concerned family and friends wondering how I'm doing since the divorce. Both Mitch and I worked in jobs that put us in the public eye. Here, I'm simply Meadow Borneman, newly divorced single mom. My past is what I share of it, nothing more or less. Sure, there are going to be bad days, but I can get through them. The hard times are going to be what I make of them, no one else.

I can do this, I think fiercely. *The only thing that can hold me back are the limits I place on myself.* I quickly dry my hair and put on minimal makeup. Deciding the worksite still doesn't lend itself to a pair of heels, I slide into a pair of jeans, a silky top, and a pair of replacement riding boots I found online for a steal. Quickly, I slip on minimal jewelry. And that's when I see it.

The ring made of woven grass that Kody made me nearly seventeen years ago resting in the back of my jewelry box.

I don't pull it out like I used to do when I'd miss him in the early years of my marriage. Much like the ring, my relationship with him is way too fragile to be repaired if something happened to it. I gently touch it with the tip of my finger and whisper the same thing I do every time I spy it: "Please be happy."

Slamming the lid down on the memories of decisions past and present, I leave my bedroom and grab my jacket, wallet, keys, and tablet from the kitchen and focus on one thing—the restoration of Nature's Song.

I can't let anything else distract me from that.

Not right now.

I'M LEANING against the kitchen counter with my tablet, and I've tucked the estimates I've received behind it so I can scoop them up once the new contractor arrives. I sneer in disgust over some of the items. "Six thousand dollars to professionally clean the Oriental carpets? I rented a truck and I'll end up paying half the price. You're not making a fifty-percent markup on my client." Using the pen I tucked behind my dark hair, I scratch the item off. "And another seven thousand for removing the wall-to-wall carpet? Give me a few days, the dumpster outside, and a box cutter and I'll deal with it. After all, if I removed all that trash, the carpet will be nothing."

"Not if you cut it up into small enough slices, no. I guess Covington wasn't joking about the amount the two of you were being overcharged with your bids."

I shake my head in disbelief. No, it's not possible. I'm just imaging his voice since I was thinking about him earlier. I scratch off the item and say aloud, "New drywall in every single room? I don't know enough about construction to know if the smells from down here would permeate the drywall upstairs, but there are those stains...?" I make a quick note to do some research online.

"If you'd turn around and ask me, I might be able to answer that for you," Kody says calmly.

I whirl around, no longer able to blame my imagination for the sound of his voice.

And there he is. All six foot two of him leaning negligently against the front doorjamb in a blue chambray shirt with dark khaki pants that I take in with a single sweeping glance. With that quick perusal, I don't miss the tool belt around his waist or the tablet beneath his arm.

When he steps inside, I want to be able to ignore the quiver around my heart when he says, "It's been a long time, Meadow."

MEADOW

"What on earth are you doing here?" My heart aches at the mere sight of him, the same way it does every time it has since the night I told him Mitch and I were married.

When I stepped into my sister's house last summer after Jed passed away and found Kody sprawled on her sofa, an easy grin on his face, all I could think was *Leave. Fast.* Before I succumbed to the same despicable behavior my husband did and threw myself at a man despite the ring I was still wearing on my finger.

No one but Rainey knew then the emotional upheaval that was occurring at home as I tried to process the emotions swirling inside. Mitch didn't wound me with a onetime indiscretion that I might be able to forgive after clawing my way out of the hellish circle of pain. No, what Mitch did was life altering. And there I was, days after finding out, faced with the man who used to watch the Alaskan sun set over the trees with a look on his face that took my breath away. I was just short of rude to Kody, despite him losing one of his best friends. I went home and both laughed and cried because, damn him, he still managed amid his own grief to tease me enough to get that smile out of me.

Through Rainey, Maris, and Kara, I know his life turned out

exactly how he imagined it. His brilliant imagination and incredible hard work put Laurence Construction on the map as one of the premier luxury custom home builders in not just the Pacific Northwest, but across the United States. Swallowing hard, I try to tamp down the jealousy I have no right to feel, recalling the amused stories they shared about Kody's serial dating but "at the end they're all friends." Maris snickered.

"No kidding. Brad says it's the strangest phenomenon," Rainey laughed, oblivious to my grip on my wine stem, so hard I thought it would break.

His hand on my arm pulls me from a hundred flashbacks in an instant and instead sends chills racing down my spine. I deliberately take a step back, not missing the cool mask that drops down over his face. "I was with the guys when Rainey called Brad."

Kody turns his back to me as he inspects the damage. I begin to fret. Damn, how much does he know? I'm about to open my mouth to ask when his next words stop me cold. "What a fucking disgrace. I spent twenty hours laying that backsplash. Each tile was imported from Italy. Well, that's not important, now. We'll find new sources. Did Covington get ahold of the insurance adjuster?"

"Wait, what? What do you mean 'you'? What do you have to do with this house?"

"Meadow, don't you know?"

"Know what?"

Turning slightly, his hand drifts down until it encases mine lightly. He gives it a gentle squeeze before saying, "One of the first construction jobs I worked on after I left Alaska that final summer was being part of this house build."

I slap my free hand against his chest, hope returning in a flash so bright, I'm barely able to get out, "No way."

The smile that still sets my heart pounding after seventeen years blooms on his face. "Way. Now, let's do a walk-through of the damage to see what we can fix ourselves and what we're going to need my crew for." Pressing a friendly kiss to my forehead, he drops my hand and heads toward the stairs.

I don't move, too startled by the uncomplicated affection Kody's never demonstrated with me before, even when we were young and had nothing but sunsets and trees lying before us.

"Meadow?" His voice shakes me out of my trance. "Is something wrong?"

"No. Nothing. Let me just get the list I started." I turn around to grab my clipboard and take a few deep breaths. Of course, with the stench still in the house, I immediately start coughing.

I hear a muffled curse. "Is something the matter?" Kody asks as I face him. He has one foot propped on the bottom step.

"I'm fine. You? Everything okay?"

"Trust me, there's nothing that can't be fixed over time. Are you ready?"

Inhaling a breath, this time not as deep, I nod.

"Then after you." He gestures up the wide wooden staircase. "Thankfully the assholes didn't trash this. I remember it took Dale, our site foreman, four months to get these custom-made. Let's head upstairs."

"Yeah. Let's do that." My voice is strained as I pass by Kody. Only I doubt it's for the reason he thinks it is.

I just never imagined in my life there would be a time Kody Laurence would say those words to me in any context.

"JED WOULD BE DEVASTATED if he could see this."

"Why?" I ask. Kody and I are standing in front of a pair of shattered glass doors in one of the guest bedrooms that overlook Flathead Lake. The damage in my layman's eye seemed to be minimal in this room, but hearing the heartache in Kody's voice makes me concerned I missed something obvious.

"He loved this place from the moment he saw this view. We rented this place a few years back..."

"I remember, for one of your reunions. Rainey used to keep me up-to-date on how you were."

"Did she? Remind me to give her hell later for not doing the same." Confusing me with that cryptic remark, he confirms, "Yes. Thinking back, it was after Jed met Dean. Our trip here was a turning point in so many ways."

I want to ask how, but I gave up the right the minute I said yes to another man. Especially when I've realized even way back to that very night, I experienced the first twinge of doubt.

"Now look where we are." Carefully, I step over the broken glass to get a better view.

"Yes, look where we are, Meadow. Crazy we've come so far." He leans against the other side of the ruined pane.

You have, but I don't voice that. Instead, I ask, "I wonder what it was about this house that called to Jed."

"I don't know. He never said." Kody runs a hand carefully around the frame of the door, frowning.

"Do you think it was because it was a part of you and he wanted to absorb that feeling for when he wasn't with you?" My question obviously shocks him judging by the way he stills. Embarrassed, I step away from the breathtaking view and head back across the ruined carpet to the entrance. "Never mind. Let's just do as much as we can so we can figure out what all of this is going to cost."

As I'm about to cross into the hall, I hear my name called out. I pause without turning around. "Yes?"

"I'd give up almost anything to know the answer, to be able to talk with Jed one last time to ask him that." Measured steps bring Kody closer until I can practically feel the heat from his body wrap around me like a warm caress. "Maybe one day when the loss of him doesn't feel as jagged as the glass in those panes, I'll be able to figure it out."

"I'm so sorry." What else can I say?

"There are some days when..."

"When what?" I can't help myself from asking.

"When all I can remember is the past. All I can see is his crazy face bellowing at me to throw an axe before a crowd of hundreds. I remember days of laughter and nights of dreams." He faces the broken window once more, and the devastation on his face causes a pinch in the region of my heart. "Right now, I guess I'm still as shattered inside as that window."

"Um, axe throwing?" Then I bite my lip. Crap. Totally the wrong thing to focus on.

That's when I catch it—the small lip twitch. "I'm a world-champion axe thrower, Meadow. You don't have to worry about needing any kind of weapon so long as I have an axe in hand," he declares with enough arrogance to make me roll my eyes heavenward.

God save me from men who think they can do things better than women.

Feigning surprise, I arch my brows. "Oh please. Is that even a thing?"

"It totally is. I guarantee I could still kick some major ass if I were to compete in the World Axe Throwing League Championships."

Deciding work can wait, I bait him by walking out of the room and calling over my shoulder, "Sure you could."

The next thing you know, my elbow is caught in his strong fingers. "Why don't I show you outside? It appears you don't believe me, and I do have my tools in my truck. I know there's a couple of axes in there."

"Sure, why not?" I agree blandly.

"You don't seem impressed."

"Who? Me? I'm sure you're going to try to totally blow me away with your manly skills, Kody." What he's not aware of is Brad taught both me and Rainey how to throw an axe so many years ago it's second nature. I might not have thrown one during the Lumberjack Show in front of screaming crowds, but I'm our combined families' reigning champ anytime we went on a trip to Zipline Adventures.

As Kody goes to get the weapons of his destruction, I permit myself a smirk, remembering how much it used to irritate Mitch when I would kick his ass. I just hope Kody's a better loser.

KODY

W hat was I expecting after all this time? That Meadow would be so thrilled to see me, she would throw herself into my arms and profess her secret love after all these years? That after seeing me, we'd kiss passionately, strip naked, and have each other within minutes of my stepping inside Nature's Song on the gross-smelling carpet that really needs to be ripped out as soon as possible? That our reunion would be just like in one of the romance novels you can't pry out of my sister Amelia's hands long enough to make her see the world around her?

Okay, maybe I fantasized a bit about that happening on the long drive from Portland to Bigfork, but the Meadow who greeted me is the Meadow who I had to charm a smile out of when one of my best friends died. And although my heart still flares with happiness every time I catch a glimpse of her face, why is there suddenly such a burning resentment burning next to it?

Because Meadow never truly saw me the way I saw her, that's why.

Greta's words taunt me as I wonder if there's something of the girl in my memories. Or did the most important part of me die long before Jed and I never realized it until just now? No. I quickly disabuse that notion. That's just not possible. I would have known; wouldn't I?

Meadow and I make our way down the grand staircase and outside. "Hold up just a sec. I have a few hatchets in my car."

"Were you planning on getting in some practice, or..."

Unsure of my footing, I answer her seriously. "Sometimes we need them for demo work."

"Right. Got it." Turning away from me, I'm blessed with a glimpse her willowy figure from behind. Carefully, I let out a measured breath. *Get it under control before you do something stupid*, I tell myself.

After a quick trip to my truck for a couple of small hatchets, I guide Meadow over to a compact wall of logs. "Since you're so new at this, I'll go first to demonstrate."

She lets out a noncommittal hum. I hand her the smaller of the two axes, not wanting her to hurt herself.

Using the heel of my work boot, I drag it in the hard earth to mark the throw line. "It's fairly simple, Meadow. Just like darts, really," I encourage her, though there is so much more to it than that.

She negligently flips the axe over and over until she almost drops it. "So, you just kind of push it toward the wood?"

I wince, wondering how much time I'm going to have to spend grinding my axe blade back to its present sharpness. "Let me show you how it's done. Lower your axe while I approach."

After verifying she does what I ask, I jog toward the pile before hearing her cough into her hand. Her eyes are sparkling with unshed tears I can spot from twelve feet away. "Meadow, are you okay?" I call out.

She waves a hand. "Fine. Just got something in my eyes from being inside too long. I probably need something to get some fresh air, maybe get something to drink."

That sparks an idea. "How about the loser buys lunch?" I toss off the challenge casually, remembering the old Meadow was feisty enough to pick up any gauntlet her sister tossed down.

She drops her head down so I can't see her face, and I fear that's it. The end. That Mitch Borneman didn't just commit the sin of adultery but also killed the spirit of his wife, leaving the world—me—nothing but the husk of what was once there.

Then she flings her long dark hair back and curves her lips. "But what if I get lucky? After all, you don't have cheering crowds shouting, 'U-S-A,' Kody."

I arch a brow at her. "You know damn good and well I wasn't some attention whore."

"True. But you did admit it was way more fun when you beat Nick because he would get more annoyed by it."

I love the fact she remembers that. Almost as much as I love being able to put my hand on her shoulders to guide her next to me on the line for instruction. "First, you're only allowed to hold the handle in one of two ways."

"Why's that?"

"Because those are the rules."

"Well, who came up with them?"

Flabbergasted we're having this conversation instead of throwing axes at some wood, my grip fumbles.

Meadow smirks. "I thought you would have a better grip on your pole than that."

Reaching for my patience, I inform her loftily, "It's called a haft."

"Oh, I'm sorry. I didn't know you only had a half. I should be much more sympathetic to your personal problems."

"Not a half, a haft." I emphasize the *t* on the end.

"Why not just call it the handle?"

"Why don't you just prepare to throw the thing?" I suggest.

"We could prepare, or we could just do it. Why not just do it?"

"Because you need to know how to handle it the right way. And while I prefer one hand, since you're new, you might want to try the two-handed method for some power to make sure you reach the target."

She tips her head to the side. "If I remember, and it's been a while, aren't men inclined to use one hand anyway?"

"Oh, God." I can barely talk because every word between us causes the shaft below my waist to get harder than the one I'm holding. And to think a few moments ago, I was afraid the Meadow I've dreamed about wasn't inside? No, she's right there just ready to break free. I grin lazily.

She visibly swallows, giving me all sorts of ideas. "So, what's the difference."

"Excuse me?" I've totally forgotten what we're doing as all the blood in my body's drained south.

"What's the difference in throwing style, oh wise one."

Right, axe throwing. "None. Except strength and experience."

"Then why don't you go first and show me how it's supposed to be done."

"All right. Step back," I warn her. She immediately complies while I get into place. "Do you see the log with the really white center?"

"Yes. Is that our bull's-eye?"

"That's what I'm trying for." I just hope Meadow's throw makes it to the log pile so it doesn't put her off from some good-natured fun.

"I'm sure you'll do great, Kody." I can't stop the way my insides warm over her praise. I keep instructing her as I get into position. "Hand holding the axe with the blade facing the target before release. And launch!" I hurl the axe toward the large white log.

My mind is on the woman standing next to me, not where the axe lands. The guys would likely howl with laughter at how far off center it really is. I can practically hear Jed taunting the amphitheater in Ketchikan if I threw like that when I was a Lumberjack as he handed the flag over to Team Canada, but nonetheless, Meadow applauds. To hell with it. I take a victory lap which triggers my favorite sound in the world. Her laughter.

Then I almost trip on my way back to her when she announces, "Okay. My turn. Get behind the line."

Scrambling, I do. I fear very little due to the nature of my work. I've seen it all from rodents to insects to blood, but an untried woman with an axe? Frankly, I'm terrified. But I'm alarmed when Meadow lines up with one arm out in front of her, the other raised over her head. "Ready to launch," she calls out.

I step back. Way back.

Seconds later, I have to pick up my jaw off the ground when she not only releases the axe beautifully, but she lands the axe in what appears to be... "Did you just get a kill shot?" I ask indignantly.

"Maybe. You'll have to measure the distance to see. I'm certain you have a tape measure handy." Her voice is brimming with laughter.

Storming over to where she neatly drove her axe beautifully between where my axe hit and the center growth rings serving as center. My shot is completely outclassed by a slip of a woman, and to be honest? I couldn't be happier.

My laughter rings out, echoing off the lake. "Where did you learn to throw like that?"

Meadow's smile eclipses the sun above us as she saunters toward me. For a moment, it's like the wheels of time are careening crazily. We're in the past, we're in the present. We could have a future. And without a doubt, I know why I'm standing here with a ridiculous smile spreading across my face.

Because much like the imposing home behind her, Meadow is everything I dreamed a home could be: strength, laughter, and most importantly, brimming with love.

Life may have changed us both, but together we can mend. Just like Nature's Song.

"Well, now that you've kicked my ass at axe throwing, how about we finish the walk-through? Then I'll take you to lunch?"

Her smile holds a note of gratitude that I hope disappears soon. I'm not doing this because of the damn house.

I'm here because of her.

"WHAT DOES milady care to dine on?" I bow at the waist as Meadow approaches from her vehicle where she grabbed her purse.

She shakes her head in silent laughter. "There's a diner a few miles up the road Russell mentioned was good."

"Your boss?"

"Yes. He mentioned in my welcome packet that he and his wife go there for breakfast at least once a week. Apparently, I have to try the huckleberry pancakes, but with everything that's been going on, I haven't had the chance. Oh, that reminds me." I stop as Meadow pulls her phone from her pocket. She scans her messages. "Russell pinged me while I was kicking your ass at axe throwing."

I press my hand against my chest. "Rub it in, why don't you."

"Just be glad I didn't take any pictures," she retorts.

"Fair point. What did he want?"

"Just an update on how things were. Any idea on when we'll be able to get an estimate?"

"What time are you meeting with him?"

"Around three."

I won't have any drawings ready, but I can meet that timeline. I think back to the estimate Greta and I built together and realize I can easily scratch about a third off based on the condition of the house. Maybe more if... My mind starts whirling. Abruptly, I ask, "Do you want to take one vehicle there? We can swing by here and grab yours before you need to meet with your boss."

"Sure. That works for me." She reaches for the door handle.

Then I remember. Crap. "Wait. Maybe, we should ride in your—" Just as she opens my passenger door and debris from my eight-hour road trip tumbles out. I can feel my cheeks warming. "I meant to clean that out."

Meadow bites her lip, but her shoulders start to shake.

"Give me just a second." Quickly, I move forward and grab an already full bag of Coke bottles and try to jam candy and beef jerky wrappers alongside.

"Here. Take these. I mean, what if you get lost and need an emergency bite to eat."

Oh crap. I was so anxious to get here to bail her ass out I forgot my truck looks like the inside of a trash can. I face her to find Meadow holding out two Slim Jims and a packet of M&Ms toward me. Her eyes are sparkling beneath the cloudless blue sky. And in my head, I can hear her voice softly saying, "Here, Kody, we were at the convenience store. Even though you didn't ask, I know how grumpy you are when you're hungry."

"Just had these on hand?" I ask, stunned, because somewhere inside her soul, she had a part of me with her—the same way I always had her with me.

"Are you kidding? I have boxes of them at home. They're some of my favorites." Then to my delight, Meadow flushes. "Why don't you hand me that trash, and I'll toss it out?"

Scooping up the last bit, I scoot back so she practically has to squeeze between me and the truck to get by. "Why don't you get in and I'll toss this in the dumpster. I'm certain it can handle a few more things."

"Smart aleck," she says primly, right before she reaches over and pulls the door closed.

Suddenly ravenous, I trot over, dump the trash, and race back to the truck to take Meadow out to eat.

MEADOW

"So, do I get a discount for kicking your ass?" I ask as I pop a fry in my mouth, moaning as I chew the bite of crispy saltiness I feel no compunction in wolfing down with vigor. "You have to try this huckle-berry ketchup. So good." I shove the plate across the table at a bemused Kody.

"I'm not sure I trust you anymore since you totally sandbagged me. So, Brad taught you to throw like that?"

"He said it was an imperative life skill. I think he just wanted to show off his skills to Rainey. He never expected me to take to it the way I did."

Kody chuckles. "How many times have you clobbered him?"

"This year alone? Oh, quite a few. It's great therapy." I swirl another fry in ketchup before chomping down on it.

Kody guffaws. "I'd have paid good money to have seen it."

"I'm sure there's video somewhere. But knowing you, you'll share it with the guys."

"Of course I will. That's what we do."

I smile before snagging another fry and biting into it.

"It's good to see you eating," he remarks before snatching one off my plate, dipping it, and popping into his mouth. "You're right. This is incredible. Want me to bring them to work every day?" he asks like it's a done deal we'll be working together.

"I eat," I protest, but it's weak at best.

"Meadow, the last time I saw you, you looked like..."

"What?" I challenge him, shoving another fry into my mouth before I snap at the man who's about to rearrange his life's schedule to help me out of a massive problem.

"You. When we saw each other last, you were a walking memory coming through Brad and Rainey's door." Even as I try to calm my heart which has problems processing his words, he continues. "So don't sit there and tell me your clothes are now hanging off you because you're starting a new fashion trend."

I turn my head to study the mountain landscape in the distance. "For now, can we just leave it as divorce isn't the easiest road I've traveled so far?" When I face him, Kody's jaw is clenched. Without thinking, I do something I've done a million times before and haven't done in years; I touch him.

My fingers slide across the table and brush his fisted ones lightly. "I'll be okay," I whisper.

"Did he hit you? Physically harm you or the kids?"

I blink rapidly before my heart softens. "No. There are different ways you can be hurt, Kody, but I swear, the sledgehammer we found next to the granite would have been used on him if he had physically touched any of us."

What's frightening to me is feeling the weightlessness as I put the miles of Juneau behind me. I haven't acknowledged until now the emotional weight I've been carrying until I could breathe again. And, my stomach settles a bit knowing as bad as things are now, they'll get better. Mitch has left such toxicity in all of us—especially Elise and MJ —that as sure as I know my own name, I know that we will heal once we have time. I'm ready to be a family once again, and I don't give a damn what tests my kids need to put me through to reach the other side. I'll take their silence and sharp words just as long as in the end, I have my children.

Kody's hand turns and captures mine with a quickness that startles me. Chills shoot up my arm at the feel of his calloused fingers against my skin. My nipples begin to tingle, and I want to curse because despite the untried feelings I recognized I had for him all those years ago, this shouldn't be happening. I treasure his happiness too much to ruin it. His face gives nothing away.

Sliding my hand away, I wrap my arms around myself. "Please, Kody. I know the friendship between us has been strained at best..."

"Why do you think that is?" he grates out.

"I always assumed you just moved on with your life." I falter.

"We'll add that to our list to tackle later as well."

That sends equal amounts of excitement and anxiety surging through me. I clear my throat. "We're making a list? Of things to talk about?"

He shrugs nonchalantly, picking up his coffee. "We'll have plenty of time."

"As I was saying... Wait, what do you mean?"

"You're looking at about eight weeks if I bring a full crew out, Meadow." My heart lurches in my chest as Kody drops a price.

"There's no way. I have just shy of half a million to cover that. And you were saying things about importing tile from Italy," I wheeze. Fortunately, I only had to refund one reservation since we're not into high season yet.

"Which is why I'm about to recommend we bring the crew in for the big-ticket construction, and then I stick around with a smaller team to help finish the job, closer to eleven weeks. You'll also pitch in."

"You? You have a company to run. And what makes you think I know how to do home repair that extends beyond putting a nail in a wall to hang a picture?" I do know some stuff beyond the basics, but what is he thinking?

Kody clutches his hands against his heart before gasping, "What? No picture hangers? You're slaying me Meadow."

Without thinking, I pick up a fry and throw it at him, nailing him square on his forehead. "I'm not a perfectionist in my home, Kody. There's no need to string up wire behind a school photo."

"There's also something called alligator clips, and they're intended to provide stability. You could have used those," he counters.

"Why are we discussing this anyway? Cleanup, I'm a champ. Even breaking down boxes, I'm good. Tell me what you want from me, and then let's see whether or not it's feasible."

But Kody isn't done. "Why didn't Mitch…"

I give Kody a look that has enough heat to set fire to the restaurant and get my wallet out of my bag. "I don't want to get into this." As I yank out some cash, I knock my elbow into my ice water, not spilling it completely but sloshing it over the sides. It drowns the remainder of my delicious fries. "I guess the conversation made sure I wasn't really hungry anyway," I try to joke as I rein in my emotions.

"Meadow." Just my name, but regret and the one thing I don't want from Kody lace his voice.

Pity.

"Mitch wasn't around, Kody. And my family helped when it came to the big things. Things that mattered like watching Elise and MJ so I could work. Yes, I was taught how to install a new toilet and lay some tile, which allowed me to redo the bathroom when Mitch was working. That money saved allowed me to go back to school. If I wanted a damn picture hung quickly, it didn't matter to me if it had a clip. What mattered was whether the picture was up. I can never repay—"

"Family doesn't expect repayment. They don't keep an accounting."

Wearily, I reply, "I know. But don't you understand? I was supposed to have someone by my side."

"And what did you have?"

Shoving myself out of the booth, I grab my bag. "Two amazing children who made my marriage worth it for as long as it lasted. Now, if you're ready, I'd like to run by the office to go over these numbers with Russell if you have an actual printed estimate and contract. Then we can get everything settled. I'm willing to do whatever I can on-site— except screw up anything at Nature's Song."

He merely stares me down until I'm fiddling with the strap on my bag. Getting to his feet, Kody's body doesn't intimidate me. No, the muscles encased in his chambray work shirt invite me to lay my head down and lean on him. I struggle against the urge because I know what a good guy Kody is. He'd let me lean on him, but that's not my right.

Sliding a pair of sunglasses on over my eyes, I make my way outside. I want to laugh at the irony of the blazing sun shining down on me while inside I'm struggling with who I am amid the tumultuous storm swirling the darkness up inside me.

Kody doesn't say a word until we get to his truck. Unlocking the doors, he helps me into the cab, but before I can close the door, he places his hand on the jamb. "We're going to be working together, Meadow. That's going to require us building a level of trust we haven't had before or someone's going to get hurt." With that, he steps back.

My response is to yank the door shut. I want to turn the clock back in order to make him understand it isn't him I don't trust. It's myself. I'm broken in the prime of my life, and the last thing I want to do is to drag him down with me.

As he walks around the back of the truck, I regulate my breathing. When he opens his door, I immediately tell him, "I'm not worried about trusting you on the jobsite."

"Then what are you worried about?" he challenges me.

"Oh, Kody." I shake my head. "If you knew the answer to that, you'd never bid on the work."

He scowls.

"For now, let's just get everything settled. Add it to your list of things to ask me about later," I suggest.

And for some crazy reason, that restores the good humor to his face. "Don't think I'm going to let you out of answering that." He starts up the truck.

I turn my head to stare out the window as we head back in the direction of Bigfork. Great, another thing to worry about—Kody Laurence figuring out my feelings.

MEADOW

"Fortunately, I know more about the way the house was originally built than any of the previous contractors who bid for the work," Kody informs us.

Russell and I are looking at the detailed bid Kody emailed to us a few moments ago which I printed out in triplicate. I'm in shock over the difference. "The floors?" I stammer. "Everyone else said…"

"That they couldn't be saved?" There's a sneer playing on his lips. "I just bet they did. Those floors are custom-made. That's why they wanted to rip them out. They don't know how to replicate the pieces to match. When the team originally laid them, the original homeowner wanted the house to feel like a log cabin. We ran them through an on-site portable sawmill to hand craft the lumber. As unfortunate as it is that you lost a few due to rot, it shouldn't be a problem for Lenny, my woodworker, to replicate them before we do an overall sanding and restain them." He frowns. "The only problem is going to be a color issue. I'd like to make sure the new owner is comfortable with the choices."

I begin to feel a thrum of excitement pulse through my veins. "And what about the kitchen?" I point to the largest-ticket item on the list.

Kody places his forearms on the table, stretching his shirt across impossibly broad shoulders. He taps his thick fingers and pulls up something on his tablet before turning it around to face me and Russell. "This is a kitchen I just finished on a recent build. The one in Nature's Song based on the pictures online was outdated. This is a perfect opportunity to modernize the kitchen with an upgrade while we're here. I could replace what you have for about half the price, but why go through the expense and not do it right when it's ruined anyway?"

That makes sense to me, but I still glance at Russell to get his reaction. "Why is there such a discrepancy in final totals?" Russell taps the two final totals.

"I explained to Meadow over lunch the higher number is if I keep a full crew here. I have to account for a stipend, hotels, and their salaries. If I send the majority of them home as I no longer need them to complete work, electing to finish the punch work myself with her assistance, then I can lower the price," Kody explains.

"What can Meadow do?" Russell asks.

Kody barks out a laugh. "Well, as long as she doesn't plan on taking a box cutter to the final product..."

I flush hotly. "That was to get rid of the existing carpet, Kody Laurence. And you know it."

He flashes a wicked grin my way before explaining. "Inevitably there's small projects like reattaching switch plates, touch up paint, attaching knobs to cabinets, and a massive cleaning. It's always things like that which are necessary at crunch time that can slip a schedule. These are just a few of the final items on our final punch list before we turn the house over to the homeowner."

"That makes sense. Meadow's already shown a willingness to pitch in," Russell agrees.

"So I heard when I learned about the job." Kody's voice remains calm, but when his eyes meet mine, there's something burning in their depths I'm not ready to explore. Dropping my eyes to the papers in front of me, I try to calm my racing heart.

Standing, Russell holds out a hand. "Let me go make a quick call. If you don't mind waiting with Meadow, Mr. Laurence?"

"Make it Kody, and no, I don't."

Russell smiles before leaving us alone in the small conference room. The minute the door closes, I turn on Kody like a whirling dervish. "Who told you about the work?"

"Brad and Jennings." I open my mouth, but before I can speak, he continues. "And before you say a single word, they didn't mean to. We were harassing my sister for going to prom with one of Nick's fighters when Brad got the call from Rainey."

"Oh." His words deflate any kind of argument I could make when suddenly I grin. "And big brother Kody couldn't let his baby sister go to prom without harassing her date?"

"Something like that," he grunts.

"How bad did the Jacks make it?" Now I'm enjoying myself as a flush begins to ride his cheekbones.

"There's only two people in the world I know who refer to us as that."

"Kara and Maris. They shared during our FaceTime and wine session we have each month."

Kody stills. "You talk to the girls—"

"Women," I interject.

"Women," he quickly agrees. "Every month?"

"No." He seems to deflate in relief. "Actually, it seems to be like every other week."

"What? How did I not know about this?" he roars just as Russell comes back into the office.

"Is there a problem?" my boss asks tentatively.

"Not at all. Mr. Laurence is just perturbed he didn't know I was the one who cleaned out Nature's Song," I smoothly lie.

I chose the wrong thing to smooth over Kody's bearlike attitude though. If anything, that seems to set him off more. "Add that one to our list, Meadow," he says menacingly.

I roll my eyes.

"Well, I'm pleased to see you both are getting your working relationship under control. Kody, I spoke with our client, Mr. Wilde. We have authorization for you to use the lesser budget plus for you to redo the kitchen. However, that will be paid for directly by him. In the event of any contingencies, he'd like to be prepared with the additional budget from the insurance settlement, and we'll have some additional cash flow by handling it this way."

"Smart man," Kody immediately agrees.

"Excellent. Then, I just need to fax the bid to Mr. Wilde. He prefers to use his own paper for contracts." Russell is apologetic. "That will take a day or so to prepare."

"That's not a problem at all. I need to look at securing housing for my crew, so I'll be around." He reaches into his pocket, pulls out a worn leather card carrier, and flips it open, then hands us each a business card. "My cell is on there as well."

"Who's your carrier?" I blurt out. When Kody names it, I shake my head. "You're going to need a cell while you're here."

"Why do you ask?" He frowns.

I shrug and look at Russell for the explanation. He smiles fondly. "Meadow isn't wrong. With the mountains, our coverage is spotty on all but two carriers."

Ruefully, Kody pulls his phone off his hip. "Well, damn. Here I was hoping it was just a peaceful day since I haven't received any hysterical calls from Greta."

"Your sister?" I burst out with. Kody's head snaps in my direction. "Umm, no one mentioned the two of you worked together."

He nods, even as his lips curve. "For about seven years. She's the best project manager I've ever had."

"That's terrific." And I mean it. Kody's as close to his family as I am to mine.

Russell clears his throat. I get a hold of myself. Right. We're here for Nature's Song. "Why don't you take tomorrow to get your affairs settled, Mr. Laurence. Then we'll all meet back here Wednesday around nine?"

Kody holds out his hand for Russell to shake. "I look forward to it. We won't let you down."

Is it wrong I'm disappointed when he doesn't do the same with me? Instead I plaster I smile on my face before I start to follow Russell out of the office.

After a quick conversation with Russell where he effusively praises me for finding a contractor of Kody's caliber, I'm standing by my SUV.

I've just unlocked the vehicle when I hear my name being called. My head whirls around, and Kody is coming at me at a fast jog. "You left," he accuses.

"Well, yes. The meeting was over." And right now, I want to go home and dissect it with a glass of wine.

"Good. Then I can finally do this." The next thing I know, Kody's strong arms are around my waist, lifting my feet off the ground. I wrap mine around his neck to keep my balance.

My purse falls haplessly to the ground. Then, because it feels so natural, so right, I lay my cheek against his shoulder. "Thank you, Kody."

"No, Meadow. Thank you for trusting me enough to let me in. And I think congratulations are more in order since we're going to be partners."

I don't know how long we stand there just like that before Kody lowers me down the front of his body, scalding every nerve ending of mine along the way. When my feet touch the ground, he removes one arm from behind me to run a finger down the line of my nose. Without another word, he turns and walks away.

Gathering my wits about me, I yell to his retreating back, "I'm signing your checks. Technically, I'm your boss."

Just as he's about to slide in the cab, he calls out, "Whatever, Meadow. Let's see who rides herd on who by the time this is done."

I'm frozen the entire time he gets into his truck and pulls out of the parking lot, but there's one rampant thought going through my mind.

Forget the glass. Tonight, I might need the whole damn bottle.

Kody Laurence is back in my life for the foreseeable future. And it's not only my heart that's pounding at the thought.

MEADOW

I call my sister the minute I walk into the front door. Before she can say a word, the words "Oh, my God" tumble from my lips.

"Is everything okay? What's wrong?" Rainey's concern is immediate.

I hear MJ in the background, and it makes my heart ache so much. I drop my head to the counter to counteract the pain of hearing my son giggling with his cousin when I apparently give my children nothing but pain. "Yes. No. Hell, I don't know." Getting a hold of myself, I sum up everything. "Kody's here. His company is going to help restore the cabin."

"That's wonderful news!"

"Of course you'd see it that way," I grumble beneath the mass of my hair. "You sent him here."

"No, all I did was call Brad and tell him what was going on. He's the one who flipped the cards and showed your hand."

"Remind me to thank him right before I—"

"Why are you upset?" Rainey interrupts me. "Someone you know—who isn't going to mess up or screw you over—is going to be right by your side."

How am I supposed to handle dealing with the man who never let a piece of my heart go every single day for the next eleven weeks without losing what's left of my sanity? Is there a way to put words to what I've held so close to my heart all these years? Deciding, no, there isn't, I reply dully, "You're right."

"What just happened?" Rainey wonders aloud.

"Nothing. I just realized you're right. I...I'll handle with everything else."

"What everything else?" Suspicion enters Rainey's voice.

"Don't worry about it. Are Elise or MJ up to talking?" Pushing myself to my elbows, I shove the dark hair I inherited from our mother off my forehead. "I'd like to hear how their days were."

There's a pregnant pause before Rainey's footsteps are heard. "Give me a second to get somewhere more private."

"What happened?" I hear the sliding door that leads to Rainey's backyard open and close. "Damnit, Rainey, tell me."

"Well, you know how one of Elise's friend's fathers was on the force with Mitch?"

"That boy she liked, Dennis," I confirm.

"Right. Well, apparently, she worked up the nerve to ask him to the end-of-year dance today. And he wasn't kind about how he said no."

"What did he say?" I brace for the answer.

"She was crying when she told me, but—"

"I hope she told him to go to hell," I interrupt.

"She did, before she called me to ask me to pick her up from school." I suck in a deep breath. Elise loves school; it's been one of the biggest bones of contentions about having to move. The whole process of trying to find new friends and fit in for a thirteen-year-old is daunting at best.

"What did he say?" I get out. Somehow, some way, I know this is about Mitch.

Rainey hesitates just slightly before she repeats, "What if you ask me now and decide you don't want to go with me later? Kind of the way your dad decided he didn't want your mom?"

"Goddamnit!" I roar. Fisting my hair with one hand, I debate the wisdom of outright killing my ex-husband for the ongoing agony he's put our family through because he couldn't man up enough to discuss the fact that maybe our marriage wasn't working before he sank his dick into another woman. "What did Elise do?"

"She's your daughter through and through, Meadow. From what she shared, she tossed her hair and said, 'Or maybe you just can't make up your mind. From what I know, little boys want to hog all the toys.' Then she walked away. It wasn't until I had her in the car that she broke down and asked me if it was true."

"I'd swear on a stack of bibles, I'm over the anger of what he did to our marriage, what he did to me; I swear I am. But right now? What his actions keep putting our kids through? I'd cheerfully sink a knife into Mitch's chest."

"You're going to have to tell her what really happened, Meadow," Rainey lectures me.

"I was trying to protect his image. She worships him," I remind her.

"I think the glow has faded a bit after today. What are the chances of you being able to fly back home and talk to Elise and MJ before the move?"

"Right now? I have no idea." Quickly I catch her up on what's happening. "But if it means their mental health and well-being, I'll quit the job."

"I don't think it will have to go that far," a familiar voice says behind me. Whirling around in fear, I find Kody lounging in my door-way. His face is completely blank, but I remember where to look to figure out his moods. His sea-colored eyes are almost jade with fury.

"How did you get in?" I whisper, forgetting Rainey can hear every-thing I'm saying.

"Covington gave me my own code into the gate. I thought I'd see if you were up to a quick walk-through. Your door was open."

"So, you eavesdropped?" I yell.

He shrugs. Rainey's squawking in my ear. "Hold on a second," I tell her.

"Is that Rainey?" Kody asks.

I nod, expecting him to pass along a message to Brad. When he steps forward and plucks the phone from my hand, I stutter, "What... what on earth..."

Kody presses a hard finger against my mouth. "Hey, Rainey. Yeah."
My fury mounts as he chats with my sister for a few seconds about the
shenanigans over the last weekend. "Listen, I don't care, I'll find some
way for the schedule to work to make a trip up to Juneau. After all, it's
not like I can't cash in one of a million favors Jennings owes me.
Right?" Another pause. "Do you want Meadow back? Okay, I'll let her
know. Talk soon. Bye."

Pulling the phone away from his ear, Kody pulls his finger away
from my mouth—which is a good thing because he was about to lose it
from my biting it off—and hands me my phone. "Rainey said she'll talk
to you later. Elise was coming to look for her."

My fury over what happened to my baby girl due to my ex-husband
and now Kody's high-handedness has a lethal edge sliding into my
voice. "If you ever contemplate pulling that crap again, Kody, I swear
to God, I'll..."

And between one blink and another, it's like someone took a drop
of blue and diluted the green back to the turbulent sea color of his
eyes. "What will you do, Meadow?"

"Well, let's just say you'll end up with one less finger for sure."

He tosses back his leonine head and laughs.

"It's not funny," I snap, stomping my foot.

"You don't have the taste for blood, Meadow."

"I'm quickly developing it," I growl, thinking about the devastating
blow my daughter was handed today. "If only I was there..."

"What would you do differently?" Kody asks me quietly.

"I'd have been their mom! Every minute I'm away from Elise and
MJ, they're happy to stay up there. Away from me." As much as I try to
suppress it, a lone tear falls down my cheek. I turn my head to the side
in case any more fall.

"You can't fix everything, Meadow. Some hurts have to be experienced to make the gifts that much more appreciated." I wait for him
to go on, but when he doesn't, I glance back up. Kody's eyes are tracing
every inch of my face as if he's trying to memorize it. With a start, I
remember he used to do that years ago. *How did I never notice?* I think
wildly.

Stepping back, I offer a wan smile. "I appreciate your support,

Kody. And you're right. Tonight would have been a perfect night to go through the house again. But I think I'm pretty done in. I think I'm just going to figure out something to eat and crawl into bed."

Not even a flicker of disappointment flashes across his face. "I understand. But there is one thing?"

"What's that?" I turn to face the counter to grab the pen and notepad I laid there for my grocery lists. My heart stops beating when I feel his strong arms wrap around me from behind. He squeezes, the gentle hug almost doing me in. "Kody." My voice breaks.

"I've wanted to do that since I saw you last year at the funeral. I've missed you, Meadow." His voice whispers against my ear.

I can't formulate thoughts, let alone words, until his warm body moves back from mine. I finally get my head together enough to tell him how much I missed him in my life too, but by the time I do, I hear the snick of the door.

He's gone.

But at least I know I'll get to see him again for a short while.

And I already know what it's like to live on the memories of that.

AFTER A GOOD NIGHT'S SLEEP, I woke up early and worked up a possible project plan I want to run by Kody after he gets his arrangements for his crew under control. But that can wait; right now, I have a phone call to make.

I dial and wait for the call to connect. He should pick up even though we're an hour ahead here in Montana.

He does with a yawn. "Meadow, do you know what time it is here?"

"Well, Mitch, I would assume eight?" My voice is like the ice in the deepest crevices of the Mendenhall Glacier. "Didn't you say you were in training?"

"Uh, yeah. We kinda had a late night."

"I don't give a shit. Do whatever you have to do to wake up," I snap.

"Whoa, Meadow. What's wrong? Is it the kids?" Suddenly Mitch is Daddy Dearest. I really wish the phone company had come through with the reach-out-and-touch-someone option. I would love to choke my ex right about now.

"You could say that." I give him a rundown of the ridicule Elise suffered at school yesterday. "Have any bright ideas how to help?" I ask.

"I could talk with the guys," he offers.

"It's too damn late for that. This has already made its way around the middle school, Mitch. What's next? The boys won't let MJ play on a team because they accuse him of cheating?" The sharply indrawn breath shows my aim struck true. "You're finally getting the picture now, aren't you? Our *children* are now suffering because of your actions. I've sheltered them as much as possible from this, and look. Now what, Mitch? What do we, as their parents, do to help?" I keep my silence as I wait for his response.

And my temper flares when he says, "I don't know."

"Well, what do you know other than how to throw me under the bus to our daughter?" I bite out.

"I don't know what you mean."

"Oh? Are you calling Elise a liar?"

"Well, no. Of course not."

"Then tell me why I've been accused of keeping secrets, when the only secrets I'm keeping are the reasons we divorced. Can you explain that, Mitch?" My voice drips acid.

"Elise must have been confused."

"Really?" I drawl.

"You know how the minds of teenage girls work…" And that's when I hear in the background, "Honey, do you want to get coffee at Wake Up this morning?"

There's dead silence on the line. Then Mitch begins talking. "Meadow, I just flew in last night. I swear, I was going to see—"

"Don't," I hiss at him. "Don't you *dare* try to lie to me. I couldn't care less if you flew in to see your girlfriend. The two of you exist for me only because *you* are the father to *my* children. *She* doesn't exist after what happened in our home. But how could you sit there and listen to what I'm telling you and the first words out of your mouth weren't 'I'll go see them'? Are you trying to demonstrate you're just as much a failure of a father as you were a husband? For once, be honest. Can you do that?"

"Yes," he bites out.

"Did you really have training scheduled for your new job?" I impatiently wait for his answer.

A significant pause before, "Yes, I do." I relax slightly before he admits, "It begins in five weeks."

I want to rail at him for not seeing Elise and MJ, but what good will it do? "If our children see you in Juneau, you had better not tell a lie to them, or I will tell them everything, Mitch. I swear to God."

"Threats, Meadow?" Then he has the gall to laugh.

"No, promises. And your child support better be in my account on the first of the month, or I am threatening I'll file a complaint in court against you that will make it to your employer." With him sputtering, I press End to disconnect the call.

I'm breathing heavily, so it's not a surprise I don't hear the slow, steady clapping until it's practically on top of me. Whirling around, I find Kody approaching me, pride stamped across his face.

I open my mouth, to say what, I have no idea. But before a word can get out, Kody cuts me off at the knees. "I fell for you seventeen years ago, Meadow Borneman. I thought I knew everything there was to know about you. I'm fucking thrilled to realize I'm wrong."

Leaving me stunned, unable to move, Kody moves past me to the door of the main house. "Are you coming?" he calls out behind him.

My heart still pounding, I face Kody. My insides quiver at the almost tactile contact from just his eyes raking over me. "I'm ready," I acknowledge. "By the way, what are you doing here?"

He reaches into his pocket and pulls out a box cutter. "Did you really think I was going to leave you to do this all on your own?"

"But how did you know..." My voice trails off as I come abreast of him and he hasn't moved an inch.

"Because I know you. Think on that. And if you have any questions, well, add them to our list." Flashing me a slow grin, he pushes open the massive door and gestures for me to walk in ahead of him.

That smile, right there? That and the fact he's here has me ready to melt right where I'm standing. "Damn you, Kody Laurence," I call over my shoulder as I sail past him into Nature's Song.

"You've said worse," he calls back. "I believe I spilled an entire beer down your new shirt."

I burst out laughing. "God, you're right. Do you remember me running after you with the hose?"

And for the rest of the day while we rip up smelly wall-to-wall carpeting, Kody and I reminisce about many of the fun times we spent in Juneau.

We call it a day early so he can get to the phone store and I can call Elise and MJ. Much to my surprise, MJ gets on FaceTime to show me his new art project.

Elise, of course, won't have anything to do with me.

Right now, I'll take anything I can get.

MEADOW

A few days later, the Laurence Construction crew is in full force. I've been relegated to cleanup duty in the upstairs bedrooms while Kody and his team begin to tackle the heavier demolition downstairs. I wince each and every time I hear wallboard being ripped away. There have been loud bursts of cursing followed by equally jovial amounts of laughter. And threaded through it all, I catch the timbre of Kody's voice calling out orders.

He was born to do this. I smile to myself as I use another specialty cleaning solution and a heavy-duty sponge to remove a substance I'm loath to name from the master bedroom wall. "Sounds like they're having a ball," I proclaim as I scrub furiously at a brown stain with an almost dissolved sponge.

"We are." I almost fall into a bucket of disgusting water when Kody's voice startles me from the door. Regaining my balance, I remain crouched but whirl to face him. "This room looks amazing, completely different than the last time I was in here."

"Thanks. I haven't made it to the bath yet."

"Don't worry. You're on schedule."

"It's my schedule!" I exclaim, ready to pelt him with what remains of the grimy sponge in my hand. I toss it up and catch it several times, debating.

Kody chuckles. "If the rest of the rooms up here come out like this one, I think we'll be able to save the drywall after all."

"Really?" I forget my ire in my excitement. Drywall saved means we'll be able to shave off more time on the schedule. And I'm certain I'll be able to fit a trip back to Juneau to see if I can convince Elise and MJ to dump the attitude they seem to associate with me and with their life in general these days. There's a lot to be said for new starts. I want the chance to show them how much this one has meant.

"Yeah." With a critical eye, he remarks, "Let the fans dry what you've done. We'll inspect it after lunch, but I don't think I'm wrong. In the meanwhile, I actually came up for a reason."

Pushing myself to my feet, I gratefully drop the sponge in the bucket to dispose of the contents later. "Oh?"

Crossing the room, he holds out one of his gloved hands. "Come on. You don't want to miss this."

I attribute the fact the hand I place in his is shaking surely because it's been cramped around a 3x2 inch sponge for hours. Using my other arm, I wipe the sweat from my brow. "What's up?"

With a mysterious smile on his lips, Kody drags me out of the room. Immediately, I'm struck by how much noise the bedroom shielded me from. "How do you not lose your hearing? It's a bit loud."

Kody plucks a plastic case filled with foam from his pocket. Pulling off a glove, he grabs one of the buds and twists it to a narrow point before sliding it into his ear. "This will help. Doesn't interfere with the hard hats."

I quickly follow suit and flick him a quick smile when the over-whelming sound dims to a dull roar. "Can you hear me?" I shout.

Speaking in a normal tone, he tells me, "I think they heard you in the next county."

"Oops. Sorry about that," I reply sheepishly.

He opens his mouth to say something but closes it just as quickly. Instead one side of his lips quirk just a bit. I remember that look—it's his "you're adorable" look.

I blush and mutter, "No, I'm not," which is how I used to reply all those years ago.

Shocked, he freezes. For a moment, there's nothing and no one here. Instead of sunlight streaming in the window, we're lying on the land warmed from the sun that's been in the air for twenty hours straight. Then a particularly vociferous curse brings us both out of the past and brings us to the here and now.

Quickly, he puts the case holding the ear protection away and slides his work glove back on. I follow suit just in time to hear him say, "Ready?"

"For what?" We make our way down the stairs that have been protected with cardboard and brown sheeting. Over by the fireplace, there's a small group of guys hovering around the built-in bookshelves.

"God, is it just me or does it feel like the smell's almost completely gone?" I'm practically bouncing in excitement.

"We hauled out all the ruined appliances and cabinets which put a huge dent in removing the remaining stench." Kody's amusement is transparent, but I don't care. This is enormous in comparison to what I was facing a few weeks ago.

"So I see." I'm in awe of what Kody and his crew have accomplished in the short time I've been trying to salvage the drywall upstairs. Then I frown. Pointing, I ask, "Where did the spray paint come from? I don't remember that during the walk-through."

"We use it to mark shit we want to demo," Kody explains.

"The bookcases—"

"Have too much wood rot from the food and spilled liquid. Based on the stench, I can only presume it was beer since it smells like the basement of my old frat house. Seriously, I don't know what's happening on the legal side, but I hope Wilde goes after his brother for vandalizing this place. Those were handcrafted oak."

I keep my lips shut, because I do know what's happening. And it makes me respect Kristoffer Wilde even more.

"But I think the ass cracked eggs on top of the beer," Kody sneers. "It really makes me want to use him as target practice."

"God, the more you tell me, the more my stomach churns. Did I need to know that?" I press a hand to stop the nausea churning inside.

Kody rubs my shoulders briefly. "Don't worry, Meadow. We'll put new ones to replace these. Lenny's a master woodworker. There's nothing he can't build."

"Oh." I look behind me up at Kody. "Is that what you wanted me to know?"

"Nope. Leroy, the hammer?" One of the muscled workers standing by with a big smile hands Kody a long-armed sledgehammer. It's not the same one Russell and I found the first day. I left it so when Kody and I did our initial walk-through, he could make an honest assessment of the damage beneath the cracks. In comparison that sledgehammer looked like it's meant to pound in a croquet stake. This one could take out, well, a bookcase.

Kody grabs it with one hand and offers it to me. Even accepting it with both of mine, I still almost topple over at the weight. "What do you want me to do with this?" I laugh at myself as I regain my balance.

Kody grins. "It's a rite of passage for any member of my crew. You get three swings to see how much damage you can do. Don't tell me you're not tempted; I've seen what you can do with an axe," Kody dares me.

Amid the chortles around us, I contemplate throwing it. "How much does this weigh?"

"Twenty pounds."

"How in the hell do you expect me to swing this?" I exclaim.

Squatting down, he says just loud enough to penetrate my protective buds, "You've carried burdens much heavier than this, Meadow. Now, use them and take out that piece of crap in front of you."

Spinning in his direction to face him fully, I almost land on my ass when the sledgehammer doesn't budge. I reach out and grip Kody's shirt to stabilize myself. "Do you have a lighter version for the newbie?"

Kody's hand slides over mine when he says, "I'll be standing right behind you to support you if you'll let me." And I know without him saying more he means more than just swinging a hammer.

"Okay." The word is out of my mouth before I give any thought to the ramifications.

Kody slips an arm around my shoulders and picks up the sledgehammer with ease. A tremble racks my body at the contrast between his obvious strength and the deliberate care he's shown me since he arrived. No, I correct myself—since I've always known him. *He's always been like this with you, Meadow.*

Nudging me forward, I'm given a brief lesson about the proper way to swing a sledgehammer so "you're not out of commission the next few days. We need you to scrub more walls," Kody teases. "Besides, you need to work your way up to having guns like ours."

And as if they were waiting for some super-secret signal, members of his crew begin flexing their muscles.

I burst out laughing.

"I don't think Meadow appreciates the fine specimen of manhood she has on display," Shane, Kody's extremely tall site foreman, grumbles.

I stumble backward due to the force of my hysterics. "They looked like..."

Kody warns me, "For all that's holy, don't say—"

"When you'd all pose as Lumberjacks after the show!" I manage to gasp out.

Kody groans just as his crew bursts out in the infamous song from Monty Python like this is a regular occurrence.

I'm screeching as the crew skips and jumps along with their off-key rendition of the catchy tune. "This...can't be...the first time they've done this."

"Not even close." I find Kody's face is lined with amusement and a hint of sadness. "The first time they ever did this, Jed was the one leading them in their shenanigans. I swear, we didn't get a damn thing done anytime he'd visit me on-site after that."

The image of Jed singing and dancing amid Kody's crew sends me into new gales of laughter. "Stop, Kody. My stomach is starting to hurt." Tears of laughter are sliding down my face.

"The first time it happened is one of my favorite memories. It's right next to Jed picking up the sledgehammer and taking out a wall alongside these guys not long after. He wasn't just a guy on-site; he became a member of the crew." He brings us full circle to why I'm here to see these antics to begin with.

Regaining control, my fingers wrap around the handle of the sledgehammer with my left hand. Amid the antics still occurring around us, Kody focuses completely on me and my safety when he shifts behind me. "Easy does it," he warns.

"I've got this." And whether or not I take out a shelf or not isn't the point. It's about regaining that sense of power I lost when I found out my husband was cheating on me. I bend at the knees and shift the weight so my right hand slides upward along the shaft. My left hand grips the bottom for stabilization.

"Choke up so your hand is just below the head," Kody reminds me.

"I've got a pretty good grip on the head." I'm focused on getting to the red X his team marked on the formerly beautiful wood. I move forward.

Suddenly silence descends upon us. "Dominant foot back; hammer no higher than your head. Then stand off to the side to avoid debris," Kody instructs.

"Why? I thought the point was to take out as much of the book-case as possible."

"You're right. It won't take out as much, but…"

Before Kody can say another word, I position myself and swing as hard as I can, crashing the hammer in the center of the X. Only a few shelves rattle before tumbling down. My eyes narrow in frustration. "What did I do wrong?"

"Not a damn thing," Kody reassures me. "That was a great first hit. You'll build up more power over time…"

I warn, "Stand back." Then I position again.

The sledgehammer comes down just as I think, *Fuck you, Mitch.*

The strike is much more satisfying, crashing through the remaining shelves and lodging itself into the cabinet below. I think I hear, "Last strike," but I ignore it. I'm taking down this fucking bookcase if it's the last thing I do today—for that matter all week.

Strike. *That's for not being enough of a man.*

Strike. *That's for betraying the vows you made to your family.*

Strike. *That's for making Elise hate me.*

Strike. *That's for MJ's pain and confusion.*

Strike, strike, strike. I lose count of the number of hits I make.

Finally, I'm not sure what gives way first—my anger or my arms. That's when I really focus on the silence around me. The sledgehammer begins to slide from my weakening fingers. Before it can fall to the floor, causing more damage to be repaired, a rippled forearm reaches from behind me to grab it.

"Like I said, I'm right here if you need me." Kody lays the hammer harmlessly at our feet before turning me to face him. Removing the gloves from his hands, he reaches in and removes my earplugs before he removes his own and randomly tosses them aside. I'm about to blast him for leaving garbage when I get my first look at the bookshelf.

"Oh, my goodness," I breathe. The doors that were on the lower cabinet are hanging on, but just barely. None of the shelf supports that are at my height or below are intact. I gape when I realize I punched so many holes into the counter that it looks like swiss cheese. "I did that?"

"You sure as hell did. Feels damn good, doesn't it?" The pride in Kody's voice is unmistakable. It's what I hoped to hear from Elise when I told her about my degree and didn't. And in hearing it, I want to grab the sledgehammer and beat the shit out of the other shelf because that's something else Mitch took from me as well.

I nod. "When can I do it again?"

He throws his head back and laughs. "In a few days." I frown, not understanding why I have to wait so long for this euphoric feeling. "Despite doing everything correctly, you're going to be sore as hell, Flower."

My heart flips over in my chest. It's been seventeen years since Kody's called me Flower. He used to say my eyes reminded him of the forget-me-nots that sprout in late June. "But 'Forget' or 'Not' are dumb nicknames, Meadow," he grumbled around a bite of hot dog in the Smiths' backyard.

"And 'Flower's better, Kody? I'll sound like a character from Bambi," I giggled back at him while we lay at the foot of the picnic table amid the fading Alaskan sunlight.

He was about to answer when Rainey called out, "Meadow, Mitch is here!"

Pulled out of my memory and back into the great room where I've just decimated a bookcase, I shrug off his concern. "Maybe, maybe not. Let's play it by ear."

Kody's eyes narrow. "Regardless of how you feel, we have something for you now. Shane? Do you want to do the honors?" He steps back, but not completely out of reach.

Shane approaches with a hat tucked under his arm. "Meadow, if you don't mind taking off that hat? It's essential we have everyone on-site properly identified."

Horrified, I raise my hands to my gray visitor hat and link my fingers over it. "I thought you guys said it was okay I was upstairs as long as I was wearing this." I back up a step, and my feet tangle with Kody's. His hands clasp my waist lightly.

"Trust me, Flower. Shane?"

"Meadow Borneman, on behalf of myself, Kody, and the rest of the men and women here today, I hereby proclaim you as no longer a visitor of this site but a full-fledged member of the crew. By massacring that bookcase and presenting you with your new yellow construction hat, you are officially a member of the Laurence Construction crew and all razzing that goes along with it."

I can't fumble the monotone gray hat off fast enough. It clatters to the floor in my haste. "I never thought yellow was my color until right now."

Shane sets the vibrant-colored hat on my head like it's a coronation. Stepping back, he tests it by pulling out a hammer and tapping it down lightly. When I feel the vibrations but no pain, it reminds me of how I'm healing from the mess of the last year.

"Thank you. None of you have any idea what it means..." Then before I break down and cry in front of the entire crew who just witnessed my strength, I haul out through the front door to have a moment in private.

KODY

Fortunately, with it being in between tourist seasons in the Glacier Bay area, I was able to get everyone into one hotel. The guys didn't even mind bunking two to a room once they saw the size of them, complete with fireplaces and kitchenettes. Shane joked, "Are you sure you don't want to open a branch of the company here? Because if you do, I'm all in."

I rolled my eyes and said, "Let's get through one job first."

Later that night after dinner with the crew in the hotel bar, I call Jennings.

"How's Meadow?" are the first words out of his mouth.

I kick my legs up on the balcony and study the lake in front of me while I debate how to answer. I admit, "If I tell you fine, I'd be lying."

"Mitch seemed like a decent guy when Meadow first met him." Jennings's voice is rife with confusion. "What on earth changes a man so drastically?"

"I can't begin to speculate. But regardless of whatever happened between him and Meadow, those are his kids."

"Meadow hasn't shared anything with Kara about problems with the kids."

"And I doubt she will, Jennings. The only people I guess who might know everything are Brad and Rainey." I can practically feel Jennings seething over the line.

"And to make matters worse, I know her heart's conflicted about not having the kids here," I conclude.

"Why aren't they? I would think she'd want them as close as possible."

"Because of the condition of the main house, she's spending ten-hour days over there right now. Meadow didn't want to have them bored in the middle of a construction zone."

"That makes sense. She must miss them terribly."

"You have no idea." The hot anger I've managed to keep suppressed from Meadow claws its way to the surface. Quickly, I fill him in on everything I've learned since my feet touched Montana soil. "And I know for damn certain that's not everything."

"No doubt. Is she sad? Grieving her marriage at all?"

"No. I think she'd be well on the way to moving on if the kids were in the same place as her."

"Well, whatever she needs, let me know. You know you don't have to ask."

Despite his tough business edge, John Jennings has a heart of pure gold. I smile in the dark. "I know."

"I think this year has shown all of us we should have done a better job of taking care of the family we made all those years ago."

"That's why I'm here."

"You're a good man, Kody," Jennings commends me.

"I don't know what else to do except to be here when she needs to shift some of the burden," I tell him honestly.

Jennings hesitates.

"What?" I mutter irritably.

"Nothing. I was just going to ask how you're handling hearing all this."

"If you thought I was furious at my parents' house when I first heard what was going on, Lord knows what I'd do if I ran into...I can't even think of the right name for Mitchell Borneman."

"Tiny Douchebag," Jennings supplies.

I sputter with laughter. "That sounds like something Jed would say, for fuck's sake!"

Jennings chuckles in my ear. "It was Rainey. She came up with it and has been socializing it among the women. Maris is apparently using it in the bar like it was his God-given name while Kara tested it out the other morning just as I took my first sip of coffee. I had to go find a new shirt since I spit everywhere."

I grin. Those women are a force individually, but together? They should terrify all of the men on the planet. My heart swells with pride when I think of the way they've all adopted each other, especially with everything that happened after Jed died. Kara and Jennings's lives have changed so much including their living accommodations. "So, despite the lack of crown molding, how's the new house?"

"Kara keeps swearing she gets lost in our bedroom. I told her I have no problem with figuring out a way stay in it longer."

"Why am I not surprised?"

Jennings's smile can be heard over the line. "Besides, I got what I wanted out of our new home."

"What? Your own office? The three-car garage?"

"No, her and Kevin living in it with me. We could have stayed in the two-bedroom apartment we were cramped in and I'd still be perfectly happy. The fact you sent a crew here as a wedding gift to custom-build it, well, that just makes it all the more special. I just wish..."

He doesn't finish his sentence, but I know what he's going to say. He wishes Jed were still alive to see how happy he and Kara are together. "Me too, brother. But you know he's watching all of us." I swallow hard right after I say the words. God, I hope he is. The idea of a world without Jed is just not something I'm ready for, despite it being almost a year since he's been gone.

"You should be scared," Jennings laughs after a lengthy pause.

"What? Why?" I'm confused.

"Jed spent a lot of time walking around Flathead Lake when we were there. Don't you have a tree house to build? When the hell are you supposed to find time to do that."

"First things first, let me finish with rebuilding what I'm here to before I turn my attention to another project."

"Well, from everything I'm hearing, you're doing exactly what she needs right now. But make sure you find time for what you need as well." Without another word, Jennings hangs up.

What I need? The thought runs insidiously inside my head. I stare out across the vast lake lit only by the moonlight. What I need is directly tied up in Meadow's happiness.

The problem is, will I get a chance to show her that before I have to leave?

On that depressing thought, I push myself to my feet and head back inside to answer some email before Greta comes out to Montana and follows me around like she used to when we were kids.

THE NEXT MORNING, I pull up to Nature's Song and find Meadow's SUV already there. Instead of being upstairs when I walk in, she's laying dozens of boxes on top of the counter alongside boxes of coffee and stacks of cups next to it. Her cheeks look pale, but still she smiles when she sees me. "Morning, Kody."

"What's all this?" I ask, gesturing to the items she has lined up on the kitchen island, the last viable surface we have to remove.

"I placed an order at the diner we went to for to-go coffee and apple cider donuts...Kody!" Meadow screeches as I yank her into my arms.

"Your job is not to feed the entire damn crew," I growl.

She shoves at my chest to put some space between us. "My job is to do whatever the hell I want it to be, Mr. Laurence. You sure as hell aren't the boss of me."

"Oh really? I'm not? Then tell me, Meadow, where's your hard hat?" I smirk down into her face as a flush immediately brightens her cheeks. "Right. The minute my company took over this job, I become your boss the minute you walk through that door until the moment you step out of it."

The flush staining her cheeks recedes as if it was never there.

Instead fury tightens her features. "Only insomuch as you get to direct my work. But remember who signs the paychecks. And if I want to be a nice human being and buy the men and women who are working on this site something to eat to say thank you out of my own money the same way I did when I was nothing more than a lowly waitress working at Donna's, then I'll damn well do it. I'm not your employee, Kody. Nor am I your wife. Hence, I don't report to you for a damn thing despite the fucking color of the hat I wear while I'm on this site."

While I stand there stunned, Meadow uses the opportunity to shove herself out of my arms and storm away. But not before I see her swipe up her hard hat, which was sitting right behind the mound of donuts she'd purchased for my team, and slams it on her head.

"Well, that was fucked-up, boss," I hear behind me. I swivel around as Shane saunters in. "Meadow's a great lady."

"You have no idea what that was," I tell him.

"What it appears to be was you giving someone a hard time for doing something nice that any number of us have done before. The question is why?" Shane flips open a box, and the smell of freshly made donuts permeates the air. Lifting two, he flips the lid back down. "And just for the record, there's nothing left to demo other than the island these are on and some carpet. I'm not certain I want you near a sledge-hammer or a knife right now. So, why don't you take a page out of the lady's book and go outside to cool off?"

Following Shane's gaze, I find Meadow's run past the debris in the backyard until she reached the grass near the water's edge. From this distance I can't see anything except the bright color of her shirt that proudly matches the hard hat she's still wearing. "I'll be right back."

"Take your time."

Along the way to get to Meadow, I'm stopped a few times by members of my team. Each time, I let them know about the treats she brought. Shane's right. Why did I have such an adverse reaction to her bringing them when any number of our crew had done the same in the past?

Because she's not theirs. She's yours. The thought pops into my head. I shove it aside because I don't dare think that way. Meadow's marriage just broke up. There's no way she's thinking along the same way I am—

that all those years ago maybe there could have been something deeper between us. Right now, I have to tread carefully because...

Suddenly, a frozen ice ball hits me in the center of the chest. "Shit, that hurt!" I yell.

"Good!" Meadow yells. She storms in my direction, her long limbs jerking in anger. And I realize she isn't broken, she's infuriated.

It sparks some deep-seated memory inside me from long ago as I approach her warily.

"Oh my God, Kody!" Meadow shouted. She was pulling her pale blue skirt away from her long legs. "I smell like a brewery."

"I'm sorry, Flower. I was aiming for, Jed," I stammered.

"I figured."

"I missed."

"I can tell."

"Can I make it up to you?"

Her icy glare raked me up and down. "Pray I don't get pulled over considering none of us are twenty-one yet."

Then Rainey snorted. "Like that will matter. Mitch would probably bail you out."

Meadow turned her withering stare on her sister. "Because that would look great. Hey, new guy I'm dating. Come bail your drunk-smelling chick out of jail."

I turned away with my fists clenched, not wanting to give in to the urge to lose the rest of my temper for not having the balls to ask Meadow out sooner. I've never even met this Mitch guy and I already hate him.

Meadow's chest is heaving as she hoists another scoop of ice in her hands. "That was for being such a dick this morning."

My eyes dart to the ball she's forming in her hands. "Then what's that one for?"

Her eyes narrow. "My revenge for the beer all those years ago. That blue dress was completely ruined."

Fuck. She remembers.

"You have that wrong, Meadow. I'm the one who deserves revenge for that." Swiftly, I get close enough to grab her wrist, forcing her to drop the ice ball.

"What...what do you mean?" Her head falls back. The yellow hard hat falls harmlessly to the ground, spinning on the hard grass.

"I'm the one who had to sit there and listen to you and Rainey talk about your new guy when all I wanted to do was..." My head starts to lower.

Her body stretches up. My hand holding her wrist loosens and slides down her arm over her side to grip her around the back.

"What? What did you want to do, Kody?" she whispers.

It's cool enough out that as my eyes are focused on her lips, I can see our breath entwine. "I wanted..."

Her eyes lower, long thick lashes temporarily hiding the deep blue color.

But just as my lips touch hers, I hear a large crash. I snarl. "Fuck. I can't do this now. I have to go see what happened."

Her eyes fly open as I set her away from me. Her fingers come up and press against her lips before she turns away.

I storm in the direction of the noise when suddenly I jerk myself to a stop. What the hell am I thinking? "Meadow?" I call to her. After she whirls around to face me, I declare, "I've waited too long to kiss you. This isn't the place for it."

From a good six feet away, I see her swallow. My lips quirk. "Now get to work. The rest of those bedrooms need the walls cleaned so they can be primed next week." I turn away.

"Are you sure you don't want an ice ball in the back?" she calls to my back.

I laugh knowing it's going to be okay. We're going to be okay.

In fact, I think we might just be better than that.

MEADOW

U sing a bandanna I picked up when I ran out for lunch that's sporting huckleberries trimmed to look like flowers, I sit back on my heels and grin.

It's done.

"Though, I feel better knowing it was grease and not—"

Footsteps announce someone's presence before I hear Kody say, "Crap?" I twist around to find him lounging in the doorway.

"Fecal matter," I toss back.

"Either way, we're talking about a lot of work to clean up a load of—"

"Kody!" I cut him off before he can say it, but I'm laughing just the same. "It was bad enough when I thought it was that. Let's not rehash it."

He takes a few steps into the room and offers his hand to help me stand, and I accept it. Our bodies are as close as they were when his lips brushed against mine after what I've been mentally calling the donut debacle from yesterday. All morning, I've used a critical eye as I ensured the walls of the last bedroom have been scrubbed. I've almost stripped the paper covering the wallboard in some places as I tried to make sense of what his intent was by that almost kiss.

Was he just being friendly? Familial even? I mean, there was nothing overtly passionate in the brush of his lips against mine. Scolding myself, I drop his hand and gesture to the room at large. "What do you think?"

"Isn't this the room where that schmuck went to town with markers he found in his niece's bedroom?"

"It is."

Kody steps away and my heart rate settles down. Until he frowns and shrugs off the overshirt he's wearing. I don't know if I make a sound, but he turns to face me. He opens his mouth. I just pray he doesn't expect me to speak.

Dear merciful God. The tight white T-shirt he had on underneath is molded to his broad shoulders and chest before gaping slightly around his narrower stomach. I wish my eyes were my fingers right now so they could trace each sinuous muscle on display.

My fantasies are going to take on a whole new meaning tonight.

"Don't you think, Flower?"

"I'm sorry. Can you repeat that?"

He frowns. "Are you okay?"

Hell no. "Sure. I might have been in here too long without a break," I lie.

"I was just saying that at the end of demo week, we normally have a small party. Now, I'm not sure if you're up to it."

"I'm up to it." Excitement begins to thrum in my veins. I haven't felt so eager since last summer when the kids and I would hang around with Rainey's family, Kara's family, and Maris in Juneau for family barbecues.

"Are you sure?" Kody moves closer. Inspecting my face as closely as he was the wall, he notes, "You're flushed."

I roll my eyes. "I've just been bent over, contorting myself, for hours. I'm fine."

"Thanks for the mental image. That helps."

"What do you mean?" I'm bewildered.

"Nothing. Never mind. Any suggestions where we can go tonight?"

I immediately think of the bar at the lodge he and his crew are staying at, but then dismiss it. Quickly, another thought pops into my head. "Why don't we have a cookout at my place?"

"You want this crew invading your home?" Kody's incredulous.

"Why wouldn't I?" Then I frown. "So long as they don't mess with the kids' rooms."

"I can guarantee that."

"Then I have only two important questions."

"Okay." He draws out the word.

"What does everyone like to eat? And are you going to be as pissy at me as you were yesterday if I leave to go and get it?" I give him an impish smile.

Kody tears the sponge from my hand. Peeling off my gloves, he begins to edge me toward the doorway.

"I guess that answers that part of the question," I mutter as we descend the stairs.

"If I answer the second part without including them, I'll never hear the end of it," Kody explains.

Touching his chest lightly when we reach the foot of the stairs, I proclaim, "You're a good person, a good boss."

"What else am I good at?"

I open and close my mouth before avoiding the question as I dash away yelling, "What does everybody eat and drink? Party at my house tonight."

I try to use fielding orders to distract me from the fact I can still feel Kody's eyes burning into my back.

I CHEW ANXIOUSLY at my lower lip as the crew begins to arrive with no sign of Kody. Yes, he mentioned there was usually an event, but maybe he got a better offer? *Stop it*, I tell myself firmly, as Shane gives me a side hug when he enters the front door with a case of beer.

"I'm not sure you're going to need that," I joke.

"Why?"

Gesturing to the backyard where flames are licking at the fire pit, I remark, "It wasn't just food I picked up at the store."

Shane's eyebrows raise up to his smooth hairline. "You didn't need to do that, Meadow."

"Maybe not, but you all worked hard, and it's appreciated."

A chill races through me when Kody interrupts our discussion. "What on earth is all of this?" We both spin around to find him holding a case of beer in one hand and a wrapped bottle of wine in the other. Sniffing the air appreciatively, he asks, "What's that smell?"

"Oh! The sides must be warmed up." Crossing the room, I grab the pot holders and pull the heavy trays of beans and rice from the oven. After sliding in the pans of skirt steak, chicken, and veggies, I set the timer.

Kody's followed me into the kitchen. Making himself at home, he opens the refrigerator to find a spot for the alcohol he brought only to be brought up short when confronted with bowls of guacamole, salsa, and a vat of queso I need to get warmed.

Quickly swiping my hand across my forehead, I nudge him out of the way. "Let me make some room. Then you all can start munching while I finish up dinner."

"We can?" he echoes.

"Yep. I just have to...Kody!" I exclaim as he swings me around to face him. I'm holding a large bowl of sour cream in my hands I bobble, which fortunately he catches before putting on the counter behind him.

"Have you relaxed at all today?" I must appear confused because he tips his head back to rest on his shoulders—something I know is a sign of frustration.

"Did we not discuss having dinner here?" I demand.

His head snaps down. "And when I got here, I would have used my corporate card to have ordered the crew food, even if it was only Taco Bell."

"They're only open until nine," I tell him automatically.

His lips curve. "Been there already?" He lifts a piece of my hair and tucks it behind my ear.

I blush remembering my confession to Kody years ago about my addiction to fast food. "Well, there and Arby's."

"Good." At my confusion, he leans down to whisper, "I want to take you to somewhere more memorable, then."

Holy hell. He needs to stop. He might just mean food, but my body is twisting every word he's saying. "I don't have enough batteries for this."

Leaning back, Kody asks, "What did you say?"

I fumble for a plausible explanation for my runaway mouth. "I didn't have enough details for this."

"Ah, got it. Don't worry. If Shane's reaction is anything to go by, then..." His words trail off abruptly. "What are those?" He points to the crescent roll puffs in my refrigerator.

"Oh, just a recipe I found online last year. You dredge marshmallows in cinnamon and sugar and bake them inside a crescent roll with sugar on top. Why, do you think they're over-the-top?"

"You made them for Jed's wake." It's a statement, not a question.

"Well, yes." And Mitch bitched at me for wasting money doing it, but I don't add that.

Kody picks up the back of my hand and rubs his lips across my knuckles. "I could barely stomach anything after the service. But Brad said I needed to eat something before I was sick. So, I thought a croissant would work." There's a pause. "I ate half the tray. They're what kept me going through the worst day of my life."

When he steps forward and presses his lips against my cheek, he whispers, "I should have known then it was you who made them. Thank you."

When he pulls back, there's a glimmer in his eyes that belies his next statement. "But I still want the receipt for all the food. Otherwise, I'll just estimate what it normally costs and take it off the house."

I can't help but smile at his laughter when the pot holder I throw at his back lands with a thunk dead center.

"HERE'S TO ANOTHER DEMO WEEK!" Kody holds up his beer. From my spot by my patio doors, I observe the crew lift bottles of beer, cans of soda, and water to toast him back with. "Once again, we've found a home that needs some help—"

"Maybe more than a little help in this case, boss," one of the guys calls out. I can't quite tell who through the smoke from the fire pit.

"True. But it makes the work that much more satisfying. And normally we'd be arguing over where we're going to eat. We wouldn't be thanked with a cookout by the person signing our paychecks," Kody jokes.

All of the men and women around the fire laugh, including myself. "It was the least I could do to repair your sense of smell," I call out.

That sets off everyone tittering again until Kody whistles to get their attention. "Okay, everyone, settle down. You may not know, but this isn't just a house for me; it's a part of my past. It holds a lot of memories because I helped in its construction. I know how it can shine, so don't be surprised if I ride you a little harder for perfection."

"When do you not?" Shane calls out, causing Kody's team to laugh again.

"True," he concedes. "But your heart never truly lets go of whatever happened with your first love—good or bad. Right now, she's infuriated she's been treated so shamelessly."

Kody keeps talking, but it's all buzzing in my head. Is he trying to tell me something? Slipping inside, I put my soda on the counter and grip the edges as tightly as I can. I think about the almost platonic kiss we shared yesterday, and I can't blame the licks of the fire's flames for the scalding heat that floods my cheeks. "Was it pity?" I wonder aloud.

"Was what pity?" I let out an agonized groan hearing Kody's voice behind me.

"Nothing." If I just avoid answering him, he'll let the question drop. At least, that's my experience with men.

But Kody Laurence is turning out to be an exception. Coming around the counter, his hand brushes my shoulder as he comes to stand next to me. "Come on, Flower," he cajoles. "You know you can tell me anything."

And those words drive a stake into the missing piece of my heart I never knew was there until yesterday. Moving back a step, I ask, "Really?"

Suddenly, the tension in the kitchen thickens so much, I'm certain it could be cut with one of the knives in the sink. I spin around and give Kody my back before saying, "Just head outside. I need a few moments."

"You need time?" he clarifies.

I nod, unable to speak past the lump in my throat. What I need and what I want are two very different things. If I could have everything I wanted, I'd, what? Do nothing different, I realize, shoulders slumping. Except maybe I'd give Kody the gift of love.

He should have known what it felt like to have someone love him unequivocally. At least someone who was free.

His hand closes on my shoulder right before he spins me around. Kody's infuriated. "And you don't think seventeen years is long enough?"

What did he just say? But before I can open my mouth to get the words out, one muscled arm slides around my waist, yanking me up so our eyes are level. I brace my hands against his biceps. "Kody." His name is a wish, a hope. And if I'm honest, a secret longing missing from my life for far too long.

"Time's up, Flower," he murmurs. His eyes still on mine, he cups my cheek with his other hand, holding my head steady as his head lowers.

Firm lips brush against mine once, twice. I twist my fingers in the overlong hair that curls just over the edge of his shirt collar, aligning our lips before starting to plead, "If you don't mean it..."

The rest of the sentence disappears as Kody tips my chin and lays waste to my mouth.

God, if I had to die right now it would be okay because even in my dreams, I'll never be able to recreate the feeling of Kody's lips on mine. I can taste the tang from the ale he toasted with under the dark sky and the underlying passion of wasted days and nights. This is a kiss of intent, not of pity. And I'm shaken to my core.

My knees weaken under the onslaught, but Kody catches me. We break apart for air, each of us gasping. His opens his mouth—to say what, I don't know—but I don't give him a chance to speak, not with words. not yet.

Instead, I tip my head back and whisper, "Again."

With a groan, he twists me until my back is pressed against the refrigerator. Smoothing his hands down my hips, he pulls me flush against his straining erection. "With pleasure."

My lips are curved as are his. Long moments pass by where the world stops and time is only measured in his arms.

We're interrupted by someone opening the slider. Both of our heads whip to the side.

"I was coming in for some more beer..." Shane begins.

Kody lets out a feral growl.

"But I think I'll just come back later," he concludes swiftly.

Even standing wrapped up in Kody's arms, now that the kiss is over, I'm seized with terror.

What did we just do?

KODY

Overwhelming regret seizes me. Not that it happened, but that I wasn't strong enough all those years ago to get over my frustration of not having Meadow in my life in some way and walking out of her life completely.

"You're thinking pretty hard there." I let go of her hip to cup her cheek.

"Regrets," she whispers.

I rear back as if she slapped me. "About this?"

"No! About all those years ago." She brushes her fingers over my lips. "Maybe some part of Mitch knew I was never going to be his, and so that's why..."

I press a kiss to them before I move her hand aside. "Then he should have had the strength to have walked away before he disrespected his vows."

At her gasp, my body surges against hers. Now that the invisible barrier's come down between us, I'm finding it hard to fight off the urge not to give in to every fantasy I've ever had about her since the day we met. My head drops until my chin is tucked neatly against the curve of her shoulder.

For long moments we stand wrapped in each other's arms,

breathing in each other. Suddenly, her phone rings. When she pulls back, her vivid blue eyes are wide. "It's the kids."

"Do you need to go somewhere to take it?"

She nods before rushing off without another word. My eyes follow her as she dashes down the hall while answering. "Hey. Elise? Honey? What happened?"

Before I can do anything, Shane pokes his head back in. "Is it safe to get another beer?"

"No." I haven't moved an inch since Meadow closed the door to what I assume is her bedroom.

"Everything okay with Meadow?"

"I'm not sure."

"Kody?"

"Yeah?"

"You're different with her," he observes quietly.

I turn my head to raise a brow at him.

He shrugs. "Just want to say, I wasn't kidding if you want to open a Montana branch." He slaps me on the shoulder before adding, "I'll clear everyone out."

"Thanks, Shane." Crossing my legs at the ankles, I lean back against the counter and just wait.

It takes twenty minutes for my crew to carry the beer and wine they brought out to their vehicles, plus most of the food Meadow cooked. But when they try to take the leftover croissant marshmallow puffs, I threaten, "Not if you value your paychecks. Those are mine."

They all laugh.

"Tell Meadow thanks. I hope everything's okay. She's been in there a while." Shane's the last one out the door.

I push away from where I've been monitoring her door to follow them out. "Will do. I'll ping you in the morning to let you know what time I plan on being at the site."

"Sounds good, boss." Shane slaps his hand in mine, giving it a rough shake before heading out. I stand in the doorway to make certain everyone makes it out of the gate, which has a small strip of lights illuminating it at night. Seeing the two twelve-foot wrought-iron structures close together after the last car, I close Meadow's front door before going off in search of her.

Walking up to her door, I knock softly and call her name. When there's no answer, I try again. "Meadow?" I drop my hand down and twist the handle. Her door opens smoothly inward.

And here I've been worrying while she's dead asleep in the middle of her bed. Likely exhaustion just took over after her phone call. I keep forgetting that even though she works as hard as my crew, she's not used to this kind of labor.

I move forward to slip off her shoes and pull a throw over her when I get a better look at her face.

Her lips are parted, her brow scrunched. But what causes my heart to clench is the streaks of dried tear tracks on her cheeks. She's curled up asleep on the bed with a box of tissues tucked closely next to her side. Wads of used ones are scattered around her spread as well as clenched tightly in her fist.

"What the hell?" I whisper, trying not to roar and wake her. What happened during that call to disturb her like this? I cover her with the soft green throw at the foot of the bed. Scooping up the used tissues, I make my way into the adjoining bathroom and toss them away.

Wishing the shadows on the walls could tell me what happened because I'm terrified the woman cradled within the bed won't, I carefully smooth Meadow's matted hair away from her face before forcing myself to leave her there alone.

After I bank the fire outside, I find her keys neatly lined up on a wall rack near the front door. There's a set marked as "spare" a few hooks down from her jacket. Without a second's hesitation, I pilfer it so I don't leave her unprotected. It's not like I don't know where to find her to return it later. Locking all the exits, I stand outside in the cold March air debating whether I should make the call. Finally worry drives me to pull up a number on my favorites.

Brad picks up after two rings. "Hey."

And that's when I realize Brad sounds like what Meadow looked like curled up on her bed, sad and defeated. I rub a hand over my chest as I open the locks on my truck. Lifting myself in and switching to Bluetooth, I offer, "Want to talk?"

"Give me a minute." I hear him murmur before his footfalls sound in my ear. "Where are you?"

"Leaving what was supposed to be a demo party at Meadow's. Got interrupted by a call though. You?"

"Somewhere between exasperated and shitfaced."

Pulling out of Meadow's driveway, I stop for the gate and finally go for humor. "What are you waiting for? Permission?"

He barks out a laugh. "No, I was just waiting to see if Rainey was going to stop crying long enough to finish the job right."

"When I locked up, Meadow was passed out in her bed. Doesn't look good," I tell him brutally.

There's an unhealthy silence on the other end of the line. "Kody, I need to tell you something. I know it's none of my business, but can you tell me what Meadow means to you?"

"We don't keep secrets from each other, but don't you think she deserves the right to find out first?" But even as those words come out, I think of the ones Jed held that rocked all out worlds. Are there any more? I wonder frantically.

"No. And not because I'm playing big brother."

"Brad, I'm thirty-eight years old. Meadow is someone I've had feelings for a long time. Are there sparks, yes. Am I interested? Without question. Am I ready to put everything into words after a few weeks?" I hesitate.

"You know the answer deep inside," he pushes.

"It's between her and I. This isn't a family affair."

"Then I can't let you know what happened tonight. You're going to have to find out what you want to know from Meadow."

I slam down hard on the brakes, causing them to squeak. "Excuse me?"

"What happened tonight is between family and—"

"Let me get what you're saying. Right here, right now, if I don't declare how I feel about Meadow, I'm cut off. That's it." What he's saying is unfathomable.

"Kody, there's things only family can know."

"And Jennings isn't that? Nick?"

"No, they are, but they're not becoming involved with someone who legally already is."

"I can't believe I'm hearing this. When has this crap mattered to you, Brad?"

"Kody..."

"You have no idea what I walked into tonight."

"I do. Rainey's in the same condition."

"But unless Meadow tells me why, I can't rely on any of you to help me figure it out." I laugh sharply.

"I'm sorry, but I have to do what I think is right to protect Meadow."

A sick comprehension smacks me between the eyes. "And I'm not it. You don't think I'm right for her."

"No, Kody, that's not it," Brad's quick to jump in.

"Now I understand why you never called when she was in trouble." I fumble for the device in my console.

"No, Kody. Fuck, you're wrong; I swear—"

I disconnect the call before he can continue. Heart pounding, hands shaking, I press the button to put my car in park before I try driving any further.

"What the hell just happened?" I ask aloud. As soon as I do, my phone starts to ring. I glance down.

Jennings.

Stomach churning, I send the call to voicemail.

"What the hell did I do to make them think I wasn't good enough for Meadow? Especially after a guy like Mitch?"

It rings again. Nick. I debate answering, but with my heart lodged somewhere between my neck and my stomach, I just can't. I send him to voicemail as well.

While I wait to see if any of them leave me a message, I pull up the one voice I desperately need to hear right now and can't reach out to. Leaning my head back, I press Play and wait for my Bluetooth to blast his voice through the speakers of my car.

Hey, buddy! Greetings from warmer climes. What's the weather like in Portland? Rainy? Dean and I took the boat out today. It's ridiculously beautiful here, Kody. You really should come visit and bring Jennings's sorry ass with you.

But enough about life in Florida. I want to know how you're doing. I just got this feeling I needed to talk to you today. So why aren't you answering your damn phone? Where are you? Off on some job, I bet, and not taking enough time to take care of you. I mean, how much did you get a chance to do that growing up? You forget I know you, Kody. You're always bending over backwards to make certain everyone you know is taken care of, you forget to take care of this amazing guy. Yeah, asshole. I'm talking about you.

Tears pour down my face as I hear Jed's robust laugh, but I don't switch off his voice. I need to hear it, hear him.

Though I don't know how some woman hasn't snatched you up by now, you handsome bastard. You're one of the kindest people I know. Besides which, in a family with six sisters? Jesus, Kody. It's like you were in training your whole life to be the best husband and father ever.

Then his voice gets really serious. *It's going to happen one day, Kody. Just like it did for me. Remember? We talked about it at Nature's Song. Don't let anyone tell you how to fall in love or who to fall in love with. Just love them with that enormous heart you've been saving all those years.*

Anyway, I really just called to say hi. Miss you, Kody. Every day. Love you, brother. Always.

I hear the click.

I don't bother to wipe the tears off my face before I tell him, "God, Jed. I miss you too. So damned much. And I'm doing exactly what I promised you I'd do the last time we were here."

I give myself a few more moments to get under control before I put the car in drive and head back to the lodge.

Tomorrow's a new day. And it's yet another in a long line where the hole keeps getting larger in my own heart since now I've lost not just one brother but four.

MEADOW

The first thing I feel in the morning is warmth when I felt so lost and alone last night after hanging up on my family. Tugging the grass-green throw closer to my chest, I roll over and stare into nothing, feeling empty.

Tears, pleading, finally Rainey shouting we'd discuss it later when everyone had cooler heads. What gave her the right to make choices for my family, when decisions were already in place? Then again, did my children consider themselves my family now? My heart felt like someone actually reached in and squeezed the blood out of it after Elise declared, *Me and MJ have decided you should let Aunt Rainey and Uncle Brad adopt us. Dad doesn't want us, and we don't want you.*

And what was worse was neither Rainey nor Brad stopped her tirade.

"Oh, God," I moan as a fresh set of tears begins to burn again. Blindly, I grope for where I was certain I left the tissues last night, only to find them back on my nightstand. Along with my cell phone.

Then I sit up in a panic. "Oh, my God. The party."

Heart pounding, I swipe away the tears and dash out of my room, grabbing my cell. Coming up short, I'm stunned to find my kitchen in practically immaculate condition. Pressing my shaking hand to my forehead, I spin toward the glass doors and find the fire was put out. Kody did this. He must have come looking for me, and I cringe at what he must have found.

Pulling out a stool, I open my cell to find it riddled with texts from my sister, Kara, and Maris. I can't handle them just yet. Ignoring them, I pull up the online schedule for work at Nature's Song to see if there's anything I can be doing at the main residence to distract me today. A quick check of the schedule disabuses me of that idea as the guys are ripping out insulation and replacing it with spray foam.

A key in the lock captures my attention. I blurt out as Kody enters, holding my key aloft, "You're supposed to be dealing with the insulation. It's too bad they can't spray me with it."

"Yeah, but we don't know if you'd survive. This isn't carbon freezing. I suspect you'd suffocate."

His eyes are bloodshot, face unshaven. There are lines bracketing his mouth that don't belong there. It's disconcerting, because this isn't the Kody I know. The normally laid-back man I've known for years is gone. Yet, for a man who has always been such a bright force, it's his darkness calling to me on an elemental level.

Without a word, I move toward him. He holds himself still, waiting. I slide my hand over his heart to find it pounding. Raising my eyes over his plaid-covered chest, to his exposed neck, the underside of his jaw, I finally whisper, "I went to bed feeling alone and cold and woke up feeling cherished. It's the first time in too many years I experienced that."

With a groan, his strong arms pull me into his body. All those times we lay next to each other talking, how did I never wonder we'd ever fit against each other like this?

"I did too," he murmurs into my hair. "Way too many nights."

I choke, realizing I spoke out loud.

Pulling back, some of the lines have eased. I reach up and trace them. "I'm sorry I flaked out on last night."

"You have nothing to apologize for, Flower."

"Are you sure?" I can't stop the uncertainty in my voice.

"If anyone has any apologies to make, it will be me to Shane."

"Oh? Why's that?"

Kody leans down and nuzzles my ear before whispering, "Because we're going to play hooky. Have you eaten?"

"No. I just got up."

"Go get dressed. I have an idea." He pulls back, and his sea-colored eyes are twinkling.

Suddenly the idea of escaping everything to be with Kody sounds perfect. "I just need a few minutes."

When Kody lets me go, I miss the warmth of his embrace. Then I freeze when he says, "I've waited a long time for our first date, Ms. Borneman. I'll wait as long as it takes."

My lips part in surprise before I turn to make a dash back to my bedroom. I don't even care that I hear his low laugh behind me.

Maybe some part of me has been waiting too.

AFTER STOPPING for some drive-thru coffee, we begin to drive almost with no destination in mind. At least I'd think that if it weren't for the voice telling Kody to make an occasional left or right before notifying us we have thirty-five miles until we reach our destination.

"I'm going to have whiplash by the time we get back," I tell him. The scenery out the windows is beyond magnificent.

He points to some mountains in the distance. "That's Glacier National Park over there. When the weather warms up, I want to take the Road to the Sun."

Twisting toward him, I declare, "So do I. But you know we can see the glacier even now."

He doesn't take his eyes off the graveled road, but his lips curve. "Sounds like another date."

And again, emotions reminding me of the days that were flood through me, and my mouth speaks before my mind can hold it back. "If this one works out, then maybe."

He begins to retort, but before he can, a call comes through. I tense when I see it's Brad. Kody doesn't hesitate before sending the call to voicemail. "I'm impressed, Meadow. You haven't asked me where we're going."

"Because I suspect I know," I tell him.

"Do you?" The phone rings again. This time it's Jennings. Again, Kody declines it.

"You don't want to answer the guys?" I'm confused. These are the Jacks. If they're calling back-to-back, something must be really wrong. And unless there's a tragedy, in which case my phone would be blowing up as well, the only thing wrong would be...

Me.

"Kody?"

"Yeah?"

"Maybe this isn't such a good idea," I whisper. Suddenly my stomach rolls as Kody whips the truck off to a scenic photo stop.

Jamming his finger to put us in park, he demands, "How did you know what they're calling about?"

"What else could it be? First, my children tell me they want to live with Aunt Rainey and Uncle Brad. Now, the Jacks are frantically calling you? It's not hard to piece together. I just want to know what I did to alienate everyone when just a few weeks ago it felt like they supported me." My eyes drift over the trees that were caught in the wildfire that made national news a few years ago that are just starting to grow again.

Kind of like me.

A painful silence engulfs the car. Reaching for the handle, I mumble, "I need to get some air."

"Meadow, this isn't about you," he begins.

And fury whips through me.

"The hell it's not," I lash out as I face him. "I don't know why you don't have children, Kody. You're perfect husband and father material. And I prayed you'd be happy. That's all I wanted for you from the moment I told you I got married—that you find some woman who'd steal your heart and make you forget all about that wretched moment between us, even if I never could."

"Maybe I couldn't either," he counters.

I shake my head because to believe him makes my heart hurt more than it already does. "I thought I knew what love was. I was so wrong."

His hands tense on the steering wheel, but he doesn't interrupt me. "But the love I have for my children is absolute. Being Elise and MJ's mom means loving them enough to sacrifice anything, including my honor. Having children means giving up on your dreams so theirs come true. And I thought I was doing that. I fought for them, and each night since the divorce, I died inside for them. Now, they want me to give them up. Apparently so do Rainey and Brad, who didn't say a damn word to stop them. Then Rainey said we'd discuss it when we were calmer. As if that would ever be the case." Even as I spit the words out, I recognize the shock on Kody's face.

"That's what happened?"

"And now it looks like they're trying to get you involved too. So why don't you give them a call back?" I gesture angrily.

And I pretend bravado when he pushes a button on his steering wheel and says, "Call-Jennings-Cell."

The powerful engine is the only sound other than the ringing of the phone. "Kody, thank God. No one can reach Meadow—"

"If you all think for one second I'm going to help anyone get her kids away from her after the hell she's survived, you're out of your fucking minds. Jed would be ashamed of all of you." Then he disconnects the call.

My lips fall open, but no words come out. I know because I can taste the tears on my face after Kody tells me, "Last night, Brad told me I had a choice. I had a choice to declare right then and there where this was going or I was out."

"No," I moan, my hands coming up to cover my mouth.

"I'm giving you the same honesty I gave to Brad. There's something between us, but I refuse to be dictated to. I'm a different man and you're a different woman than we were all those years ago." His head ducks and the sunlight bounces off the gold streaks of his hair. I want to sink my hand into it to pull him closer, but is that my right? "I want the chance to explore that. He said it wasn't good enough. What you just told me? Everything's worth that."

"Forget what I have the right to do." I flick off my seat belt and launch myself at him over the console.

He clutches me to him. "What do you mean by that?"

"I wanted to hold you while you were telling me about the Jacks. I wasn't sure if I could. Should."

Letting out a sigh that blows across the top of my hair, he admits, "Should. This absolutely goes on the should list."

We sit there for a few moments holding on to each other before he eases me back into my seat. "Come on. Now, I really want to get where we're going."

"Which is?" I don't bother to hide wiping my fingers under my eyes.

"Supposedly the best bear claws in this part of the state." He glances over. "Are you buckled up?"

Quickly, I snap my belt in place. "Yep."

"Then let's get going."

The rest of the ride to Polebridge I spend asking him about his crew. What I get are a crazy riot of stories that have me in stitches. "There's enough material here for you to write a book!" I screech at one point.

Just as we pull into the small gravel lot behind a sign indicating the unincorporated community of Polebridge, Kody flashes me a wicked grin. "Maybe one day when they can no longer aim power tools at me. Now, wait for me. I'll be right around."

As Kody slides from the car, I reach for my cell. Pulling up the list of activities I was waiting to share with my kids when they arrived in Montana, I almost hit Delete on the whole damn thing. Instead, I look at the third item on the list and just remove it.

Go to Polebridge for huckleberry bear claws

Instead of experiencing this unique place for the first time with my children, Kody and I are about to step into the unknown together.

KODY

I knock on the wall outside the room so I don't startle Meadow where she's priming the walls with Kilz. She's rolling the paint on the walls while humming along to some song I don't recognize. It's catchy and if it's any indication of her mood, she's in good spirits.

That's perfect for what I have planned.

"I know you're there." Meadow executes a perfect spin while holding the roller full of the thick primer as she attacks another spot in the small room Jed used to love that overlooks the water. It was a great surprise to us both to come back from Polebridge and find new doors replacing the shattered ones.

"That was the idea. I didn't want you to..." I'm stunned speechless as Meadow begins to use the roller as a microphone before dipping it back into the paint tray. "Whatever you had this morning, I want some."

A smile lights her face. "I just feel good in this room now that the windows were replaced. Don't you?"

Come to think of it... "You're right." Approaching her from behind, I grab the roller out of her hand as the song tells us to move. Laying my hand on top of hers, I absorb her laughter into my soul as I help her paint the wall. When we drain the roller dry, I pull it from her hands and toss it into the pan.

Amid drop cloths and paint fumes, I spin Meadow in a tight circle, careful not to step in any obvious globs of paint.

"You know how to show a girl a good time, Kody."

"Well, thank you, Ms. Borneman. I sure do try, but I think I can do better." I waggle my eyebrows.

Meadow's hand slaps against my chest. "Stop before I end up falling on my butt in a paint puddle."

Glancing around, I roar over the amount of Kilz on the floor. "How much have you actually got on the walls, Flower?"

"The job said to get the walls covered. There was no requirement on how much I had to avoid hitting the floor," she informs me loftily.

"Remind me to have one of the guys do the ceiling, or you might have to shave your head."

"So, I'm a sloppy painter. What are you going to do about it?"

"Hmm. I was thinking about asking you out on our second date."

"Fifth," she corrects me.

I frown down at her. "We've only been to Polebridge, Meadow."

"And we've been together every night since either at my house or here."

"Those weren't exactly dates."

She bends down to pick up the roller, and I let out a small groan of appreciation. Twisting her head, her hair comes perilously close to landing in the pan. "Why not?" she demands.

"You cooked while I sat at your kitchen counter. I brought subs here while we went over work. And last night..."

"We had leftovers. But the real questions you should be asking are did I want to be there, and did you kiss me good night?" She straightens, brandishing the roller like a weapon.

I growl, "I hope the answers are yes and hell yes."

"Since they are, then they count as a date. Now, I'm on a tighter schedule than I thought I was since I have an important date to impress and you're a distraction, Mr. Laurence."

Bravely, as she's still holding the roller, I get back into Meadow's personal space. "I'll pick you up at six."

"Six. Okay."

"Meadow?"

"Yes?"

"You okay?"

She stops. For a moment, the joy disappears and I see what's beneath the dancing—a woman who's fighting to find her happy. I want to kick myself for taking that moment away from her.

"I'm an idiot," I rasp.

"According to Shane, you are for ordering the wrong kind of nails, but that appears to be the kind of thing I don't know much about. I can't wade in to save you."

"I think you may already be doing that." And without thinking, I pull Meadow in as close as I can. My lips brush hers once, twice, before settling down for a longer, more intense kiss that leaves us both breathless as we pull back.

Meadow licks her lips. "Whoa." Then she goes to raise her hand to her cheek and whacks herself smack in the lips with the roller. "Oh, gross." She begins spitting.

I'm wheezing as I clasp my knees in order to stay upright. As Meadow paces around swiping her face, it reminds me of Jed the first time a girl at the Lumberjack show pounced on him and kissed him. For just a second, I'm transported back to Ketchikan with Jed clomping around the apartment we shared, spitting out mouthwash in every available sink and demanding, "Do I look like the kind of guy girls should throw themselves at? Christ Jesus, if you got that axe in the right spot, they'd have crawled all over you, Kody."

Right then, remembering Jed, remembering that time with him, makes me stalk Meadow amid her grumbling and place a huge kiss right in the middle of the splotch of primer. "Get your groove on, Meadow. I'll pick you up at six."

"I'll be the one that looks like an art project!"

But even as she starts to paint again, I still hover for a few moments to make certain she's okay.

❄

A FEW MINUTES AFTER SIX, I pull up to the guest house. Ringing the bell, I hold the flowers to the side so she can't see them. I thought the florist's head was going to pop off when I went in a few days ago with my request. "But they have to be blue," I stressed.

"There's a whole bunch of lovely flowers here," she tried to dissuade me.

I started to make my way to the door.

"I'll have to special order them," she panicked at the thought of losing a sale. "You do realize many people don't think of them as flowers at all."

"I'm not one of them. As for cost, just bill my card." I pulled out my wallet to hand it to her.

I hope Meadow appreciates them. As for me, they remind me of roads in Alaska that would be dotted with them, reminiscent of Meadow even when I wasn't able to see her because of my obligations in Ketchikan.

The bouquet was originally wrapped in paper. When I first took it from the florist, I knew something was wrong about it. Finally, after dressing in jeans and a dressier shirt, I realized what it was. I tore the paper off and grabbed the natural twine I had in my suite, careful not to damage the beautiful blue buds. Using careful fingers, I tied a simple bow around the bouquet.

Now, it's perfect. It's something I would have given to her seventeen years ago as well as now. I don't want her wondering how much it cost; I only want her knowing it came from one place.

My heart.

When Meadow flings open the door, I forget about the damn flowers. Hell, I forget my own name. There's nothing in my head except the glow emanating from her. Forget spending time removing the primer from her skin, Meadow worked some secret woman magic—the kind I know my mother passed down to my sisters—to turn into the siren standing before me.

"You're beautiful," I manage to get out. I've always thought so, but the young girl has only evolved into an evocative woman who tantalizes me more than I ever thought anyone could.

Even Meadow herself.

I was right, I think fiercely. I couldn't tell Brad how I feel about her, even if I caved, because I'm just learning. What I feel for Meadow is so much more intense than what I felt all those years ago. It's a hundred times more intense as I stare at her in simple leggings, boots, and a blue top that's fitted yet slouchy with a dropped neckline.

"And you're charming. Come on in." She backs up, and I enter. "I just have to grab a jacket, and then I'll..."

"What is it?"

"Kody, what are those?" Meadow's voice is trembling.

"These?" I lift the bouquet for her inspection. "Just a little something I picked up in town."

"Forget-me-nots," she whispers. "You always said the name was stupid."

"Maybe the name was but never the meaning. After all, there was never a time I forgot about you, Meadow." I present the bouquet to her.

But unlike other women who have received flowers from me, Meadow doesn't make a fuss over them. She immediately tosses them on the counter in lieu of something much more important.

Surging into my arms.

Wrapping her arms around my neck, Meadow pulls herself up enough so her lips can find mine. She presses her lips against mine sweetly at first before tracing the seam of them with her tongue. My lips part in surprised pleasure, and Meadow quickly takes advantage, drawing the bottom lip between her lips to suck on it a moment before completely fusing our mouths together.

I groan before wrapping my arms around her to hold her right where I want her—against me.

For long moments, neither of us move beyond shifting our heads slightly to deepen the kiss or to take a necessary breath. Finally, I pull my head back just a bit and rest it against hers. Gasping, I manage, "That's a thank-you for flowers?"

"No," she pants. "That's for remembering the good and not hating me by having to remember the bad."

"I don't know if that's possible," I tell her. But something shifts next to my heart, a longing for those years that we didn't have.

"Still, it's nice to see tangible proof."

"I just wanted to do something nice."

Her fingers tug at my hair, making my insides quake. "It was more than nice."

I clear my throat before pulling her gently against the erection straining my jeans. "Flower, I'm trying to be gentle. On the other hand, if you want to forget about that..."

Her pupils turn to pinpoints. "Maybe I should put the flowers in some water." Her voice is breathless as she steps back and picks up her bouquet.

"And maybe I should feed you."

"That'd be good since I practically ate mineral spirits in order to get the Kilz off my lips."

Smacking my lips together, I make a face. "Well, now that you mention it, I was wondering what that taste was."

Meadow throws a cut stem at me even as her slightly swollen lips twitch with amusement. Turning around, she quickly searches for and finds a pitcher. Sinking the flowers in, she leans over to smell them. Over the tops, her eyes open and meet mine. It's as if the land has sucked all the air from my body. I feel my lungs inflate with something, but it's not the natural cycle of oxygen shared with the plants, the trees, the earth. It's something so purifying, I'm helpless. I want more, yet I'm afraid to take another hit.

Because it could give me everything even as it destroys me.

I just saw the soul of the woman who was somehow born to be mine despite the years and distance between us. And even as my heart rejoices, my mind cautions me because I don't know where she's at.

And she has to take that step to bring us closer.

MEADOW

I moan. "This may be the best thing I've ever put in my mouth."

Kody chokes on the drink of water he had just taken. "Seriously?"

I flush. Then, thinking about it, I don't take back what I said. "What can I say? It might be about the right size, but it sure as hell didn't have this same flavor." Quickly, I dunk the huckleberry barbecue chicken wing into the extra sauce I coaxed out of our harried waiter a few moments ago.

Kody mumbles something under his breath before reaching over to grab one of the wings on the platter between us.

We're at the lodge bar eating with a magnificent view of the Bigfork Lake in front of us. Somehow, we managed to get a seat up against the window where the lights from the lodge and the houses on the water reflect down, casting glows against the ripples of water.

When we got here, Kody wanted to take me to the more formal dining room, but I was captivated by the view as the dredges of the sun was setting.

I lift the glass of pinot noir to my lips and take a sip. "Have I said thank you yet?"

Kody stops massacring the chicken wing to ask, "For what?"

"For not pushing when you know you could have? For not asking the questions I know you have? For being an amazing man?"

Dropping the half-eaten wing to his plate, he wipes his fingers on his napkin and uses a wet wipe before reaching for mine. Lacing them together, he tugs me forward. "Meadow, I'm not going to pretend like I don't know things."

Even though my heart's hammering, I respond calmly, "I figured you might."

"It's been four weeks since we came back into each other's lives. It's been years of silence. We have a lot of time to work our way up to the answer of what happened in the years in between."

Before I can stop myself, the words are out of my mouth. "How about we tackle one per date?"

"One for you and one for me?" Kody's work-roughened fingers begin stroking in between mine, the sensation sending off signals to my long-neglected clit. God, if the man's hands ever got in that region, I might go off like a sparkler on the Fourth of July.

God bless America.

"I like that idea. This way, we can move past barriers without fear. When did you get so smart?"

"Is that your question?" I tease.

"Just making an observation, Ms. Borneman." He lifts my hand to his lips and brushes his lips across it. "Can I go first?"

"Sure." I figure Kody has the right to ask me anything he wants.

"Why didn't you take your name back after the divorce? Why did you stay Meadow Borneman?" His lips brush over the indent where my rings rested that's slowly easing as the days pass.

"Does it bother you?"

"Is that your question?" His face doesn't reveal the answer one way or the other.

I shake my head to indicate no, it isn't before I give him the answer he's looking for. "If it was just me, I'd have paid any amount of money to have removed his name from me. But I left it as is because of the kids."

Kody appears frustrated.

"Hey, what is it?"

"I want to ask you more, but we said one question each."

I dip my head in rueful acknowledgment. "I think this is getting to know each other on a deeper level, Mr. Laurence. If learning about each other isn't so cut-and-dried, then we ask questions, we give answers."

"That's fair."

"I'd like to think you'll answer the same way when it's your turn."

"I'd like to think I don't have secrets," he counters.

I reach over and pat his cheek condescendingly. "That's so sweet, and I bet if I asked anyone who knew you—and there are plenty around—they'd tell me otherwise."

He pales. "Christ, this was such a good date."

I giggle just as our server comes up to remove our appetizer and plates. When he does, Kody leans forward. "Why would you have cut so much history out of your life? You—" He swallows hard before he forces the word out. "—loved him a long time."

I give myself a moment to think of the best way to explain it. And all of our hard work at Nature's Song flashes through my mind. "You know how possessive you were of Nature's Song when you saw the damage to it? There was a piece of your soul tied to it, even after all the years, despite the misuse?"

"Yes."

"That's how I feel about Mitch." Kody rears back as if I've slapped him. I squeeze his hands hard and try to make him understand. "We're bound, Kody. We have children, the most indelible tie there is. From now until the end of time, we'll share memories with them—providing he can prove himself to be the father he used to be with them. And before all the lies and the games, he was a good one. He was an important part of Elise and MJ's lives, and for their sakes, I hope like hell he can get over..." I release Kody's hand to wave mine in the air. "Whatever this selfish bullshit is. Otherwise, he'll lose them."

"He's doing a bang-up job."

"Aren't we both?" The devastation of the last few weeks lives in my words. But I finish with, "But in short, I kept my name not to alienate my children."

I sit back and take a long drink of wine.

Kody slides off his stool and comes around the table. "I think that's one of the most courageous things I've heard you do for your children when your own pain could have led you to be destructive. You could have withered; instead you sought out the sun. Just like any flower would." Bending down, he brushes his lips against mine. He moves back to his side of the table, leaving me reeling.

"For months, I've had questions and uncertainty running through my head about everything. And it seems like everyone I've talked with has an opinion that differs from my own. For just a moment to have someone support something I've done means everything."

Flame that has nothing to do with the flickering candle between us leaps into Kody's eyes. "I haven't walked in your shoes. What right do I have to play judge and jury? And really, let's be honest. I just wanted to know if I was facing competition from your ex." The wicked leer he shoots me sends me into gales of laughter just as our mains arrive.

I'm dabbing tears from my eyes. "Oh, Kody, if you only knew..."

"Knew what?"

I smile but don't answer. His time for questions is over. Just as he takes a bite into his burger, I ask innocently, "So, is it really true you're friends with all your exes?"

Kody begins coughing as the bite of food goes down the wrong way. "Where in sweet hell did you hear that?"

"Maris, of course."

"Damn. That means she heard it from only one person."

And together, we both say, "Jed."

Pushing back his burger, he demands, "Do you really want to hear this?"

I fork up a bite of my salmon and nod. "Kody, I was with the same man for a long time. And you know what's terrible?"

"What?" Eyeing his burger like it might be his salvation, he braves another bite.

"Every time your name was mentioned, I think I missed you more than I missed him. Me and you? Well, we were...special."

"Meadow?"

"Yes?"

"While I'll admit I've never ended a past relationship poorly, I don't plan on ever being your friend ever again. Ever." His voice rasps out the last word, penetrating sea-colored eyes pinning me in place.

I squirm in my chair, certain I'm either having a heart attack or an orgasm. Either one is a likelihood.

His sexy laugh floats between us. "I'm certain you'd know if it was a heart attack, and I'm damn certain I'd know if it was an orgasm. Now, let's finish up and get out of here."

"You don't have to tell me twice." I chunk off a bite of salmon and hold it to his lips.

He accepts the bite. "Delicious. But not quite the taste I want in my mouth right now."

Forget the heart attack. I know damn well the pounding of my heart is due to the ache between my legs.

ON THE DRIVE BACK, I've been amusing Kody as I sing along to the '90s channel on his satellite radio. After a while, my voice drifts off when I realize how many songs I've sung along to reminded me of Kody and the nights we spent at the Smiths' instead of the early memories of my marriage.

"What are you thinking so hard about over there?"

"It's amazing how it took being forced to break away for me to realize I wasn't happy—and not just with my marriage. In so many ways, there were things wrong with my life in Juneau, but it took the worst kind of experience for me to be able to make a change. What does that say about the woman I am?"

"That you're human," he replies simply before reaching for my hand. "You said it yourself at dinner, if it was just you, maybe you would have taken a chance a lot sooner. Don't blame yourself for not doing so now. If we all had the ability to look back and make different decisions, don't you think there are those I wouldn't choose to do over?"

"What would you do differently?"

"There's two that will haunt me." Kody's voice sounds hollow.

Whoa. This wasn't what I was expecting. I reach over and turn down the radio, thinking Britney isn't the best background for this. "Will you share them?"

His hand tightens on mine. "The first is never going to see Jed in Florida. He asked time and again. If I could have broken away, he would have been so happy. Did he resent having to come to us? Did he understand it was always just about poor timing? And now that I know everything, how many lives would have changed?"

"Oh, Kody." My heart aches. "I don't doubt for a minute Jed loved you."

"Did I tell you he gave me a gift certificate to stay here at Nature's Song?" For just a moment, there's a wholly amused smile on his face. "I can just see bringing the guys back for a reunion and having you at our beck and call."

I try to tug my hand away. "Now, that's just cruel. Why would you end a perfectly lovely evening by ruining it that way?"

Kody laughs. "I don't think even Jed could have planned this, sweetheart. Despite his machinations with Jennings and Kara, there's no way he could have foreseen this."

"True." Then, "You'd come back after you leave?" I whisper almost inaudibly.

My comment has the desired effect. Kody growls. "Oh, yeah."

Silence envelops us for a few moments while I dream of what could happen if Kody came back. Then he wipes my mind blank with his next words. "My other regret should be obvious by now, I imagine. I waited too long to ask a beautiful woman out, and she slipped through my fingers." He slants a glance in my direction while I gape at him. "I'm trying not to screw up my second chance."

I'm almost numb even as my body absorbs the rush of feeling everything. He hasn't let go of my hand, but now even that simple touch has me wanting more, wanting him. And what's even more precious than that is believing I'm worthy of it.

In a thousand different ways since I first knew Kody, I convinced myself this would never happen. First, he was destined for so much more than I could be; then I was married. But since we've met here as equals, I've never questioned the force of emotions that keeps trying to grow between us.

"Maybe it's finally our time," I say aloud in the darkened vehicle.

"Maybe it is. Are you ready for it?" He brings my hand to his lips, not to soothe but something else. Something I shied away from years ago.

Kody Laurence wants me. And the hell of it is, I've wanted him back.

As we pull up to the gate at Nature's Song, I lean forward. "Yes. Are you?"

The security lights give just enough light into the car so I can see the strain on his handsome face. "I've been waiting a long time, Meadow."

As soon as the gate's open, Kody drops my hand to turn his attention to driving. Making the turn off to my house, we're soon pulling up to my door.

But my mind is made up.

I want this man any way he'll have me for as long as it will last.

Tonight's a good start.

MEADOW

"Would you like to come in for a few?"

Kody turns off the engine. His probing gaze finds mine before he nods. "Wait and I'll be around to help you down."

He slides out of the cab, and my blood begins pumping through my veins so hard I can feel it, hear it. I'm overheating just at the idea of us alone.

As the door is opened, the cool night air blasting me is a welcome reprieve. "Thanks."

His eyes narrow, until I feel like I'm nothing more than his prey. "You're welcome."

I let us both inside before shrugging off my coat. I'm immediately drawn to the flowers Kody gave me a few hours before. "Honestly, I'm not sure what I have beyond wine, water, coffee. Does any of that work for you?" Is that my voice all high-pitched and squeaky? Nerves come at me out of nowhere.

Each metallic zip of his jacket coming undone holds me in place as surely as if he'd drawn his hands across my skin. "Or if none of that works..." My voice trails off as I feel Kody's hands shift my hair aside before his lips nuzzle the nape of my neck. My head bows forward, exposing even more skin, more of my soul.

Kody's lips trail down over each vertebra while his hands grip my arms firmly. His hands are the only thing preventing from falling down with the sensations rioting through me.

When his teeth graze in the hollow between my shoulder and my neck, my head falls back against his. When I twist my face upward to kiss him, we're so close we're breathing in the other's whispers and dreams so they land perfectly where the other needs them—safely in the other's heart.

Kody spins me in his arms before backing me up against the wood pole in the foyer. "All I want is you." His calloused fingers drag through my hair, occasionally catching, until they wind up over the pounding of my heart. "Do you want me?"

I thread my fingers into his reddish-gold hair and tug his head down. "Yes." Such a simple word for such an overwhelming need.

Kody braces an arm on the column above me, wrapping the other around my waist. Hauling me against his body, I shiver when I feel the contours of his erection against my leggings. "Thank fucking God. I was starting to develop Flower Power again."

I sputter, "What the hell is Flower Power?"

He thrusts his hips against mine, and I let out a soft moan.

Kody puts his lips to my ear before sharing something so earthy, so male, something that makes my insides quiver even as I feel my knees weaken. "It means grabbing a hold of my own dick and pretending it was your hands on me."

Oh. My. God.

"While it builds up a man's arm strength over time, it will never substitute for the single woman he craves who drives him to that condition. The benefit is"—his voice is a sexy croon—"imagine what my hands will do when they're all over your body."

Should I be appalled? No, the thought of him touching himself while thinking about me is devastating.

"I have a lot of practice, then and now." He pins me with the strength of his muscular thighs, leaving his hands to roam over me freely. I feel his fingers deftly working the small buttons of my shirt. "I can't wait to touch you, to taste you, to finally sink my cock inside of you."

This close to him, I can feel the heat of his body sear me through his dress shirt. Almost hypnotized by the feral look on his face, I raise my hands to the top button of his dress shirt. I fumble with the first one, the second. "I'm so out of practice." My voice comes out shakily as my fingers descend toward his waistband.

"There's no amount of practice that could prepare me for you." I'm about to shy away from the pretty words until Kody holds out a hand for me to see. There's a fine tremor setting it in motion that settles something inside of me.

My head collides with the pillar as Kody skims his hands lazily up and down my now exposed torso. I'm only wearing a bandeau bra because of the sheerness of my shirt, which Kody impatiently tossed to the floor. Meanwhile, I'm drowning every time his fingers touch me. The years of hard work that have callused his fingers brand me, leaving fire in their wake. The seam of my leggings is getting soaked at the thought of him using them around my clit. But... "Do you want to go to bed?"

"Maybe for round two," he mutters as he fumbles for something in his pocket. When he whips out his multiuse tool, my eyebrows skyrocket. "Stand perfectly still," he warns me. Then Kody Laurence shows exactly how impatient he is for me. He cuts the top seam of my bra and my leggings before tossing the tool aside.

I follow it as it lands with a clunk. Then I lick my lips in anticipation, in provocation. I'm not sure which. All I know is by the feral hooding of Kody's eyes, it's as if his own inner control has snapped.

With one tear, he renders my bra useless. My gasp and the rip of material occur within milliseconds of one another. He quickly tugs the material away, my breasts falling heavily into his waiting hands. I don't know whether to be exhilarated or terrified. After all, they're no longer the same pert breasts as the twenty-two-year-old he knew. I'm in good shape, but motherhood changed my body in all the best ways.

When I tip my head back to gauge his reaction, there's nothing but reverence in his expression as he rakes his thumb over the turgid tip. "Exquisite," he utters before lowering his head.

The minute the heat of his mouth surrounds the tip of my breast and Kody sucks it firmly, a whimper escapes. I can't control it any more than I can control my reaction which is to be as close to him as I can.

Now.

Pushing against the pillar, I wrap one leg around his strong back, wanting to feel his skin against mine. I shove frantically against the shirt blocking all those muscles I've dreamed about from my view. I can only be grateful he didn't button his shirtsleeves as Kody helps me by shrugging one arm and then the other out of the material. It too lands somewhere.

Meanwhile, Kody's switched nipples, sending pleasure tearing through my senses. But I push back. "No, Kody."

He rears back, standing stock-still until I run my hand over him from the joint over his shoulder, through the thatch of hair. "My turn. You're not the only one who's waited."

Then I swing him around until his back is up against the pillar. I begin to trail kisses everywhere I can reach over the breadth of his chest, spending particular time swirling my tongue over his nipples which are as hard as mine. Taking a small nip, I'm startled when I hear him cry out.

"Fuck." The curse is bitten out as his hand slams back against the hardwood behind him. The other is threading into my long hair as I trail my tongue down over every box of his cut abdomen. I can feel him fighting for control. I think I love him more because he's not wresting it away from me but letting me explore his big body.

Soon, my tongue is darting along the impossible V a man his age shouldn't be able to boast of having as I undo his belt and fumble with the clasping of his jeans. But my leggings are useless to soak up the moisture that floods me when I find out Kody Laurence goes commando. I'm just about to lean forward to brush my lips across his bead of fluid that's escaped when I'm suddenly hauled to my feet.

"Not yet," he hisses. "I haven't dreamed all these years for it to be over this fucking soon."

Lowering his head once again, Kody's kisses work much like his words do. They drag me to a place I've never been where I'm wanted and cherished for being nothing more than me. I'm not sure I ever want to come back from it.

Using the strength he demonstrated to dispose of my bra, Kody renders my leggings to much the same fate. He lifts one foot and manages to work the remains off one ankle boot. Then while I feel each and every shift of his powerful muscles, he boosts me against the smooth wood with nothing at my back before looking down. A carnal smile touches his face. "I see we have the same taste in underwear."

I begin to stammer, "I couldn't find my thongs. I thought I..."

He lays a thumb across my fingers. "Trust me, Meadow. Don't bother finding them." He rolls his barely covered cock against my naked pussy, and I moan.

I absorb every single sensation: the feel of Kody's bare chest against mine, the roughness of his jeans abrading the inside of my thighs, and the calloused thumb tugging my lower lip down—maybe in preparation for his kiss? The feel of his powerful muscles shift beneath my fingers. I can't stop touching him, and it leads to more.

I have to taste him. I do. It's a primal need. Opening my mouth, I draw his thumb inside and do what I wanted so badly to do to his cock earlier. Kody stills his movements as I draw from him, rolling my tongue over the head of his thumb. I lash it with little flicks back and forth, much like I would have the slit that was just beginning to leak fluid.

"God, Meadow." His head drops forward, breathing ragged.

But Kody's no passive player. His lips begin to wander from my bare shoulders to the tops of my breasts. I arch into his lips, gasping, which frees his thumb as his other hand spreads my folds and dances along my clit.

"Kody. Don't stop!"

"Wasn't planning on it," he says, the guttural sound of his voice another layer of sensation.

And then when his fingers dance easily over the opening of my sex, I bury my face in his shoulder. I'm shaking. "I'm so afraid, so everything, I could fly away."

"Then fly, sweetheart," Kody says just before he takes my mouth and pushes two fingers into me.

Shudders of pleasure tear through me. Kody makes a small adjustment of his fingers that has me bucking against him. Tearing his mouth away from mine, he says, "I can't wait to feast on this pretty little pussy in round two. Are you going to want that, Meadow? Just like I always imagined, you spread out before me, naked, my mouth...right...here." Then Kody presses the heel of his hand down against my clit.

My clit is throbbing against the pressure of his hand as each thrust of his fingers causes my walls to clamp down tighter and tighter. Finally, with a keening sound, I detonate around him.

I don't know how long his sheer strength has held me just like that while I come down from the clouds, his fingers still buried deep inside of me, twitching gently to keep me aware of him. "Like I need a reminder. If you think I don't want what's hiding behind those jeans, you are so wrong."

Kody laughs, a sexy, predatory sound. Reaching for his face, I pull him close and kiss his forehead. Then I kiss the bridge of his nose, each brow, before laying my lips against his. "Thank you."

"That is never something you have to thank me for." Slowly, Kody pulls his fingers from me. While I watch with a mixture of shock and arousal, he slides his fingers into his mouth and sucks them clean. His eyes narrow. "That taste will have to do until I get you on a bed."

Boldly, I reach down between my legs which are still wrapped around him. I find his cock head damp with fluid. "Can't wait?"

Reaching behind him for his wallet, he pulls out a condom. Tossing the leather billfold somewhere onto the pile of our discarded items, he shakes his head. He fiddles beneath my hips for a moment before surging against me. "Time's up."

Kody pulls his hips back slightly. Lacing our fingers together over my head, he uses his other hand to wet the crest of his cock in the juice still dripping from my orgasm. But it's my heart that splits wide open waiting for him to take his rightful place when before he connects us, he whispers, "Are you sure?"

I use my free hand to draw him in for a deep kiss. I can feel the strain he's under as his body shudders beneath my hands. When I pull away, I whisper, "With you, I'm sure of so many things. Take me, Kody."

Kody begins easing himself inside me, parting me. The feeling of ecstasy, as much from the emotional intimacy as the physical, causes my neck to arch. "God, Kody," I gasp.

He ducks his head down and begins to place small kisses on my lips as his hips shuttle back and forth as his thrusts take him deeper, stretching me further. My legs tighten around his hips, my arms around his shoulders, as I feel the power of him, the power of us, unleashed.

"Tell me it's not another fucking dream" he groans.

I don't know how he's able to talk. I'm fighting for each breath as a new round of sensations threaten to drown me. All I can do is tip his head back and press my lips to his. I absorb the furious thrusting of his hips, and yet, he still hasn't let go of my hand.

My anchor in a storm that's determined to destroy us both. It's ripping apart every coherent thought but one.

Him.

Kody's other hand is buffering me from the pillar from the brutal pace of his hips. It also leaves my hand free to roam across his skin. Finally, when I feel the crazy-hot tension start to snap inside me for the second time, I cup his cheek. Forcing his eyes to meet mine, I manage to get out, "I don't want to wake up," before I snap my head back.

Kody's hips jerk once, twice more before he grinds his hips against me. "Neither do I, baby."

He leans against me for long moments as we try to regain our breath. Finally, after separating our bodies, he carries me to my bed.

After we catch our breath, it doesn't take much for round two. But despite the phenomenal sex, it's the feeling of Kody rolling me to my side and sliding his legs behind mine before whispering, "Go to sleep," that sends my heart slamming against my rib cage.

Instinctively, I reach for the phone to text Rainey to tell her all about it. When I can't, silent tears fall down my face.

How can life demand the highest of highs and retaliate with the lowest of lows? It's with that thought I fall asleep, never knowing the man behind me waits until I do before he brushes away my tears.

KODY

It wasn't a dream. I'm certain of this because even in the best of dreams I've had about Meadow Borneman, they've never extended beyond sinking my dick inside of her.

What's happening now is better than anything sexual. Meadow wrapped around me, her head nestled against my chest. She's still sleeping, but her fingers are tangled in my chest hair. Her leg is hooked high against mine, leaving her moist heat to ride against my bare thigh.

And my morning wood.

"What a douchebag," I mutter into the silent stillness of the room. Mitch Borneman was a complete idiot, but I almost want to send the guy a thank-you card for being such a fucking moron. "Does Hallmark make cards like that?"

"Hmm?" Like a cat, Meadow stretches against me.

"I was thinking about your ex," I admit.

Meadow's head jerks back. "Way to snuff out the postcoital glow, Kody!" she snaps. She flops over to her back in a huff.

I roll her way and grin when she glares up at me. "I was thanking him for being an idiot. Does that count?"

Holding on to her grudge for two seconds, Meadow laughs before slapping a hand over her mouth.

I frown. "What's wrong?"

"Mworningbweath" comes out as a jumble from behind her hands.

I smother a chuckle, before saying with complete sincerity, "I have a cure for that."

Her eyebrows raise, but her hand doesn't move.

I don't say anything. Instead, I merely fling the bedclothes off us both. My aroused cock springs up from the nest of hair I keep neatly trimmed. I've been used to waking up in some semblance of this condition since my preteens but never this bad.

I blame the woman in bed with me.

My cock is already begging for attention this morning when it should be dead after the workout Meadow and I gave it last night. But it's like it's punishing me for all the mornings I took matters into my own hand when I'd wake up hard and aching after dreaming about the woman who's staring at it as if it could be breakfast, lunch, and dinner wrapped up in one.

God, I hope so.

Meadow's hand falls forgotten from her mouth as she clears her throat. "Do you always wake up like that?"

"Like this? Not quite like this. This is the very definition of Flower Power."

"Do you...do you plan on doing something about it?" Her eyes flick up to mine and away but not before I miss the look of interest in her eyes.

"Well, I'll be damned. Did hearing about that turn you on last night, Flower?"

Meadow squeezing her thighs together doesn't escape my notice. "Fuck, if you want to see me stroke myself, who am I to deny it?" I lower my hand and grip the flesh just below my head.

A small bead of fluid escapes. Right along with a moan from Meadow.

I prop my legs a bit. If I'm going to put on a show for her, then fuck if I'm not going to be comfortable. Meadow scrambles around the end of my feet for a better view, heedless of her own nudity and how her bouncing tits wreak havoc on my self-control.

She's breathless as I apply another stroke, two. I use my thumb to spread the fluid escaping over the head of my cock. Almost of her own violation, Meadow leans down to get a taste, swatting my hands away.

"That's it, sweetheart," I groan as she drags her fingers up my inner thighs. I shift my feet apart some more to make room for her.

Meadow's lips suck the entire head of my cock into her mouth. She swirls her tongue, much like she did over my nipples last night. Pulling back, she drags her lips down the shaft until she finds the sacs beneath. With a mischievous glance up at me, she carefully pulls one into her mouth, treating it to the same gentle suction.

"Son of a bitch," I curse. My hands fist the sheet beneath me.

Releasing me with a pop, Meadow taunts me, "Hmm. You're right. I guess I don't think I have to worry about morning breath. But I guess it's time to rinse."

Then using her lips and hands, she proceeds to destroy my senses until I erupt in her mouth.

When she's done, I roll her over to her back and proceed to show her the importance of good oral hygiene between partners goes both ways.

We don't leave the bed for quite a while.

"SINCE TODAY'S A DAY OFF, you know what might be nice to do?" Meadow has just come out of her bedroom in jeans and a sweater. Her long hair is still wet from our shared shower.

I'm wearing the same jeans from last night but have yet to slide into a shirt. I was too intent on coffee. "What's that?"

"How about heading out to Glacier National Park? The roads are clear at least to Lake McDonald."

My back's to her when I say ruefully, "We'll need to run by the lodge. I was prepared for certain possibilities last night, Meadow. I certainly wasn't ready to do the walk of shame." I snicker.

I expect her to laugh along with me, but I know something's wrong when I hear nothing. Whirling around, I find her eyes downcast. Forgetting about anything else, I make it to her in three large strides. Cupping her face, I demand, "Tell me what's wrong."

"It's just, I wouldn't call what we did shameful." Pride-filled blue eyes lift to meet mine. "If that's the way you feel, then maybe…"

I don't let her finish that sentence. I'm too busy wrapping her up in my arms. "No. It's not. It's a stupid expression that has nothing to do with the intimacy between two people who exchange something as beautiful as what we did last night and this morning."

"Oh."

"God, I need to remember that your ex did a number on you," I grate out.

"Actually, Kody. In this case, I wouldn't blame Mitch. I only had one lover, I never experienced this 'walk of shame.'"

But her words fill me with a savage heat. "Are you telling me that Mitch was your first? And there's been no one since?"

"Well, yes."

"And you want to go to a glacier?" I ask her mildly, my mind already thinking of all the ways I can take her. I start stalking Meadow until she's backed up against the counter.

Nice. I can work with that.

Meadow lays a hand in the middle of my chest. "Easy there. How about giving my parts time to adjust to your more sizable ones." She flushes to the roots of her hair.

"You realize every time you keep opening your mouth, any comparison between me and your ex keeps ending up in my favor?" But now that she's mentioned it, between last night and today, I've used up my supply of condoms. And, I admit silently, I'm not as young as I used to be either.

It takes Meadow a second before she bursts out laughing. "Can't deny that one, but I'm just saying, it's been a while and I need a short rest."

Dropping my head down to hers, I pluck a kiss from her lips. "So, how about this for a plan? We head back to lodge, get me some clothes, and then go for a ride. Then, if you don't mind, I'll stay over."

"Honesty?"

"Always." Everything about making this chance between us work hinges on honesty.

"It sounds just about perfect."

*

AFTER MEADOW OOH'ED and aah'ed over the suite I have at the lodge, I grabbed enough clothes and my tools so I wouldn't need to come back for a few days. After stopping to let the desk clerk know I'd be away for a few days, we set off for the west entrance to Glacier National Park.

We make great time even with Meadow punching me in the arm repeatedly to stop at the Huckleberry Patch. "Just to do a little shopping. Come on, Kody. They have pie," she tries to wheedle.

"Flower, let's go to the park first. I'm sure the store will be open." Because God help me if they're not.

"You realize you will be driving back out here if they're not."

"So noted." We're at a stoplight, so I lean over and press my lips to her pouting ones. Then I wonder aloud, "How did you know they have pie?"

Meadow freezes. Her voice breaks. "Not now. I'll answer that question when we get inside the park, okay?"

She's fiddling with her phone, so I can't take her hand like I normally would. Instead, I lay my hand on her leg as we begin moving. "Okay." It's all I can offer her right now.

Her mood has shifted from exuberant to subdued as we pay for a pass and follow the navigation to the Going to the Sun Road. I heard the warning of the park ranger about the limited drivability. "There's no way we're getting past Lake McDonald today."

"That's all right. There will be other days to make it all the way. Won't there be?" The anxiety in Meadow's voice is like a punch in the gut.

I find the first pull-off for a photo opportunity. Turning to her, I assure her, "There will be," but she's blind and deaf to what I'm saying.

"Kody, look. Just, look." Within seconds, she scrambling from the truck. I'm quick to follow.

Grabbing her hand after she comes around the hood, we check for traffic before dashing across the street and carefully make our way down the embankment to the water's edge. And there she is.

The Continental Divide.

"It's magnificent."

"There was a reason I wanted to come here first."

"Why's that?" I face her, but she steps back carefully.

"Give me a moment. I need this picture of you. Just like this. Then I'll answer the question you asked me earlier."

I still and let Meadow take a few pictures on her phone. Then she fiddles for just a moment with it before telling me, "Did you know Lake McDonald is the largest lake in Glacier National Park? In fact, it was glaciers that carved the valley the water sits in."

"I didn't. I'm impressed you do."

"Oh, I cheated. I looked it up. It's right here." She holds up her phone. "I have a whole bunch of facts about the park ready for when..."

I take a step forward. "For what?"

"I thought if I brought the kids here, it might help them make a connection to home. You know? We had Mendenhall there, and maybe if we made it all the way up to the top of the Going to the Sun Road, they'd realize home isn't that far away. I have this list of things to do with them when they got here, but that's never going to happen now, is it? I don't know what to do yet about the pain that's causing me, and yet, there's you." Meadow clenches her jaw before giving me a ghost of a smile. "So, you see, I needed to take a picture of you to keep myself from pitching this phone into the lake." And that's when I'm witness to a strong woman breaking.

Tugging her into my arms, I hold on as she weeps. It's the storm I've been expecting since I arrived, but not for the reasons I anticipated. It wasn't the harsh realities of a new job. It isn't the anger over a marriage ending. It's the heartbreak over children she filled with her love turning their back on everything she sacrificed.

And now that I'm holding on to the one woman I always wanted, I want to fix this for her. But can I set aside my anger and pride to reach out to the men who can help me do it?

She sniffles and pulls back. "I apologize. Sometimes I need to cry to be able to figure out where to start over again."

"I never gave much thought to having children," I find myself saying.

Her lips part, but no words come out.

"Jed used to think I needed a houseful. He said whether they were my own blood or not, didn't matter. They'd still be mine. I thought after having six sisters to look after, I was done with having that responsibility."

"I understand—"

"I've always liked kids." I talk over her as if Meadow hasn't said a word. "Loved them in fact—maybe with the exception of Sandra in her teens because she's Satan who has my parents demonized to do her evil."

Meadow gives a hiccuping snort. "I feel like I have to meet her."

I wrap an arm around her and haul her against me. In my life, I never thought watching the way a woman's pupils dilated would be as arousing as the press of her breasts against me. But everything about Meadow has changed the way I think and feel. "Children weren't something I thought of before, but now I get why the brother of my heart understood I would have them. Because if they're anything like their mother, I have little doubt my feelings for them are going to be strong." Meadow goes to speak, but I gently hush her. "That's for later, Meadow. Not now."

The air is thick, despite the crisp cold of the Montana air. I've just laid out everything I ever wanted to say to Meadow from the time I was a young man. And all around us is silence. I have no regrets though. I start to pull back when I hear her voice.

"For years, I told myself I wanted you to be happy. I wanted you to forget all about me, to find love."

"How could I?" I'm about to say more when she lays a cold finger across my lips.

"Because I needed to tell myself that, Kody. Otherwise, how was I supposed to stop feeling guilty for being as uncommitted in my heart to my marriage as my ex was? Do you know what the truth is?"

"What?"

"You were right. Ever since that night. So, was there really a differ-ence between my feelings for you and the way Mitch cheated on me?"

"You're damn right there was."

"How?" Her voice is so lost and bewildered.

"Because otherwise, you would have let me do this on any of the number of occasions we saw each other over the years."

I jerk Meadow so hard, her phone drops from her hands. Then I'm kissing her so long beneath the cold Montana sky, I lose track of time. It isn't until we hear another voice say, "Oh, my! Harold!" that we break apart and begin to laugh.

Scooping up her cell, I hand it to her. "I don't ever want to hear you compare yourself to him again, Meadow. You were faithful to the vows you took."

She touches her lips. "Okay."

"Come on, it's time to get you some pie."

Once we climb the embankment, Meadow declares, "Maybe we should get it to go."

God, I love the way she thinks. Then again, I just plain love her.

KODY

Meadow's breathing is even, but I can't manage to sleep. Even after I made love to her and she pulled on a ridiculous shirt with a bear proclaiming "I'll be your huckleberry" we picked up at the Huckleberry Patch—as well as the most delicious pie I've ever laid waste to—I can't get my mind to relax.

Maybe it's the fact I'm lying here fighting loneliness.

Even though I've started to let my mom in on what I'm feeling about Meadow, I should be able to let Jennings, Nick, and Brad know how I'm feeling. That's the way it was as Brad took his ribbing about Rainey. Jennings lived falling in love with Kara out in technicolor. And Jed? Jesus, tears drip down my face when I remember sitting on the back porch at Nature's Song while we discussed his falling in love with his future husband, Dean.

If we were on the same page, I'd have sent them one of the goofy pictures I took of her using strands of huckleberry licorice as a microphone as she sang along with the '90s channel on satellite radio as I made rude comments to Britney and the Spice Girls, but I couldn't help lending my voice to Bryan Adams's ballad from *Robin Hood* which —as I lie here reflecting on the lyrics—perfectly echoes everything I want to give to the woman in my arms.

Maybe that's what I need to do. I need to talk with one of my brothers.

Sliding away from Meadow, I wrap her arms around my pillow. Scooping up my clothes as quietly as possible, I carry them out of the room. Quickly I slip on my jeans and button up my shirt. I'm tying the laces of my boots when I hear her soft, hesitant voice. "Going somewhere?"

I look up and there she is, the woman I'd give up anything for, even friendships that were supposed to last a lifetime. Her hair is smashed to the side of her head. She's still holding the pillow I slid into her arms a few moments ago. Walking straight to her, I bend down and kiss her lightly. "I need to talk to Jed." It sounds slightly crazier when I say it out loud.

Moonlight casts a soft glow over her skin as she drops the pillow to the floor in order for her hands to frame my face. "I'll be here waiting."

I kiss her fiercely, because that's how I love her. "I'll be back soon." Then I turn and grab my coat off the back of the couch.

Soon, I'm heading up the main road to Nature's Song. I use my codes to unlock the front door before flipping on a minimum of lights and head right out toward the back deck. Easing open the slider, I see the outline of where the furniture used to be. I walk around to where I was sprawled in the love seat that day and say exactly what I said to him that afternoon. "How did you know?"

"Probably the same way I know a lot of things, Kody. I watch people."

My head turned and looked back over my shoulder into the house where Brad and Nick were arguing over who had caught the biggest fish. "You don't think he knows, do you?" The last thing in the world I needed was for Brad to realize that I'm in love with his sister-in-law.

Still.

Always.

Jed barked out a laugh. "There are some things you all have to figure out on your own, as much as I want to dunk your heads under some ice-cold glacier water to get you all to see what the hell's right in front of you. Nothing about love is perfect in this world, Kody. Sometimes, we have to wait a lifetime to find out why we suffer through it."

"She's the love I waited a lifetime for, Jed." Tears dry on my face as fast as they're coming. "I knew Brad wouldn't understand. Remember, I even worried about it. But if I have to choose between brotherhood and love, I choose love. I know you understand that.

"You were right about so many things, buddy. I can see it all with her—the house, the kids. The whole shebang. And for Christ's sake—what the hell are you going to do to take down Tiny Douchebag?" A reluctant smile crosses my lips. "Rainey's nickname for Mitch is pure genius, though I'm royally pissed at her too. Well, I suppose you can see what's going on. I'm barely holding on when all I want to do is to protect my woman."

My email pings, but I ignore it. I'm too busy talking with the one brother who I know is still talking with me. "Just...watch out over Meadow's kids, buddy? I've got her covered." Then realizing what I've said, I groan aloud. "I mean protect her, you pervert. I'd do anything for her." Then a stupid smile crosses my face. "Not that the other isn't ridiculous, but don't be pulling some kind of poltergeist shit and showing up in the middle of things with those damn flamingo shorts on. Okay?" My throat gets tight when I picture him spitting his drink at me. "I love you, Jedidiah. Always have. Always will. My love to Dean."

Just as I'm about to leave the porch, my phone reminds me I have an email. I frown when I look at the time. It's after 1:00 a.m. I close the slider as I fish my phone out of my jacket pocket. Then I fumble it when the sender and subject come across my screen.

Sender: Kara Malone

Subject: FAMILY. URGENT. PLEASE OPEN!!!

"Oh, God. What happened? Jennings? Kevin?" Quickly unlocking my phone, I open Kara's email.

Kody,

I hope you're reading this. We're all getting desperate.

First, let me state, Brad and Rainey are NOT trying to take Meadow's children away from her. The kids were about half a heartbeat away from having a breakdown. To keep them from doing something desperate after their father met them at the school bus the day Elise called Meadow, they permitted the call. They had no idea what Elise was going to say to her mother. And from what I'm being told, MJ is just going along with whatever his big sister is doing because Elise is the only touchpoint in his world throughout this godforsaken mess.

Second, Brad's an idiot. No, he's a foolish moron for demanding information that's not his right to have. Even Rainey's pissed at him for that. You're just an idiot. How you could possibly think that the Jacks would give up on your friendship after Brad had an epic case of open-mouth-and-insert-foot? You must be in love. That's the only way I can excuse such a smart man being so incredibly stupid. Jennings is losing his mind worrying he's lost another brother. And damnit, Kody, how dare you? After losing Jed? How could you put them through all of this? Brad, well, like I said, he's a moron. But Jennings? Nick? Didn't you all make some sort of sacred vow while sacrificing the guts of a sheep? Oh, sorry, no wait. That would be before you all came into the funeral of two men I loved more than anything other than my son and mean-mugged me over their ashes. My bad.

Even though years separated us, I remember Jed urging me time and time again not to give up on Jennings, that he wasn't the same man I knew back in the day. Well, we need you both to not give up on all of us. It's your turn to show Jed you're still a part of this family.

By the way, we're all still pissed at Brad. And Nick's mad at all of us. We won't talk about Maris. That's too much for one email.

Please respond when you get this.

Love,

Kara

I look out the window and can practically see Jed shrugging his shoulders as if he's saying, "What can you do?"

I hit Reply and type out a quick message because all I want to do is get back to Meadow.

Kara,

Could I reply to this rather lengthy email tomorrow?

And for the record, I'll always love you guys. I just won't let Meadow be hurt anymore.

Kody

Her reply comes in less than one minute later.

YES!!!!!!

I don't reply. All I do is shove my phone into my pocket and get into my truck. When I get back to Meadow's, I shuck my clothes and crawl beneath the covers. She immediately turns into my arms.

Half-asleep, she asks, "How's Jed?"

Truthfully, I respond, "A pain in my ass."

Her lips curve up even as she gets comfortable. I pull her tighter. I hear her murmur, "Then everything's just fine with him."

My heart clenches when I realize she's absolutely right. With that, I close my eyes and I'm finally able to sleep because maybe things are moving along with a little help from up above.

KODY

Today I feel like celebrating. We're about 50 percent complete with the major renovation. Lenny is applying the final stain to the built-ins in the living room. All of the doors and windows are repaired. The new wine cellar racks have been installed. And the kitchen cabinets were delivered. They're even better than I imagined, and I'm eager to get them installed. The distressed two-toned cabinets fit in with the rustic appearance of the cabin without screaming pretentious. With the solid surface counters, this kitchen will hold up with minimal maintenance for the Wilde family and any renters. And damn if I'm not debating replacing all of my appliances with the ones we ordered.

But every time I try to get Meadow's attention, she's on the porch with her cell up to her ear. While my crew's been working for over two and a half hours, she hasn't taken the damn thing away from her ear. I wonder what's going to give out first, her hand from a cramp or the damn battery.

As this is the last major project the majority of them will be involved with before hightailing it back to Portland, she needs to get her ass inside and show her appreciation. In just weeks, my crew brought Nature's Song back from the brink of disaster to being almost complete.

I stomp off in the direction of the porch to find out what the issue is.

"No, Mitchell. This isn't a damn joke, nor is it a play for more money. If I'm willing to speak to a counselor to help our children, why won't...ah. Your job. The job you lied about needing to be at so you and your girlfriend could spend some quality time together?" There's a pause. "Frankly, Mitch, I don't care for my sake; I care for Elise and MJ. It's one thing to lie to your wife—excuse me, ex-wife. But to persistently lie to your children? Who's next? Your boss? Are you going to falsify evidence to put away someone because...hello? Hello? Goddamnit!" Meadow's face is flushed with fury.

"I take it you were on the phone with Santa Claus making out your wish list?" I try to lighten her mood.

"What is it, Kody? Is it urgent?" Just as I open my mouth to answer, Meadow bites off, "You can't fix this. It's not the house where you have the right to butt in and take over. This is my family."

And hurt overrides common sense in that moment when I reply quietly, "You don't get to say things like that to me."

Remorse immediately eliminates her anger, but the plug has been pulled and I can't rein myself in. I point at Meadow's phone. "I'm not him. What have I done to you to deserve to be treated like that except love you longer than you ever imagined?"

"Kody," she begins, but I need her to listen to what I'm saying because as much as she's lost her family, I lost a portion of mine. Because I know the best days are the ones we'll build together. We'll work out the problems at each other's side but not by spitting and spewing at each other to do it.

"I've been the man who's been by your side when the world fell apart around you. I'm not the schmuck who caused it. You don't get to dismiss my very real concern when the man who you chose to bring into your life, the man who is the reason why I'm navigating a field of land mines to love you, causes you even more agony. Because no matter what happens, I'm the one who is here, the one who will always be here. I'm yours, Meadow. But don't you dare shove at me the shit you want to hand him."

Meadow hasn't moved a muscle. I'm not certain if she's angry or upset, but as much as I love her, as much as I stand behind the lifelong commitment she has to her children, I just can't be her punching bag. I'm not Mitchell Borneman. I'm not the man who broke her. I'm the man who will be the rock at her back, who will move Heaven and Earth to give her what she needs.

Just not at the cost of hating her for it.

"Listen to your heart and ask yourself if you doubt there's anything I'd sacrifice for you. Then think about treating me like your ex again." With those parting words, I slam out of the screened-in enclosure and storm off toward the tree line near the lake.

I need a break. And right now, that means putting as much distance between me and Meadow as I can before I do or say something I'll regret.

Spotting a tree not too far from the water's edge, I use my upper-body strength to haul my lower body up enough so I can brace my booted feet on the knots. Scrambling quickly to a notched V that cradles my length, I brace my hips and wonder aloud, "What have I done to make her think I'd ever hurt her the way Mitch did?"

The rustling of the trees calm my fiery temper down, much as it did when I was a kid. I let the cool breeze off the lake whistle through the leaves when I remember Jed struggling to climb a tree with me when we were last here.

Huffing and puffing, he glared at me. "You're a royal pain in the ass."

Taken aback, I demanded, "Me?"

"Yes. You're a sensitive guy, Kody."

I scoffed at him.

"Think what you will, but you rarely put your soul forward anymore. You think I don't know why?" Jed clapped me on the shoulder and smiled sadly— right before he almost toppled out of the tree. "Christ, how am I supposed to get out of this thing without breaking my damn neck?"

I smirked and dipped my chin. "The same way you came up. Just don't fall."

"Maybe a fall would do us both some good." Before I could reply, Jed grinned one of his crazy smiles. "You know what this place needs?"

"I'm sure you're going to tell me," I drawled.

"A tree house. How cool would it be to come up here and cast a few lines with a few beers?"

I bellowed out a laugh. "Dude, we're like 300 feet from the water. You can't cast a line that far. And by you, I mean you personally."

Jed just kept on smiling, ignoring my insult. "A man can dream about many things, can't he, Kody? Good fishing, a tree house, and happiness are just a few." Without another word, Jed began the descent down the tree.

Frozen, I shove aside a few branches and look out over Flathead Lake, which is what I did after Jed left me alone that afternoon to let my ire cool.

And before me is the same thing I saw that day. A two-story stone structure that's been abandoned for as far back as our first visit here. And on the shore are two trees that, from a distance, would make the perfect structure for a tree house.

I choke on the lump in my throat as I remember the words of Jed's will.

"To Kody Laurence, I leave my travel journals, sketch books, and drawing kit. There's also an open-ended monthlong trip paid for at the retreat we went to in Montana. Inside one of the journals, you'll find a drawing of a tree house I thought would be perfect there. Make that happen, will you? Sorry, Kody, the sketches suck. My skills were never up to yours. If I could wish anything for you, it's to see there's so much more than houses that need your magic touch."

Build something... Did Jed mean the tree house, or did he realize I'd sit here where he once pulled me from a dark mood and would recognize the potential in a home behind it? *Or maybe I just thought you'd finally see the potential I always knew you had inside yourself,* I can hear the crazy bastard whisper. Fighting the burn I tell myself is due to the glare of the sun off the lake, I whisper, "You always did have more faith than I did."

That's when I hear the rustling of the branches below me. Then a muttered curse before "It's never you I didn't have faith in." First, her hard hat pokes up. Then, a flushed, heartbroken face. My heart aches at the realization of how delicate Meadow's heart actually is. She reaches for a branch to pull herself up and winces as bark scrapes against the sensitive skin on her palms.

I'd offer to help, but her words from earlier still rattle me. I'm not trying to take over her life, damnit. I just want to become a part of it. Okay, a permanent part, but to be compared for an instant like Mitch Borneman set me off.

When Meadow gets settled, she doesn't say anything at first—probably waiting to see if I have anything more to say. But any of my sisters could tell her once I speak my piece, I'm done. I begin to see the benefits to arranging a meeting between the women related to me and Meadow, and not just for them to spill all my secrets. Maybe Brad and Rainey will help me with the same? Then I chuckle—well, Brad maybe. Rainey will never sell out her sister.

"Is it okay for me to be here?" Her voice is so soft, I might have missed the undertone of hurt as the leaves rustle.

"Yes. I finally separated the boyfriend who wants to make everything perfect in your life from the irrational idiot that spewed crap at you when you're already so stressed—which is what Jed used to call me when we talked about your marriage. Now, I'm ready to be the man you need me to be."

I've shocked her. While she's trying to formulate a reply, I reach for her hand. "I'm not trying to challenge you when it comes to Mitch. At least," I continue when she starts to squawk, "I wasn't trying to."

Her fingers twine with mine, cradling my hand much like the branches of the tree hold us both. "What you said was low, Kody. I haven't compared you to him. I haven't turned away from my problems or my responsibilities. But damnit, I have to deal with him, and it's so frustrating because nothing seems to get through the selfishness."

"Why haven't you said anything before now?"

Meadow pulls her hand back. I feel the loss when she wraps her arms around herself, protecting herself from another blow. I want to curse myself because I know pain isn't just physical. More often than not, the mental anguish leaves scars that are worse to overcome.

And I just added to her suffering by being an insufferable jerk.

"You don't have to answer that," I jump in before she can respond.

She shakes her head, her lips pressed tightly together. She shifts, and for just a second I'm terrified she's going to leave. Then, her words practically have me falling out of the tree to the hard earth below.

"No marriage is perfect. There's always something you question whether it's about you or your spouse. That's normal; people are human. But when your child is placed in your arms for the first time, there's this expectation of perfection you feel you need to live up to for them. Your humanity takes a back seat to doing everything humanly possible to making their life superior to your own. While everything on earth would have made you happy, nothing but climbing a mountain will do—no, I take that back. Handing them every star in the sky if you can manage it."

She takes a deep breath before continuing. "When Mitch betrayed us, the sky came crashing down on all of us. He was their father. He was the sun their world revolved around. Should I have ruined that for them when everything else was falling down around them?"

"So, you said nothing," I conclude.

"I said nothing," she emphasizes. "I have no control over what Mitch said and did. But for the first few months, barely a civil word was shared between me and Elise. MJ hardly spoke to me at all."

"And now?"

Her face contorts. "Now, they're hearing the right things from the wrong people. Maybe it's selfish, but I want to be their soft place to land. I want to wish all of this away, and it has nothing to do with you, Kody. It's because I want to be on a plane home to Juneau to hold my children for the first time in three months and tell them it will be okay. We'll be okay." She dashes away the tears underneath her eyes. "In fact, I think we're going to be great." Her hand, still damp with her tears, stretches across the divide between us.

She hasn't given me the verbal reassurance I was hoping for, but her actions tell me everything. This isn't an affair, a moment out of time. What I'm feeling for her is real. And like life, the more real love is, the more complicated it can be. Should be. Especially when it matters. "Meadow, I'm sorry for what I said."

"I'm not trying to hurt you or keep you out. I'm just trying to figure out how to rebuild a life for the two of most important people to me, this time with their feet on the ground."

I tug her hand gently. She carefully picks her way across the thickly woven branches, much like she's navigated our relationship. When she's resting fully against me, I whisper in her ear, "I don't plan on going anywhere."

And in that moment, when her heart thuds so hard I can feel it bounce against mine, I mean every word.

MEADOW

I've focused my energy on Nature's Song as the kitchen's progressed with cabinets being installed and the space has been measured for solid surface countertops. I wish I could hug Lenny a million times, even though he's gone back to Portland. Every time I pass the bookcases, I'm awed by his talent. He proved himself to be the artist Kody said he was with the new handcrafted bookcases I think are more beautiful than the originals. And I've enjoyed the hell out of shopping for new furniture—a mix of old and new.

Kody and I attended a furniture auction near Missoula to an overnight adventure that still has him sending me salacious glances. And I might occasionally fan myself in memory of what that man can do with a slatted headboard.

I've ignored every attempt my sister has made to get a hold of me these last few weeks. I can't stop myself from reading the few emails and texts she's sent to make certain the kids aren't dead, but other than that, I need time to think. Because I have to decide if Elise was lashing out or if I truly have to approach Mitch with her request.

God help me if I do.

Kara and Maris have tried to reach out as well, but after the way the Jacks have shut Kody out, I don't feel right responding to them either. For the first time, I feel like I can only rely on my heart to decide what's best.

And that's terrifying because what's best for them may destroy me even as happy as I am with Kody.

I took the day off from working at Nature's Song so I could think, really think. Ever since Kody left, I've been sitting in a roomful of Elise's things still packed up in boxes. Since I wanted her to be a part of the process to turn this into her new home, I labeled each box carefully so I only undid the ones necessary without invading her personal space. Fortunately, that means I know exactly what's in what box.

Shoving and grunting, I find the box I'm looking for. It's one I packed labeled "Pictures and Memories," but inside it contains everything from Elise's footprints to her school pictures. Albums of our lives sit next to mementos carefully wrapped. There are boxes inside boxes.

Flicking open a box cutter, I slowly cut it open. As the knife penetrates through the packing tape, every word she screamed at me slices through me.

Dad's cheating is probably your fault.

I don't want to be a part of any family with you in it.

I'm old enough to say what I want and don't want.

The knife nicks me at the very end. I don't feel the pain, as numb as I am. But as the contents of this box may be the last tangible items of my daughter's I hold, I don't want them marred. Quickly, I grab a tissue from the box I brought into the room with me and wrap it around my finger before reaching for the folder labeled "Elise – Infant."

And there she is—my baby girl. "You weren't even a day old," I whisper, my fingers dancing over the page. "So tiny. Your dad could hold you in his arm like a football. I was afraid the jackass was going to drop you on your head. Did I ever tell you he did once?"

"Maybe you should tell her that?" Kody says from the door.

Somehow, I'm neither surprised nor angry he's here. He's become a part of me I never want to let go. I'm just terrified to admit it with the fear of losing everything else I've loved.

Ever since we went to Polebridge, and then made love the first time, we've spent all our spare hours together. Yes, there's the rush of lovemaking, but there's so many hours we just spend talking. It's never about the big things, but about what it was like for him at school, and about how I liked online classes after all the years in between. Did he truly enjoy living in Portland? Did I miss Juneau? And shockingly, how much we both loved living in Montana even though it had been only a short period of time.

Yesterday, I thought I was going to pee on myself after he took a call from his mother. We were lying on the sun-warmed grass next to the lake, both of us grinning at the complaints from the crew because the cool mid-fifty degrees felt like shorts weather to us both. Kody was still wearing a smile when he wrapped up his call saying, "Love you too, Mom." He paused, pressing a kiss to the top of my head before saying, "I'll tell her you said hello. Okay. Bye." Tossing his phone to the ground, he announced, "Mom says hi."

Tightening my arm around his middle, I nuzzled my head against his chest before murmuring drowsily, "Hi, Mom."

"So do Candy, Vicki, Greta, Amelia, Alissa, Sandra, and my dad. Apparently, Mom has shared the news with everyone I'm seeing someone."

My lashes flicked open. "No pressure there."

"Nope. None at all." He ran his hand over my back, relaxing me again. "Just keep on being you, Flower. Things will be just fine."

Taking him at his word, I simply enjoyed the moment. Then, my curiosity got the better of me. Shifting upward, my long hair formed a curtain around his face, blocking out the fading sun. "There's always been something I've wanted to know, especially now that I've had children."

Reaching up, Kody tucked a strand of hair behind my ear. "You know there's nothing you can't ask."

I smiled. I do now. "But this isn't about you exactly."

"Oh?"

I braced an elbow on his broad chest before propping my chin on it. Then curiosity won out. "How did your mother name so many kids?"

Kody roared with laughter, practically bucking me off him. "I'll let you ask her that one day."

"Deal," I answered, before plopping my head back down and enjoying the rest of our time before we had to close down the house for the night.

Even though we've circled each other's lives for forever, I feel like neither of us are in a rush to push our relationship at some breakneck speed just to suit someone else's timeline. But seeing him standing there—ready to protect me even from my own heartache—makes me feel cosseted, protected. Cherished. My anger also flashes because how could Brad make him choose?

"Would you have listened to your mom when you were twelve?" I ask him instead of responding to his question about Elise.

"I don't know. I'd like to think so, but I'm not twelve anymore."

"Thank God," I murmur.

He laughs softly, and I finally rake my eyes over his boots, up over his jeans, to his flat stomach covered by an untucked flannel, to the broad chest that holds a heart I'm just getting to know all over again. Finally, I tip my head back against the bed until I see his face. He's frowning. "What is it, Kody?"

"Why Elise? When I got her birth announcement, I tried to figure it out, but I never could."

I recall the frustration during what should have been one of the happiest times of my life. I try to hide it, but Kody notices. He crosses the room and squats down next to me. "Hey, I didn't mean to bring up any bad memories."

"Not bad, per se. Just emotional ones. Do you remember—" I swallow hard before I say my sister's name. "—Rainey or me talking about our Aunt Alice? The one who moved to Connecticut years ago?"

"The shrink? Of course. Out of all the stories Brad ever told, those were some of the best. The lady sounds like a whack job."

"She treats whack...patients, Kody. Anyway, she's great. We've always been close. But when I wanted to name the baby after her, Mitch had a conniption fit. He thought the name was too old-fash-ioned." Kody makes a rude sound I appreciate. I finish with, "So, I found a variation that meant the same thing."

"What does Elise mean?" He reaches out and takes the hand I hurt, laying a gentle kiss on it.

"Noble, brave. Dedicated." My eyes drop to the photo I'm holding. "And she's all of those things. She's not going to change her mind about this." A sob erupts from me. "I'm going to lose my baby girl because...because..."

Before I can crumple the photo, Kody pulls it out of my hands before he wraps his arms around me. "Shh. Let it out, Flower."

"What did I do, Kody? All I did was refuse to let him walk all over my pride." I cry into his shoulder.

Then I freeze as an unexpected voice says from the doorway, "Damn straight. And if you answered one of our texts, maybe we could have told you we agreed with you."

"What?" I pull back and find myself facing a seriously pissed-off Maris Smith and Kara Jennings. "What are you two doing here?"

Maris goes to open her mouth again, but Kara lays her hand across it before saying, "We're here because Rainey and Brad can't be."

"And because Jennings is an idiot," Maris says as she flings Kara's fingers away. She grins at Kara. "I haven't said that in way too long."

Kara merely rolls her eyes. "Please. You say that to him all the time."

My lips quiver as I burrow into Kody. His lips hover over mine. "Trust me, even if you can't feel like you can trust them right now."

And because I know down to my bones he wouldn't harm me, I nod.

That gets me a hard kiss right in front of the two women who both go, "Aww," before Kody glares them into silence.

"There's way too much estrogen here. I'm going to work." Pulling me to my feet, he brushes my hair back. "Call, text, whistle if you need anything. Otherwise, I'll be over after work with dinner for everyone."

"Bring wine," Kara suggests.

"But I have..." I start to say.

"And we'll be long through it before Tinkertoy can get back from work," Maris concludes.

"Tinkertoy?" I bite my lip before darting a glance at Kody, who's trying to hold in his own laughter.

"It was that or Lincoln Log, but we haven't got to that part of the conversation," Maris explains.

"And I'm out. None of you need wine," Kody declares. "You're dangerous just as you are."

Kara grins, but it's Maris who bats her lashes. "We're irresistible."

"Jed used to call you insufferable, but I guess you're that too." The two share a warm look as Kody makes his way past. After he gets past them, he mouths, "You'll be fine," before disappearing from sight.

I track him as long as I can. When my eyes return to Kara and Maris, it's to find Maris tapping her foot. "Listen, your next email was going to be my announcing I'm pregnant."

Kara's droll "By what? Immaculate conception?" has me roaring when that was the very last thing I expected to do in this room today.

This. These women were what I needed. And Kody gave it to me. He set aside whatever is going on between him and the guys to give it to me despite my never asking for it. And even without him here, I feel myself teetering over the edge into something so dangerous, it makes Wonderland appear tame. My head spinning, I tune back in to find the Mad Hatter and the Cheshire cat still arguing.

"Don't kid yourself, Kara. I'm debating having a child," Maris declares.

Kara tips her head back and begins murmuring. Confused, I look over to a grinning Maris, who explains, "She's talking to Dean in Heaven begging for some divine intervention."

"Maybe if we're all lucky, one day he'll answer me," Kara sighs. "In the meanwhile, it's way past time for you to get your ass over here and hug us."

Quickly scrambling to my feet, I do just that. And if I feel like there's a part of us that's missing, well, that might be because I still don't know exactly why Maris and Kara are here.

I really hope Kody brings a lot of wine. I have a feeling I'm going to need it.

"HE DID WHAT?" I screech as the glass of white spills down the front of my shirt as I surge forward from where I've been listening to Maris and Kara.

"Met them right at the bus stop," Kara confirms. "And during that time, he explained 'his' side of the story."

"In other words, he lied," I say flatly.

"But see, that's the thing, Meadow." Maris puts her glass down. "He lied just enough to confuse the kids even more. What they're hearing are rumors from kids at school, garbage from their father, and silence from their mother. The only people who are giving them any kind of stability are Rainey and Brad."

God, her words hurt. "You're right. I've been so busy trying to make their lives perfect for when they get down here that..."

"You hoped things would calm down with Tiny Douchebag out of the picture up there?" Maris suggests.

Even though I want to laugh at my sister's nickname for my ex, I'm so emotionally exhausted all I can do is nod. "I just wanted them to have a chance to have some peace before the upheaval started again."

Kara's thoughtful. "I'm not certain that ever happens."

My heads whirling. Mitch's actions have forced me to leave the past behind. But my children aren't the past; they're my everything. And it's time I take a stand a fight for them. I clear my throat before I ask, "You both said I only needed to ask and you'd help?"

"Of course," Maris replies.

"Anything," Kara says generously.

Taking a deep breath, I release it slowly before saying, "I need to pack. I want to see my children. It's time to explain what really happened."

Kara's eyes go wide while Maris is bouncing in her seat, ready for action.

"And if all goes to hell, at least I know I have the two of you to pick me up when I land." I reach out a hand to each of them.

"And Kody," Maris reminds me.

"And Kody," I agree.

Maris gives a huge shout while Kara just curves her lips in a knowing way. Meanwhile, my heart thumps in in my chest. Kody. How do you thank a man who can look beyond a disaster and find something beautiful amid the mess to salvage?

I'll figure out some way.

But first, it's time to fight for my children.

KODY

"You make me look smart."

"Fuck you, Nick." I've said it at least twice during this call, but I really can't think of anything else to say.

"Did you really think Brad was giving up your dumb ass because you're falling ass over elbow for Meadow? Hello? Did the turpentine finally get to you?" He leans forward and knocks with his hand against his phone. "Maybe you should open the windows instead of sniffing that shit."

Jennings laughs next to me where the fire's roaring in my hotel suite. "I'm just glad you actually decided to read Kara's email. I was getting close to having Brad call Covington."

Putting Jennings's phone onto the stand on the coffee table so he can see both of us, I yell, "How would you have felt? What if that was Jed saying shit like that to you after you found Kara again?"

Both men sober quickly. I go on, pressing the advantage. "I understand why, now. But honestly? Could he not have shot me a text? An email? Could one of you? I might have been able to have done some damage control over the last few weeks. Instead, the two of us felt like we've lost our families."

"You're right," Nick says.

I blink, not certain I heard those words come out of his mouth. "Excuse me?"

"You heard me. But in my defense, I didn't know until afterward. I did try to call you, but I get you shutting every one of us out. And, I let them both have it because we all know who would have lost his mind, don't we, Jennings?" He throws our friend completely under the bus.

Jennings leans forward, bracing his forearms on his knees. "Jed would have, for sure. While I was flying here with Kara, I kept talking to him, pleading with him not to take out his frustration with my stupidity on her."

"Well, you made it alive."

"I still have to make it back home."

The three of us laugh. I sober quickly. "So, what's going to happen next?"

"That's entirely up to Meadow. The women are telling her what Tiny Douchebag did to the kids."

"He's such a piece of..." There's a knock at my door. Frowning, I stand. "Are we expecting anyone?"

Jennings's brow lowers. "Kara said she'd call."

"Then who..." I peer out the peephole before turning around and glaring at Jennings and the phone, though there's no way Nick can feel the force of my ire. "Are you sure this wasn't a setup?"

"What are you talking...?" Jennings's voice trails off just as I fling the door open to reveal a haggard Brad.

He tries to step over the threshold into my room until my hand slams into his chest. I still haven't quite forgiven him. "What are you doing here?" I demand.

"Flying commercial sucks. Let me in and I'll tell you. I couldn't get a hold of..." Then he spies Jennings over my shoulder. "Why are the rest of you here?" Brad demands.

"Trying to fix your stupid, big-mouth mistakes," Jennings drawls. He tips his head to the phone before twisting the stand so Nick can wave his fingers at Brad. "Apparently, even Nick's got a more golden tongue than you do."

Nick waves his tongue like it's a damn flag at all of us. It's like he's humping the damn phone with it.

I open my mouth to blast Brad, but instead, wheezing comes out. "He...didn't."

Brad's tension-filled countenance starts to relax. "Stupid idiot. Of course he did. Never knew when to keep it in his mouth."

Then from the wall that's Brad, a feminine voice announces, "Oh, Nick must be on the phone. We got here just in time." Maris shoves past him and strides into the room, owning it the minute she steps in. "Nice digs, Kody. Meadow, have you seen these yet?"

"Yes, I have," comes Meadow's voice, but I can't see her.

Kara strolls in after Maris, and Jennings sighs in frustration. "I thought you were going to call?"

"And I thought you were going to answer?" she retorts. Spotting the phone on the coffee table, she rolls her eyes. "Now I get it."

Sheepishly, he stands. "Sorry, Owl. I thought your text would break through. How did you all get here?"

Meadow brings up the rear, rolling a small suitcase behind her, which startles me. "We asked Kody's foreman for a ride. Besides, I don't want my car at the airport." She comes up short when she realizes Brad's in the room. "Hello." Her voice turns arctic. I think the water we saw at Lake McDonald might be warmer.

Brad's face crumbles.

I reach for her hand, and much to my delight, Meadow doesn't just take it, she slides her arm under mine. "Taking a trip?"

"I'm going back to Juneau."

"Why?" I ask her.

"It's time to lay my cards on the table to the kids. I thought what I was doing was right, but parenting is full of mistakes. I've made a big one; it's time to correct it." Meadow's blue eyes are lit with a combination of fury and despair. But the passion in them is undeniable. This is the woman I've never been able to forget.

"Meadow?" I tease a piece of hair away from her face.

"Hmm?'

"If you see Tiny Douchebag, don't kill him. You're building a life down here, okay?"

Her lips curve. Even if the smile doesn't reach her eyes, I can feel the determination in her. "Anything you want me to keep an eye on while you're gone?" I ask to divert her emotions.

"How about finishing the bathrooms?" She bumps her hip against mine, knowing damn well that's weeks away. We've just barely finished the tile in the showers.

"Listen, Flower. Be grateful if I finish the grout before you get back." I press a kiss to the side of her head. Then I pull back. "Unless you plan on being gone weeks?"

She shakes her head. "Couple of days max. I just need to book a flight."

Jennings coughs loudly, as does Maris.

"I mean I need to ask Jennings if I can ride back with Maris and maybe see if he'll have someone fly me back? Maris has already said I could stay with her." Meadow adjusts her plans quickly.

Jennings beams and nods.

Brad's face tightens, as if he's holding back tears. "Meadow, could I have a moment with you? Please?"

And I don't know who in the room—or on the phone—is the most surprised when Meadow replies, "Are there secrets here? Weren't we all supposed to be a family? Or did that end the night my children told me they didn't want me as a parent?"

Brad groans, "God, I'm so sorry. Neither me nor Rainey expected that. We didn't know that was coming. We swear it. We wanted to warn you Elise was upset, but we didn't have time to let you know."

Meadow absorbs that information before nodding. "I'll be dealing with that once we reach Juneau. But here's my problem with *you*, Brad." And she pulls out of my arms to face off against her brother-in-law.

"You put Kody in the position of having to answer to you about our developing personal relationship when that had no bearing on anything. In your overbearing concern, you tried to manipulate Kody into admitting feelings he may not be ready to admit to you, me—hell, to himself! I know you want to protect me from being hurt again, but you almost lost two members of your family with that move—a

brother and a sister. So, tell me right now, Bradley Meyers, why?"
Meadow demands.

As the words flow from her mouth, my heart tumbles clean out of
my chest to fall at her feet. She only needs to reach down and pick it
up. It's hers. It's always been hers. It will never belong to anyone else.
Ever.

Brad begins to stutter, and Meadow gets right in his face. "Not.
Good. Enough." Whirling around to face me, I realize the years in
between when we met and now don't matter. All they did was
heighten the longing I have for her. I want to throw each and every
person out of my room so I can tumble her down on one of the luxu-
rious beds and show her exactly what I'm feeling. If the flush riding
her cheeks is anything to go by, she knows where my thoughts have
gone.

"I owe you an apology, Kody," Brad chokes out behind us.

Damnit. I'd forgot he was still in the room.

And then the clapping begins from the device still connected on
the table. Just as I'm about to blast Nick, Maris snaps, "Jesus, will you
shut the hell up, Nick? God, you can be such a jackass."

And the look of shock on his face is almost as funny as the fact as
he actually does it.

MEADOW and I are sitting together at one of the lodge's high-top
tables while Brad, Kara, Jennings, and Maris devour a plate of huckleberry wings in the corner. We keep getting interrupted between Maris
and Kara groaning over the wing sauce and Jennings and Brad laughing
at them. Each time it happens, Meadow's lips curve in remembrance of
the first time she tasted those wings.

Me? I'll never forget a damn moment I've ever spent with her.

"Do you know what you're going to say to the kids when you're
with them?"

"I packed some of the photos I moved down here with me. I plan
on leaving them there. In my haste, I took everything assuming they'd
be with me soon. That was a mistake."

"You're human, Flower. You couldn't have predicted what would happen and the decisions you'd have to make," I point out.

"No, but I'm certainly not blameless in this situation. Kara, Maris, Rainey, they all tried to encourage me to tell the kids the truth." Meadow turns her head and stares out the back deck over the lake. "I didn't want to tarnish their memories."

"And what's changed?"

"Nothing. I don't plan on doing that. I plan on giving them facts. Casting blame is up to them." Turning her head around, Meadow slides her hand across the table.

I reach for it and instinctively twine my fingers between hers.

"If Elise chooses to hold on to her feelings of hate, I'll have assessed the situation so I can have a serious conversation with not only Mitch, but my attorney."

Whoa. "Meadow, are you saying..."

"I'm saying I'll always be their mother. But I refuse to let them be unhappy. There's an enormous difference. And I refuse to let my ex bounce in and out of their lives at whim. I'm not just going up there to talk about what happened; I'm going up there to discuss full custody. He doesn't get to play these games anymore."

My heart stops just as my thumb scrapes over the ridge where her rings used to sit. "Does that mean you'll be moving back to Juneau?"

Her hand slides from mine. Pushing away from the table, she stands and walks around until she's standing directly in front of me. I twist until my back is to the windows.

Meadow braces her hands on my thighs. "Someone special made me a grass ring a long time ago. I kept it safely tucked away, and not just in my heart. To me, that tiny piece of land represented everything he wanted it to be: dreams, hope, and chances. But when I slid it on my finger today, it reminded me I have a new beginning here. Do you really think I'm giving that up?" Stepping back, she cups my cheek. "That's something else the kids and I have to discuss."

Swallowing hard, I manage, "What's that?"

"That if they come with me, home means Montana." Just then, Maris calls her name. Meadow calls back, "Is it time?"

"Yep. We have to meet the driver out front," Maris says.

Meadow's hand slowly starts to drop, but before it can, I surge upward. Uncaring of who's watching, I wrap my arms around her waist and pull her body to mine. Our lips meet tenderly. Still touching, I whisper against them, "I'll be waiting for you to come back."

"I'll call you when I can." Then Meadow tears herself from my arms and grabs her coat, purse, and bag.

Signaling to the bartender I'll be back, I follow the crew out to the front entrance of the lodge. Hugs and kisses are exchanged all the way around. Brad and Maris climb into the hotel's airport transportation first. I hold the door for Meadow.

I'm about to close the door, but before she goes, she needs to know, "Seventeen years is too long for our hearts to be apart. Can you come back quicker this time?"

A sob escapes her lips. She opens her mouth to respond, but I just close the door.

It will give her something to think about on the plane ride to Juneau other than worry about the kids.

MEADOW

The afternoon after we land in Juneau, I walk into my sister's house as if I own it. Only Brad doesn't look shocked to see me. I've already spent all morning with my attorney discussing my custody agreement, obtaining the necessary paperwork to ensure the adjustment for Brad and Rainey's temporary guardianship for the kids and making sure Mitch's actions have been noted. I want everything documented in the event I can sue for full custody one day, but it left me in one hell of a mood. Isler commented, "Meadow, it's going to be a fight regardless of what happened in your marriage. That is, unless he shows fault as a father."

As I reminded Isler, Mitchell Borneman's fault as a father was because he was a failure with what he was doing to his children. The question I was asked in return was, how can I demonstrate it?

As a result, I'm emotionally drained even before seeing the kids.

Rainey immediately starts to run in my direction. She halts when I hold up a hand. "I'd like to speak to Elise and Mitchell privately for a few moments. You're, of course, welcome to supervise."

Rainey's eyes—the exact same shade as mine—go wide. "Josh, Sophie, why don't you two go with Dad into the backyard."

"Aw" and "Come on" come from two kids, who are currently

kicking butt on a video game. But my two children are staring at me as I'm a stranger.

And I might as well be. I'm sure as hell not the same woman who left over a month ago. I realized that last night.

Yesterday evening, I called Aunt Alice in Connecticut for the first time in forever to ask her advice about the situation. After being lambasted for not asking for help sooner, I took copious notes on my laptop and bookmarked websites she recommended.

After, I spent some time in Maris's sunroom writing letters to both of my children. After speaking with my aunt, I prepared myself for the fact they may not listen to what I wanted them to hear. So, I wrote both Elise and MJ long letters.

Now, I'm cataloguing every change in each of my children's features without saying a word. Elise's hair is growing longer, just like mine. MJ is getting leaner, losing that little-boy chubbiness. I missed this because I didn't want to push them into accepting the divorce. I straighten my shoulders. I won't miss anything else.

Rainey is practically quivering, her eyes darting over to me. I frown. Her head ducks, and she lets out a shuddering breath. God, I want to hug my sister so hard, but I can't. Alice prepared me last night: "Elise and MJ see her as someone they absolutely trust, Meadow. You can't show her any preference or that could set them into a tailspin." Fortunately, I did warn Brad in text just before I walked in.

Brad, who's standing behind everyone, gives me an understanding nod before dragging his kids outside, closing the door firmly behind him.

Once he does, I begin to speak calmly. "Since we've had some time to digest our last phone discussion, I felt it prudent to have a family sit-down about it."

Elise immediately snaps, "What's there to discuss? Why are you even here? Me and MJ want to—"

I slide my bag off my shoulder and pull out several manila envelopes. "Elise, please. If you could refrain from your dramatics right now? I've had about enough of them over the last year. It hasn't exactly been the easiest time for me either."

My daughter's jaw drops. Her eyes fly over to Rainey to determine how she's supposed to react.

Rainey's face is impassive except for the tiny wink she manages to get at me from her right eye.

Bingo. Here we go.

"I suggest the dining room table for this conversation?" With the three files in my hand, I take the head of the table. Rainey takes the foot, deliberately I'm sure in order to force Elise and MJ to sit in the middle as we discuss their lives.

Last night, my aunt reminded me that yes, I lost my marriage, but I sure as hell didn't lose the pride-filled titles of mother, college graduate, and businesswoman. "And, young lady, I want to know where all that courage went to that made you fight every single day that you dedicated for each of those?" she snapped.

That's when Maris whispered loud enough for Aunt Alice to hear, "Dear God, the stories about her *are* true. I'm going to get some chocolate."

And all three of us laughed then, but I'm not laughing now as I reach for the first file inside the first manila envelope. "Rainey, here's a copy of my divorce decree and my attorney's information. You'll need this information if you plan on seeking custody of the children." I slide the folder the length of the table.

My sister nods. "Everything is in order?" She knows it is, but so easily, she's picked up my game.

"Of course. It cites the reasons for the divorce as well as all of the information about the custody agreement between me and Mitch." I bite my lip. "It also identifies the codicil about the move to Montana, the mandatory distance until they're eighteen, and his pension. How is that going to work for Brad if..."

"Well, we haven't discussed that part yet. We're hoping Mitch will be reasonable," Rainey says with a completely straight face that I know must cost her.

I snort. "Good luck with that. It cost me thousands of dollars just to get him to agree to college payments. Don't you remember? And I was married to him for sixteen years."

"God, that's right. Well, we'll figure it..."

"*What are you talking about?*" Elise screeches.

I barely spare my daughter a glance. "Your aunt and I are discussing the battle I went through to ensure you and your brother would be financially secure after your father and I ended our marriage. The problem is, there are certain rules in place. For example, certain aspects about my life have to be maintained since he fought over the custody agreement—such as the distance to where your father plans on living with his new job in Idaho. However, things like contributing to your college funds?" I shake my head. "That's determined based on income. And your aunt and uncle make more than your father and I did at the time we signed the documents. So, I suspect they'll have to absorb that cost."

"But...Dad said he was solely paying for college." Elise's voice trembles. "No matter what."

Rainey and I exchange a long look. "When was that, darling?"

"A few weeks before Mom left. He took us out to eat and said Mom was putting money aside for a secret, but he had one of his own." Her face is much paler than normal. I want to reach out and reassure her, but I pretend indifference.

"Everything I've told you is a court-ordered mandate. You do know what that means, correct, Elise? You've heard your father say that at the dinner table enough."

"It means the court is making someone do something," she whispers.

"That's right. So, Rainey, back to Montana. I don't see why you have to move to Bigfork, but anywhere within ninety minutes of Bonners Ferry should work."

"Is there ocean access?" she asks, knowing damn well there isn't.

I shake my head. "No. Lakes are aplenty, but no ocean."

"Oh. But I don't see that as a major problem as Mitch has been here. Maybe we can sit down with him to discuss it."

Now it's my turn to act shocked. "He has? He was supposed to start training for his new job. That's why we all agreed to let the kids finish out the school year with you and Brad."

MJ speaks up. "Dad came up for a few weeks. Said he had the dates wrong, Mom."

"Well, that must have been good for you all to see him. Did you speak with him about your desire for Aunt Rainey and Uncle Brad to..."

"No. We, uh, didn't think that the timing was right." MJ's frantically trying to catch his sister's eye, but hers are locked on the stack of papers Rainey's holding.

"Sorry, Rainey. He'll have to sign away his rights in order to—" I begin, but Elise shoves back her chair.

"What are you doing? Don't you want us anymore?" she yells.

This was what I was looking for. "I have wanted you from the very moment I knew I was carrying you, Elise. And everything I do in this life is to make certain you are happy and healthy. Even if that means"— my voice breaks—"walking away. I will let you and your brother hate me if that's what you need right now to get through this. But if you're going to hate me, you will do so knowing the truth."

"I don't have to listen to this," Elise declares. MJ starts to rise.

Rainey corrects her, "Yes, you do. Now, sit down. Both of you."

Elise and MJ quickly listen. Their heads avert when I start speaking. "I will apologize for a few things. That first is I didn't do a good enough job reassuring you that this wasn't your fault. That somewhere deep inside you may think you were the cause of this divorce. Neither of you were."

I push away from the table and begin to pace back and forth. "Your father did something that broke the foundation of trust to our marriage." Elise opens her mouth, but I shake my head. "You may have heard rumors or people talking about it. I'm sorry I didn't discuss those reasons with you, but it goes back to the first one. What good does it do to tarnish your father's image to his children? Did he break his vows to you? No, he did that to me. Me." I slam my hand against my chest.

"It was my decision not to drag the two of you into it, to not make it ugly. I tried to preserve that love you each had for him. I encouraged you to go out with him to dinner, to spend as much time with him as you could. So, maybe this is all my fault. Maybe all of this confusion and pain does lie with me.

"I tried to hide my initial anger and sadness that my marriage, that the family dynamic we lived for so many years, was ending. I was dying inside, but I didn't want to burden you with it. You're my children, and it's my job to protect you from that and from messy discussions like the one your aunt Rainey and I just had. Thank God for her is all I can say." My eyes are brimming with tears as they meet my sister's. Hers are overflowing. "I don't know how I would have survived those first few months when I *did* try to piece together our family before I decided that my—*our*—future had a higher value than what was being offered."

"What does that mean?" Elise asks.

I shake my head. "One day when you're old enough, I'll explain. But right now, you need to experience your feelings and your emotions in your own timetable. Just know that it has to do with the adult part of your father's and my relationship. Okay?"

Elise quickly nods. I slide the rest of the first folder in Rainey's direction. Rainey looks up in surprise. "What's this?"

"I had a long talk with Aunt Alice last night. She said for you to read all of that and to call her. There's some good information in there. And when they're ready—" I slide the two envelopes with photos and letters for each of my children across the table. "—well, you'll know what to do with those."

"What? What are those?" Elise queries. Her voice is less antagonistic than when I came in.

"Yeah, what are those, Mom?" MJ asks.

I hold my sister's eyes. I can't walk out without telling her, "I love you."

"I love you. And I'm sor..."

"Don't be. There's no one to blame."

Rainey's lip is trembling, but she doesn't say anything more. She just slides the folders aside.

With a sigh, I know I'll never make it to the door without possibly outdoing some of my children's healing. *But at least things will be better between you and Rainey and they'll know that,* I tell myself. And besides, I need to hug my sister before I leave Juneau.

"I'm just a phone call or a text away if you have any questions. And, God, I hope both of you know, I love you more than anything in this world, in this life. I'd give up anything so you both will be happy." With that, I begin to make my way around the table and through the dining room.

I feel my heart squish under my boots when I hear MJ ask Elise in confusion, "Wait? Where's Mom going? She's not staying?"

"I... Don't ask me that now!" his sister snaps at him.

My hand is on the door before I'm whirled around. I can't see her face, but I know it in the place in my heart where the sun always shines and the grass always grows. There's always a piece of rain there.

That's my Rainey.

Her arms squeeze me so hard, I can't breathe. "I love you, Meadow. I hoped you understood what was happening. Then you wouldn't answer. So, I had to..."

"Shh. It's okay."

"I'm seeing you for all of twenty minutes and I know you're doing better. Tell me you're better."

Over Rainey's shoulder, I catch a glimpse of Brad coming inside with the kids. In my sister's ear, I whisper, "Ask Brad," knowing that will drive her nuts. Squeezing her hard because I know it will have to last for a long time, I turn and make my way out the door where Maris is waiting to take me back to the airport.

I figure I can break apart just as easily on the plane waiting to take me back.

KODY

Jennings and Kara stay overnight, which is a welcome distraction. I show them around the property and explain all the repairs the team is making to the main house. Jennings is surprised at how far we've come in just a few short weeks.

I snort. "Don't ever underestimate Meadow. She could give Greta a run for her money."

Jennings's brows raise to his hairline. "She's that good?"

"Better. She's ridiculously talented as a negotiator, and she doesn't shy away from getting down and dirty. By the time I'd first walked in the door, she had this place cleared out in order to get rid of some of the 'ridiculous upcharges.'" Jennings snorts remembering his comment about the crown molding. I go on. "I always knew she was strong, but I never knew she was this determined. There's an inner strength inside her I've seen in only a few people."

Jennings opens his mouth to reply, but Kara elbows him in the ribs. "I don't think I'm breaking any confidences by reminding you she's also full of so much insecurity still, Kody," she says.

Yanking off my hard hat in frustration, I run a hand through my hair in frustration. "After everything she's been through, I think I understand why."

"No, I'm not sure you do," Kara corrects me gently.

I frown at her.

Jennings and Kara exchange a complicated look. "Sometimes, it isn't because they don't want to share, Kody," Jennings begins. "Sometimes it's because there's deeper burdens the person you care for isn't quite ready to unload."

Kara curves her body closer to his in silent agreement.

"I hope Meadow is beginning to understand I'm here for anything she needs to share." Hasn't a part of me been lying dormant for almost two decades for the chance? A tiny bit of bitterness fills my mouth at the thought, but I shove it aside.

"In one sense, you're better equipped than most," Jennings starts.

Mocking him, I arch a brow and throw an arm out to the side where the team's left large saws neatly aside to rip drywall down in the morning. "I'd say my equipment is pretty impressive."

We all laugh, but Jennings continues. "You understand women."

"Should I be here for this?" Kara asks impudently.

"Because of his family, Owl. Kody might have some latent estrogen floating in his aura and not know it."

I roll my eyes. "Cute, Jennings. Can we get back to what we were discussing?"

Kara takes pity on me. Stepping forward, she reaches for my hands. "All I'm going to ask you to think about is this: Would it have worked out all those years ago? Are you both the same people now that you were then?"

I open my mouth immediately to say yes, but my voice gets stuck.

"For years, she's had a life. So have you. And now, you're at a crossroads. It's so familiar it's like I—we—" Her head tips back to look at Jennings, before she continues. "—are living it with you. It hurts us because while we don't know, we *know*."

Understanding slams into my heart stronger than any punch Nick could ever throw. "Brad..."

"Is trying to figure out how to protect everyone from getting hurt. It's just not possible," Jennings confirms. Devastation crosses his face. "When he realized what he said, how badly he screwed up, he called me and said, 'I feel worse than the night we lost Jed.'"

I turn away and brace my hands against the cabinet frame. Too many thoughts and emotions are tangling together. "Do you know what she's doing?" I finally ask.

"No, but she'll be back by tomorrow night." I spin around, shocked. Jennings is holding Kara clasped to his side. "I got a call from Lou"—Jennings's partner in Northern Star Flights—"to send Jasper to pick her back up in Juneau tomorrow afternoon. So, whatever is going down is happening quickly."

I'm absorbing that information when Kara suggests, "Let's head back to town and get something to eat. Then we can plan on heading out early ourselves? I want Kevin to sleep at home instead of at Brooks's tomorrow. He has a physics test the next day and doesn't need to be blowing up things all night. What? You Jennings men don't think I don't understand you?" She rolls her eyes up at her husband.

Jennings taps her nose, and for just a moment, I'm riddled with envy over the ease of their relationship—not that it wasn't a hell of a ride to get to where they are now. "Those are manly secrets. Besides, he's studying while playing."

"Really?" Kara's tone is dry.

"Well, that's how he explained it to me."

Leaving them to bicker it out, I move through Nature's Song to close off lights until we're all back in the truck.

After dinner that night and having given each of them long hugs goodbye since I won't see them in the morning, I'm standing at the balcony rail, thinking of the questions Kara asked me.

Would we have worked out all those years ago?

Pulling out my phone, I decide to call someone whose honest opinion I can always rely on.

My mom answers immediately. "Kody? Is something wrong?"

"No, I just wanted to hear your voice."

"Ah." And that's all she says until, "What's going on with Meadow?"

Dragging a chair next to the deck rail, I prop my booted feet onto it. "Is it a sixth sense, or do you have a wire on me?"

"Sweetheart, you're a grown man—one your father and I are proud of every single day. But for you to call at almost eleven o'clock at night means you have something on your mind. Since I very much doubt it has to do with the job since I don't know how to put those thingies on the back of a picture frame—"

I can't quite hold back my laugh. Mom doesn't take any insult but continues. "—then I can only imagine it's something to do with this woman you're seeing."

I take a deep breath. "She just isn't any woman, Mom."

"I know."

"How?" Even to myself, I sound like I'm whining.

"Because this week I've had calls from Jennings, Nicholas, and Bradley all asking if I've heard from you. The fact they haven't called you is very telling, darling," she chides me.

I tell my mom everything, starting all the way back with falling for a young Meadow Jones back when I first met her in Juneau while visiting the Smiths' with Jed, Jennings, Brad, and Nick. I explain how we'd spend hours talking, and I tell her about how Meadow was dating someone. Finally, I tell her about how brokenhearted I was when Meadow told me she'd become Meadow Borneman and I'd lost my chance.

"It's not like I haven't lived, Mom."

"Certainly, no one can accuse you of that," she replies dryly.

We both laugh. "But Kara asked me something tonight that's been churning me up inside," I admit.

"What's that?"

"Are we the same people we were back then? Would we have made it?" Before I can reply, I plow on. "It's obvious Jennings and Kara have made their peace with that part of their lives."

"And you feel you need to before you can move on?"

"Something like that." It feels good to admit it.

"There's only one problem."

"What's that?"

"Maybe's there's no answer, Kody."

"What do you mean?" I demand.

"I fell in love with your father when I was seventeen and he was nineteen. That love has changed, yes. It has. Every day it becomes something different. When you add children, arguments, laughter, and life, love changes. And that's the love you were raised with."

"So was Meadow." I think back to the Joneses' marriage and to Brad and Rainey's.

"Then she had an unfortunate experience. But what you want is for someone to answer whether she'd have had a better life with you. Kody, that's just not possible. That's what Kara's trying to tell you. Don't you understand? It has nothing to do with whether you would have made it then; the question is can you set aside the past to have a chance at your now?"

I feel like I just walked face-first into a solid plank that was just run through the portable sawmill at the site. "Someone's going to get hurt," I say softly.

"In love, someone always does. If love doesn't hurt just a little, how do you know it matters?"

Pulling my feet down, I rest my forehead on one hand while still holding my phone to my ear. My mind flashes back to what Meadow said just before she left. "She kept a ring I made for her from some grass," I whisper as if it's a secret.

"Then it sounds like to me, she may have been a little bit torn in her feelings too. Hold them precious for what they are, but live in what you find today."

"Tomorrow. She'll be back tomorrow." And I plan on giving her one hell of a welcome home.

I don't know what my mother hears in my voice, but I hear her murmur something to my father before saying, "I love you, Kody. Call soon."

"I love you too, Mom. Same to Dad." Then I disconnect the call.

Tapping the phone against my lips, I send a quick text to Meadow. *You're on my mind.*

She has no idea of how true that statement is.

I don't hear back from her before I go to sleep, but with the flight and the time change, I'm not surprised. When I pull up to Nature's Song, my phone pings with a text from Meadow that has the device falling out of my hands into the center console in shock. "Whoa."

And you're on mine. Last night, I sat outside in Maris's backyard and remembered us. I have strength today because of a foundation of yesterdays. Thank you for being part of that.

Then she sent me a flower emoji.

Then Jed's words filter through my mind. *Don't let anyone tell you how to fall in love or who to fall in love with. Just love them with that enormous heart you've been saving all those years.* Shutting off my truck, I vow, "That's exactly what I plan on doing, brother. And I think you'll approve."

Striding through the front door of Nature's Song, I find the guys milling around, concerned. Shane pipes up. "Hey. Have you seen Meadow? Normally she's here by now."

"Family issue. She'll be back later today or tomorrow." Then I clap my hands together to get all their attention. "While she's gone, let's try to get ahead of schedule? Let's get the rest of the green board up in all the wet spaces so we can start tiling. Lenny, how are we with the repairs on the floor?"

"Just about finished with the final millwork, boss. Should be able to start laying planks today. Tomorrow at the latest."

"Great. Everyone, you know where you're supposed to be. Check in. I'm also going to see if there's a place that can deliver lunch today." My crew leads hoot and holler. "Christ, she's spoiled all of you with a few donuts," I gripe.

They all nod. "Getting the hint?" Shane jokes as he takes off to finish the drywall plastering in the last room downstairs.

"Just get to work!" I call out.

But I am getting the idea. In more ways than one.

MEADOW

The return flight from Juneau, I don't have Maris trying to distract both me and Brad by saying outrageous things like, "I'd make a damn fine mother," or "Can't you picture me with a child in my arms?"

Brad, unable to hold out long, retorted, "Don't you want to be married?"

Maris shrugged and said, "It'd be nice, but it's not a requirement," shocking him back to silence.

But on this flight, I was left with ample opportunity to think about where everything went wrong, not just recently but years ago.

Life has a way of showing you just what you need at that exact moment. Sitting in Maris's backyard, I was bombarded with memories of Kody I hadn't allowed myself to have in years. Shivering, I recall the gorgeous MIT student who I was attracted to, but I never expected could feel anything for me. I ignored what in hindsight was obvious flirting. I blindly turned my head away from the lazy invitation Kody Laurence offered me time and again because I was afraid of what?

Myself. Of not being good enough.

The answer is so incredibly obvious now.

I thought settling with Mitch and a life in Alaska was all I deserved. If I didn't go to all the places I once dreamed of, I wouldn't know there was something missing. Looking back, I started my marriage with a hole in my soul. I used so many things to cover it up: sex, kids, work. And as each one began to fail or change, then what was I left to rely on but the very thing I needed the most?

The only thing I was supposed to be able to rely on in the first place. Me.

I swipe my hand under my eyes, grateful there's no one else riding down to Kalispell with me on this flight. I didn't even consciously recall what made me decide to put my dreams aside all those years ago. When Alice asked me, I couldn't answer her. "Meadow, it was never my place to say..."

"What wasn't, Aunt Alice?"

"All those years ago, Rainey and Brad? Their marriage never shocked me. But you and Mitch?"

"It surprised you?" The amount of disturbance in my voice must have startled Maris, because she reached over and took my hand, squeezing it hard.

"Honey, you wanted something different. You wanted your own path. At twenty-one, had you even had a chance to live to figure out what it really was yet? I don't know what it was that changed that." Alice's voice held a note of apology that she didn't step in and voice her concerns.

"We all take our roads, Aunt Alice. I guess, I just took the wrong one." By this point, there was no hiding the tears either from Maris or from her.

"A path is never wrong. There's not a right or a wrong one. There's just yours. And look at the treasure you've found along the way."

"The kids." Maris soothed me.

"Elise and Mitchell Junior," Alice reiterated firmly. "They have their own path to travel, but trust me. Unless your heart is cold, all paths do the same thing."

"What's that?" I managed to sniffle out.

"They can lead you home."

Now, even as Jasper announces our approach into Kalispell, I vow to spend some time closing that hole in my soul. I can't do that by patching it up with the wants and needs of other people.

I have to pray for my children and while I'm doing that figure out who their mother is.

THE HOUSE IS dark when Jasper drops me off. Unlike the first night when I experienced a flicker of excitement, right now I'm just left with an overwhelming need to sleep. Giving him a wan smile, I say, "Thanks. For the flight and for the ride out here. Are you sure there's nothing I can do…"

"Meadow, you know Jennings better than that. I'm all set." He jumps out of the car to grab my bag.

I take it from him. "Right. Then safe travels back to Seattle."

He tosses off a salute. "I'm sure I'll be seeing you soon. Be well."

"You too." I stand off to the side until he slides behind the wheel. Then, I quickly punch in the code, which illuminates the house.

My nose scrunches as smells begin to penetrate. Oregano. Sauce.

"Pizza?"

Then a voice startles me. I whirl as Kody turns the corner from the kitchen. "Do you know what a pain it is to keep from eating all of this when I'm…"

My bag crashes to the floor as I fly into his arms. He immediately catches me against him, pressing my head tight against his chest. My arms wrap around him as far as they can reach.

He tips my head back. For long moments, nothing is said. Nothing has to be. Pain is shared. And now I'm reaching for something I feared all those years ago. "A chance."

"Hmm?"

I sigh in pleasure. "You're here."

His eyes turn stormy. "I was going to wait to do this but…"

His head lowers until his lips touch mine. Just a touch, a brush. Kody's not pressuring me in any way. But by the time he pulls back, my hands are sliding up his chest. "Welcome home."

"All paths lead to home," I murmur into his chest.

"What was that?"

"Nothing. At least not for now."

Taking my hand, he guides me to the table I haven't used yet which is lit only in candlelight. "You did all of this for me?" My free hand comes up and covers my mouth.

"I'd do anything for you."

He said that long ago, and I didn't believe him. "You said that before I married Mitch. Once before."

He stills. I let go of his hand. "I didn't believe you then. I couldn't understand how someone who was as smart as you, who looked like you, could ever..."

"Meadow?" His voice holds a note of pain I've never heard.

"I was afraid, Kody. What was so special about me?"

"Everything." One word, but it's like a lash the way he whips it at me. I deserve to feel the lick of pain from it.

"I didn't believe it."

"Because of me?"

"No, because of me. I ran away. And in the process, I hurt you." I'm standing close to the windows now. Turning, I face this beautiful man. "I wanted you to forget about me."

"Why?" he rasps as he moves closer.

"So you could be happy. That's all I ever wanted for you was to fall in love." I duck my head.

Kody's standing directly in front of me. He grasps my chin and pulls my face up toward his. "I already was. I've been in love since the first time you made me laugh. You had just finished telling me the freezing cold land under my ass was warm, and I was telling you that you were full of shit."

"But that was the first year you met me. You were maybe eighteen?"

"It took you a while to catch up." Kody yanks me to him. "Are we finally on the same path?"

I barely manage to whisper, "Yes," before his mouth settles on mine.

This kiss is different than our first, which was pure fire.

Each time our tongues entwine, it isn't to incite passion but to further the intimate exploration of our hearts. The hunger of that first kiss is tempered by an emotion I wasn't ready for until now. Sliding my fingers into his thick hair, I relish the way the thick strands feel as I hold tight. As I pull back, my fingers savor the texture, brighter than the million rays of the midnight sun we spent with each other in the past. But before I can say anything, Kody's lips are touching mine again.

This time, I arch more fully against him. My arms wrap more firmly around his neck. His response is to bring me flush against his strong body. For a long while, a soft sensuality envelops us. My body clenches as he trails soft kisses from my cheek down the side of my neck. A soft groan rises and falls between us—I don't know who it comes from. But as soon as the moment the sound hits the air, Kody pulls back after dropping one more kiss on my upturned lips. He wraps his fist in my hair and pulls my head back so our eyes connect. Slowly, he runs his tongue over my lower lip, capturing our taste before tugging me forward until our hearts align.

My head rests against his neck, and I hear the irregular beat of his heart. For long moments, we stand there. Kody rocks me back and forth before he says, "Come on. Let's get some food in you. It's been a long trip."

Pulling back, I frown.

He bends down and rubs his nose over mine. "I haven't just waited for pieces of you. I want it all. So, tonight, I want to sit with you, talk about what happened in Juneau."

"Kody." His name is the only thing I can get out because of the tears welling in my eyes. Finally, I manage to get out, "Are you sure?"

We both know I'm not asking about sharing.

He nods. "You need to know I'm here for you, Meadow. The way I never could be all those years ago."

"I'm afraid," I blurt out. That hole inside me yawns widely.

Eyes steady, he asks, "Of what?"

"Of finding the real me. In the end, what if I'm not enough? What if the kids..."

His hand cups my cheek. "Don't. Go into this knowing you are enough. And be grateful in the end that out of all the people you could have been, you're you. And that's the woman I love."

The air between us is thick, but I find the strength inside me to give him the words I've said a million times in my heart. "I love you too."

"Damnit." Kody bends down and lifts me high against his chest. "Tell me you're really not that hungry."

"Right now, you're all I want. You're everything I need."

There are so many things unsaid, but right now, that's no less than the truth. Kody carries me over to the sofa and lays me down upon it. I stretch out beneath him as his mouth slants down and drives me out of my mind. But after he lets me up for air, his mouth has another job. It captures whispered secrets of love I finally feel safe releasing. I touch his cheek, dragging my fingers through the smooth edge of his beard as every emotion I've held in my heart comes pouring out.

His head drops down to my quaking heart. I run my hands through his silky hair. Suddenly, his head snaps up. "Let me show you everything I've dreamed of doing to you."

My lips part. It's barely a breath, but I whisper, "Yes."

Kody sits up, chest heaving. His fingers make quick work of my shirt, deftly unbuttoning it. Each time his knuckles rake against the slopes of my breasts as more of me is revealed, I cry out. In between my spread thighs, I can feel his erection growing and thickening. It's not physically possible it's becoming harder than the previous times we've made love. I tell him so.

"Shh, baby. It will be fine." Then he pulls the tails of the shirt from my pants and tosses it away. Using just the tip of one finger, he trails his finger along the lace edge of my bra. "So beautiful. I've always thought so."

My hands are smoothing up under his sweater, feeling the satiny skin covered by rough hair. "Take it off. I want to feel every inch of you against every inch of me," I plead.

Within seconds, Kody's sweater is flung somewhere. There's a sound of something crashing to the floor. I don't care as he lowers his torso against mine, bracing most of his weight against his forearms. He fiddles behind me, and soon there's not even lace between our bodies.

I fight for breath as he scrubs his chest back and forth. A moan of anticipation escapes my lips.

"You were made for me," Kody swears, just before he lifts away.

I start to protest until he shifts and his head is aligned with my breasts. Then I still at his words. "I can picture your children nursing here. I hate it was him who got to see it, but just the idea you nourished a child from these sweet tips..." Kody's hand plumps up one of my breasts before he captures a nipple between his lips.

I cry out. My thighs tighten involuntarily around his waist. I'm grateful I'm still wearing my panties and jeans as a rush of wetness floods them when Kody rakes the nipple in his mouth with his teeth, his free hand capturing its twin and twirling it between his thumb and forefinger.

Then, God help me, he switches sides. And I can't help but call out his name. "Kody!"

He relents, briefly, but only to slide his hands to the snap of my jeans. Kneeling between my legs once again, he makes quick work of the zipper. I wiggle and shift my hips, helping him slide the material off my hips when he stands to shuck his own.

Handing me a packet, he crawls back between my legs. "Hold on to this."

I barely have time to process what he means before my legs are thrown over Kody's shoulders and I feel him part the folds between my legs. His lips caress me there like he's kissing my mouth. I whimper, arching into his mouth as his tongue dances around my clit. But I begin to shake and tremble as he slides first one, then a second finger inside me.

"Please, Kody. God, I can't take it." I'm begging him to do something.

And he does. Spectacularly.

Pushing my thigh down with one hand, Kody proceeds to lap at me like I'm his last meal. He places his mouth over my clit and sucks as he makes a come-hither motion with his fingers, sending me soaring. I arch my back and come, open eyes sightless. The only thing I need to see, to feel, is his heart. And I don't need vision for that.

As I recover, Kody plucks the condom from my hand and sheaths himself. I wrap my legs tightly around his hips, and he aligns his cock and pushes past the still-pulsating muscles. Deep. So deep and hard. I shiver when I feel his pelvis against the most intimate part of me.

"Don't hold back," I beseech him, scoring my nails up his back, love binding me to him in all ways.

Kody lowers his head, his tongue tracing my lips. I can taste myself on him, that lingering scent from an act so intimate driving my hips upward. His eyes roll backward before he slams his mouth down onto mine and grinds his hips downward. Shifting his weight, his hand seeks mine as we unite our bodies, our hearts, our souls.

Finally, it's too much. I tear my mouth away, gasping for breath. He ruthlessly finds my lips again. "Now." Then he shifts and his pubic bone rubs my clit again. Again. A third time, and I feel like I've lost my senses. I cry out, but the sound escapes into his mouth.

A self-satisfied grunt comes from him as I clench again on him. My hips jerk as his semen spurts inside the condom. Even with Kody, it's never been like this. Where the emotional connection between us swells inside me as much as the physical shattering. I give myself over to the sensation and just hold on.

Kody collapses off to the side, but he wraps me up in his arms tight. Grabbing the throw off the couch, he gently pulls out. "Now I have everything I ever wanted."

I almost do. If the kids were here, it would be perfect. Nuzzling against his chest, I drift off.

I'M WOKEN by the sounds of my stomach protesting to my lack of food. I flush when Kody bursts out laughing. "I take it that's my cue to feed you?"

"I wasn't exactly hungry before."

"How does twice-warmed pizza sound?" Kody stands and wraps me in the blanket we were dozing under. Quickly dealing with the condom, he slips into his jeans, before excusing himself a moment. When he returns, he drops an arm around my shoulder before bringing me over to the dining room table. The candles are almost burned down, but the effect is still perfect.

"Delicious." Then I frown. "How did you get in here?"

"Great question, Flower. Once again, I helped myself to your spare key. I borrowed it the morning I left to go get Maris, Kara, and Jennings from the airport. You know, you really shouldn't just leave it there for anyone to borrow."

"No, but you're not just anyone."

"Who am I, Meadow?"

I fumble with the answer under his penetrating stare before I state what I know to be true in my heart. "You're mine."

"Just like you're mine. Now, I don't know about you, but I'm starving. I was attacked by this sexy as hell woman when she got home." He stills. "Can that be a part of our nightly routine? Can it?" His voice sounds like a little kid who's pleading for a new toy.

I whack him in the chest, smiling when I didn't think I could tonight. And that's when I realize what Kody did for me tonight. He wasn't just here when I got back to my house.

He was here to welcome me home.

The real question is, what will I do when he's gone? How will I survive when he isn't?

MEADOW

A few weeks later, I wake up in Kody's arms with a sick feeling in my stomach. For the first time since we began sleeping together, I wish he hadn't stayed over. There's a part of me that wishes he'd just leave me alone all day to sink into a deep depression, but that's not how we work. Especially since I inadvertently hurt him so badly the other day after hearing from Mitch.

In the pale morning light streaming through the windows, I study his face. It's something I used to do from afar when we were young. I never was afforded the chance to scrutinize every flicker, line, or breath as something to be treasured—which it is. But regret still tugs at my heart over the time that's been wasted in both our lives on the path from then until now. "So much heartache. So many changes," I breathe.

In the straight line of his nose is the determination of the boy; his jaw holds the fortitude of the man; and his lips are the gateway to the heart of them both. "What did I do to deserve you?" I trace a finger along his brow, not to wake him but just to reassure myself he's not a dream. After all, today of all days I need a little reassurance of how I'm worthy of a man like this when my own children won't even speak with me.

Settling back, I tuck my hands beneath my head and wonder what Elise and MJ are doing right now. Are they up with Rainey and Brad's kids cooking breakfast? It's so quiet here. Is the house in Juneau filled with secret giggles and laughter? I blink rapidly, remembering other Sundays where I'd overhear similar preparations before I'd wake up "surprised" with a concoction full of love laid in my lap to eat.

Not today. Maybe not ever again. But I love them enough to give them the world they want.

The jaggedness of emotions that lives in me is cutting me up inside. Maybe over time, much like the way water slowly wears down a rock edge, it will ease up. But not right away. The hurt is too new and fresh. It's been four weeks since I flew to Juneau and still nothing from the kids. Rainey's been in constant contact via email about how the kids have settled down now that I've put Mitch in his place and threatened him with a full custody suit. But beyond that, nothing. And as each day ends, the hope of a reconciliation dwindles as my children find their peace. A lone tear trickles down my face.

And of course, today being what it is, it makes it so much worse.

"Keep looking like that and I'm going to begin to wonder if I did something wrong." Lazy blue-green eyes flutter open. Behind him, the sun is barely up over the horizon.

"You didn't do anything."

"Then what is it?" His finger traces a line from the corner of my eye over my cheek as I speak.

"It's just... I'm used to being woken up by little voices singing. Balloons. Not that I expect that from you," I hasten to add. "It's just ever since Elise could talk, it's the best part of the day. And it just hit me today I'm not going to have that."

A confused frown appears between his eyes before his "Shit. Come here" breaks me. Rolling into him, I sob.

Because it's not just any Sunday; it's my birthday.

And I immediately regret my earlier thoughts about it being easier if he wasn't there because, Kody holds me against his chest tightly, not saying anything while I cry.

It isn't until much later when he's stroking my back as my head's resting on his heart that he says, "Mom called me once crying on her birthday. She said all parents have a tough time with letting their kids go, no matter what age. I felt guilty as crap."

I give a hiccupping sob. "How old were you?"

"It was three years ago."

I can't suppress the giggle that escapes. "I really want to meet her one day."

He smiles against my hair but doesn't say anything. "If I had to make a guess, I bet she does this to this day with Dad—crying about all her babies being out of the house. Well, except Sandra. Hell, for all I know, she might be crying because Sandra's attempting to cook her breakfast as part of her gift."

Even though I haven't met Kody's baby sister, I slug him half-heartedly. "Not nice," I chide him.

"You're right. *She* probably convinces my father my mother deserved a day out now that there isn't nine of us to feed."

"You know you love her."

"I love all of them, even though they're responsible for all my gray hair."

There's a significant pause, and then I manage to say, "I will always love my children, Kody. I just hope they know that."

He rolls me over so he becomes the only thing in my vision. "I hope they do too."

I nod. I love that he doesn't lie to me. Pushing at his chest, I manage a half smile. "I guess it's time to get up."

"In a bit." Then he lowers his head and brushes his lips against mine.

It's a long time before we both decide to crawl from the warmth of our bed.

AT THE MAIN house later that afternoon, my temper is frayed. "These outlet plates are supposed to be ivory. Right?"

Kody frowns. "That's what the invoice says. Meadow, I can just run into town and see if they have new ones—"

"And it will take an hour by the time you get there and back.

Besides, these were a special order; I doubt they're going to be in stock."

"Probably not. So, that sets us back how far?"

"A few days at least," I grumble. "Now do you understand why I wanted to go through everything before we started tomorrow?"

"I get it, but don't you want to take a break for lunch?"

I press a hand to my stomach. "I'm just not that hungry, Kody. If you feel like anything, then we can stop."

"Flower..." But whatever he says is lost when my phone rings from where it's sitting on top of the new quartz countertops. Because it's a ring I haven't heard on my phone in months. Not since I was in Juneau.

I dive for it, just to make sure I'm not hallucinating.

MJ would like to FaceTime

Before he hangs up, I quickly swipe my finger to the right to accept. After a moment, there's my baby boy booming, "Happy Birthday, Mom! Sorry, I couldn't call before now, but you know how whacko Uncle Brad gets on the weekends. We were up at the crack of dawn doing chores. Then we took a hike. I just got out of the shower, and this is the first second I had a chance to get to call. By the way, did my package make it there yet? And whoa! Is that our house?" He's speaking so fast and so animatedly, I'm not certain he's taken a breath.

I know I haven't.

"Hi, sweetheart. I miss you" is all I can get out before my eyes start leaking.

"I miss you too, Mom. I put all of that in my letter to you though. Aunt Alice said it would be good for us to talk, so I'm going to try to call more often, okay?"

"I would love that. So, so much."

"So, seriously? Is that our house? And hey? Why's it under construction?"

"No, sweetheart. This is the main house on the property. This is the house that was really damaged. Uncle Brad's friend Kody—"

"I remember Aunt Rainey and Uncle Brad talking about Kody. His job is super cool. Builds a lot of homes and stuff."

My eyes flick over to the man in question, whose face is as shocked as mine is. "Well, the house was so damaged, I had to hire his team to help repair it."

MJ gets really quiet. "That sounds like a lot of work, Mom."

"It has been." But I'm quick to add, "It doesn't mean I haven't missed you every moment though. I want you to know—"

MJ talks right over me, just like he used to. "That's really nice of you to do, Mom. I bet the people who own that house appreciate that."

I make a choking noise. "I hope they like it when it's done."

"How soon is that? Elise said we get to move when you're finished. I caught her going through her stuff the other day."

Elise said... Even though MJ's telling me this, I can hardly breathe at the gift he's just given me. But I'm cautious when I reply, "I don't want to rush you both. You take as long as you need."

He looks down at the floor and then directly into the phone. "What I want is to give you a hug, Mom. Next time you're here, can I have one, please? I'm sorry. I'm so sorry." His lip starts to tremble.

My son's face disappears behind the veil of tears. "MJ, there's nothing to apologize for. I swear."

"I love you, Mom. I just wanted you to know that." He hears his name being called. "I have to go."

I wipe my eyes on my sleeve. "I'll keep an eye out for a package. And I love you too, MJ. Call me whenever you want to."

There's a mixture of adult and baby teeth in the wide, toothy smile he gives me. "And be sure to save your teeth for the Tooth Fairy," I remind him.

"Yes, ma'am. Happy Birthday!" He starts to sing off-key. It's perfection to my ears. Then when he's done, my screen says Call Ended.

I'm still frozen holding my phone until Kody walks up to me, plucks it from my hand, and pulls me into his arms. "Did that really happen?" My voice is dazed.

"It sure did, Mom. How do you feel?"

"Like I could fly," I tell him truthfully. And between one second and the next, I'm airborne as Kody spins me around in circles. I grip his neck so tightly as a mixture of tears and laughter pour out. My heart is still soaring when he stops spinning and just holds me. I clutch his shoulders.

He opens his mouth to say something, but before he can, my phone bleeps with an incoming text. Kody lowers me to my feet. But his eyes bug out when he glimpses what's on the screen.

"What? Is it Maris telling us she's pregnant?" I tease, because it's laugh or cry.

He doesn't say a word. Just hands my phone to me. Quickly unlocking it, I immediately see what Kody did. It's a selfie of Elise. There's some kind of filter on the photo making her appear like she's wearing a tiara—just like in her baby photos. Her right hand is giving me a slight wave. But beneath it is a simple "Happy Birthday, Mom. I missed you today."

My knees begin to shake. It's not the enthusiastic conversation I had with MJ, but it's a message from my baby girl that's not filled with vitriol. "I don't know what to say back."

Kody smooths the hair away from my face. "Just tell her she was missed. It's nothing less than the truth."

I type in the words and hit Send.

But I have to sit down when just a few seconds later, Elise sends me hugs and kisses. I send her a quick XOXO. Immediately I tell Kody, "In all the years to come, I don't need anything for my birthday. All I want is this."

He squats down next to me. "What's that?"

"To hear from the kids. No matter where they are. Even if it's just to know they're thinking of me."

"I can accept that. Do you know why?"

I tip my head to the side. "Why?"

"Because you just said, 'In all the years to come.' Trust me, Flower. I'll make certain the kids touch base." Pulling my head up, he presses his lips to mine. "That's a promise."

"Kody." I rest my hands on his leg as his lips continue to brush against mine.

Finally, he stands and pulls me to my feet. "Come on. Let's check on those outlet covers. Then we can decide what to do next. I have this slave driver of a boss who wants to keep us on schedule."

Slipping an arm around his waist, I tell him seriously, "She does. But nothing is more important than celebrating the little moments in life. So the outlet covers don't match? Who cares? Do you know what I really want to do?"

"What's that?"

"It's a beautiful day. Let's go find a spot to talk, Mr. Laurence. I just want to be with you."

Without another word, Kody undoes his tool belt and places it carefully on the ground. Then he takes my hand and leads me out the front door, making sure the house is locked behind us. Together we wander around the back of the house toward the lake so we can find a spot where the sun will warm us for a while.

We still have a lot of our hearts' secrets to share. And plenty of years to make up for.

KODY

I told Meadow I'd be taking a personal day to wrap up some business. With the crew working on easy items like trim and paint, she laughed and told me to take the week off. "I've got this covered, Kody."

"Smart-ass. You know this is what you're paying us for."

"Only to a certain point." Her voice turned serious. "There are certain aspects about my job I need to handle on my own."

I wonder how much she's going to miss it when we're all in Portland. Maybe what I'm doing today will help make up for that.

"The house was built in 1996, Mr. Laurence, but it's really the land that holds the most value. Most of the people I've shown the property to are concerned with the cost of tearing down the house," the Realtor informs me, but I'm barely listening to her.

The two-story stone home has been neglected for years. Carefully, I step over missing floorboards on top of potentially rotting floor joists. "It will require a ton of work to get it back into shape," I comment offhandedly.

"Why would you want to do that?" she asks blankly.

Why would I?

Mentally tearing out walls, I make my way to the rickety sunroom so I can view the sloping lawn. Across the water, I see the glory of Nature's Song across the way. Over the last three months, Meadow and I have put in a ton of sweat equity to demonstrate that if you love something enough you fight for it.

And then the trees catch my eye. Jed's tree house.

"Because I'm a builder, Ms. Rupi. I believe that with a little love, you can create something built to last." Turning around—carefully, so I don't sink through to the hard earth below—I demand, "Now, let's talk about price."

"As is?" she confirms.

"As is, and to sweeten the deal, my company will pay cash. I don't want to wait a second longer than I have to. The building season is short enough here in Montana."

"I think you should be able to take full ownership in a matter of weeks. Why don't we head back to my office to iron out the details?"

As I drive to downtown, I wonder what Meadow will think when I tell her I bought us a summer house here in Bigfork. This way, she won't miss Montana as much when we have to leave to head back to Portland. "And I'm sure Elise and MJ will love the city as well," I muse aloud.

Within a few hours, I've signed all of the papers and Ms. Rupi has faxed my offer to the owners, a family who inherited the home from their deceased parents. Meanwhile, I'm on my way to Nature's Song.

When I step in, I grin at the first thing I see. Meadow and Shane are engaged in a paint war. Meadow's sneaky, I'll grant her that. She's just slashed a streak of beige through Shane's long hair. Deciding to help my foreman out, I wrap my arms around her. "Go for it, buddy," I encourage him.

"Oh gross," Meadow squeals as Shane uses the roller with the same color up the side of her face.

But I'm the one she kisses—right before she sticks the paint brush in my ear and runs for her life.

I pause before I chase her out into the yard when I spy the house across the lake. Yeah, I'm never letting her go.

Not for any reason.

"WHAT MADE YOU BECOME A BUILDER?" Meadow asks as she slides her hand up over my chest beneath the blanket we're wrapped in.

We're lying on the grass near the water's edge at Nature's Song watching the sun come down as the carpet installers finish the last of the rooms. My fingers tangle in the ends of her ponytail as I contemplate the answer.

The build is just about wrapped up. There's not much left, even on the punch list. The last of the crew has gone back to Portland, though Shane reminded me again that he'd love to be the foreman of an office here in Montana. I practically had to shove him into the truck after Meadow smothered him with hugs and effusive thanks.

"Growing up with so many sisters, I was dragged into all these girlie things."

"Tea parties?" Meadows voice is overflowing with amusement.

"Those I actually tolerated. Mom fed me cookies." I grin over her head at the memories. "It was the dolls. All I wanted to do was play with skateboards and bikes, and instead Candy or Vicki were shoving a doll in my hand for me to dress." I shudder in remembrance.

Meadow is bravely trying to hold back her laughter. I tip her face up to mine and drown in the love shining from her eyes. And in that moment, I realize no home is as important as the one we're building right here between us. Pressing a kiss on her nose, I recall, "All their friends had these whacked-out doll mansions, RVs, and pools for these plastic toys. But we didn't have a lot of money. So, I remember asking my dad if we could make something for Vicki's birthday."

Meadow presses up on an elbow so she's looking down at me. "What did you make?"

I bark out a laugh. "A swimming pool that originated from Vicki's old baby tub. Dad and I built a box around it from 2x4s and painted it white. We even painted pink flowers on the side."

"What happened when you gave it to her?"

I tuck my arm under my head, the memory burned in my mind. "Nothing."

"What?"

I pull her back down where I want her and finish the story. "She was entranced with the Princess Victoria doll my parents got her, sweetheart. It was about a week later, after I refused to play with any of my sisters mind you, that I heard Vicki screech at one of our neighbors, 'I'm sorry. That pool is exclusive only to Princess Victoria's dolls. It was created by the Crown Prince Kody.' I ran to my window, and there was Vicki, chucking some girl's doll across the lawn."

"Oh," Meadow mumbles before breaking into gales of laughter. "What did your mom do?"

"She shut down the pool and all its occupants due to a virus outbreak for a week. When it reopened, 'Princess Victoria' had suffered amnesia and poor thing had become a mere commoner."

Meadow rolls to her back dying with laughter. "I. Love. Her. Does she take in strays?"

Rolling onto my stomach, I capture her face between my hands, "Meadow, you're hardly going to be a stray after we're married."

I think you might be able to hear the fish jumping in and out of the lake after I bungled that proposal.

Meadow squirms out from beneath me and sits up. "Married?" Her voice is caustic, and the look on her face makes my gut churn.

"Where did you think this was going?"

She scoots back. "I don't know. But Kody? Marriage?"

I get to my knees. "I'm in love with you. I've told you that."

"I love you too. But Kody, it's not just me." My heart begins to relax.

A smile breaks out across my face. I grab her hand and press it against my heart. "I'm well aware of that. Don't worry about Elise and MJ, my love. They're going to love Portland."

"Portland? We can't move to Portland." Her voice takes on a high pitch I haven't heard in a long time and—my heart thumps loudly in my chest—usually only when she's dealing with her ex. "Our lives are here."

I open my mouth to tell her about the surprise of the vacation house I purchased so she understands we're not going to lose the toehold on this place where our love began again, when she holds up a hand. "Stop. Stop right now. I need you to listen to me."

Sitting back on my haunches, I mentally brace myself. It's a good thing I do.

Taking a deep breath, Meadow whispers, "This year has been one of the worst in my life. I lost everything I put my faith in. I may not have gone into my marriage being completely in love with my husband because there was a man who held on to a part of my heart, but I'm not certain I want to jump back into another one so quickly. I need to know who I am before I accept a man into my life, present one to my children."

"You didn't seem to have a problem with that the last few months," I bite off.

Meadow winces but continues. "I am tied legally to Mitch and our custody agreement until MJ turns eighteen. Until such time I take him back to court and fight for sole custody, which I am not in a financial state to do, I am bound by that agreement. That hasn't changed. So, moving to Portland? That's out of the question."

"I have enough money to..."

"It's not your fight." Her words stop me cold.

"What do you mean, it's not my fight?" I reach out to brush a piece of hair away from her face, but she jerks back. My heartache is just about to kill me.

Then again, so do her next words. "Why the need to ask me now? What's the big rush?"

"Maybe because I stupidly waited for seventeen years?" Somehow, the words make their way past the lump in my throat.

Her face pales. "No one asked you to. You're the one who walked away telling me to be happy."

I can't stay near her. If I do, I'm going to crumble. I made a hash of it, yes, but for the second time in my life, I've laid my heart at Meadow's feet and she's turned it away. Pushing myself to my feet, I get a few feet away before I turn back. Meadow is still where I left her. She hasn't moved a muscle. "Is this what you want, Meadow?" What lies between us is so much more than land. What lies between us is what has been there from the beginning. The past.

This is what Brad warned me about. Suddenly, it hits me with such clarity, I want to fall to the grass and turn back time and have never met Meadow Jones. Anger floods my system. And yet, everything I learned about loving a woman comes from her. I try one last time. "Once I leave, I won't be back."

She pushes to her feet. The blanket falls to her feet. "If that's what you need to do, Kody. I have to do what I need to. Please stay. Talk with me. Try to understand."

Moments ago, we were laughing. Now, she's wearing her vulnerability, her pain. And just like the last time, I put them there. "Damnit." God. I turn away, pressing the heels of my hands to my eyes. "Is this what you want?" My question is torn from my soul.

"I have to deal with the repercussions of the man I married. And you? All I want is for you to be happy."

I feel her hand on my shoulder, warm and strong. A shudder races through me. Her fingers tighten in response.

Turning, I meet her luminous eyes. There's an expression on her face I don't understand. With it comes this urge to apologize. I open my mouth, but she just lays the finger of her other hand on my lips.

Then she destroys me.

"I have to tell you once while we're standing in the shadows of the place we rebuilt, that like our love, it withstood the test of time. I only hope that today, tomorrow, twenty years from now, you'll understand why I'm saying I can't marry you. But always understand I'm going to be in love with you long beyond that."

Even as I fight shedding tears, Meadow reaches up and brushes a kiss on either side of my cheek. Lingering for just a moment, she whispers, "Be happy, love," before she steps back.

"Meadow?"

"Yes?"

"Next time you need a friend to rescue you, don't count on me. I'm not sure my heart can go through this a third time."

As Meadow physically recoils away from me, I tear off.

This time, I don't look back. I wouldn't be able to see if I did.

❄

BACK AT THE LODGE, I'm throwing my stuff into bags as quickly as I can. I'll sort it out when I get back to Portland. There's no way I can stay here and finish the house now.

My phone rings with Greta's ringtone. I answer it without saying hello. "I'll be back in the office tomorrow."

She has the nerve to laugh. "That's cute, Kody, but that's not why I'm calling."

"I'm not kidding, Greta. Find someone to take my place out here. I'm on my way home."

Greta sobers. "You're not kidding. What happened?"

I shake my head. I don't want to talk about it. Everything's too raw. "She said no."

"You asked her to marry you?" Greta screeches in my ear.

I actually have to pull the phone away. "As monumentally stupid of a decision as that was, yes. And"—my body starts to shake—"God, G. She said no." The dam bursts, and raw sounds come keening out of my throat.

For a few minutes, I can't breathe. I don't know if I speak. All I know is the pain that's causing me to bleed inside is coming out my eyes. "The last time I felt like this, I spent the better part of a week drunk with the guys because Jed had died," I confess.

"You're not driving in this condition," my sister decrees.

"I have to. If I stay, I'll beg. I'll do anything."

"She's an idiot."

"Maybe it's me." My head is in my hand. "Christ, I can't breathe."

Greta says fiercely, "It's not you. And that's it. You're not driving. I'm calling Jennings."

"I can't leave my truck here," I argue weakly because the truth is, I want to leave. I want to put as much distance between myself and Bigfork, Montana, as I can.

After a few minutes of silence, Greta decides, "Jennings can have one of his guys fly someone back there who can drive it home. The most important thing is getting you here. Okay?"

"All right," I agree because right now, I can't do much more. "Thanks, sister."

"You're hurting. You'd do the same for me."

"If you'd ever tell me who hurt you, damn straight I would," I rasp, alluding to the man who had broken my little sister's heart in the past.

She lets out a sad sound. "Some hurts, Kody, just can't be fixed."

"That's kind of how I feel right now."

"I won't let you down."

It might be small, but there's a kernel of light in my heart. Family can get you through anything, even the sacred hell love inevitably brings. Knowing I can do exactly what I did when Jed died and begin drowning my sorrows in a bottle, I make my way to the mini bar. "Why did you call?"

"I'm not so sure I should tell you now."

Twisting off a small cap to a bottle of scotch, I toss my head back and finish it with one pull. The burn in my stomach matches the one in my heart. "Go ahead. I can handle it."

"The Realtor in Montana called. The papers transferring the property across from Nature's Song to become the property of Laurence Construction were completed."

My stomach churns. I race toward the bathroom. I begin retching over the porcelain toilet as the drink I just downed comes hurling back up. "Not now, Greta!" I manage, to stop her screeching through the phone.

After all, a man has a right to have his heart break in peace especially when all of the jagged pieces are slicing through him.

MEADOW

As I struggle to move a wing chair through the front door, I catch sight of the sun glimmering off the fishing boats on the lake.

I wish it was pouring. It would match my mood.

I can't even take pleasure in the restored Oriental rugs I paid to have delivered with the extra money. There's one spot that wouldn't come out, but according to Mrs. Jobber, "That stain appears to be as old as the rugs themselves. To remove that blemish would be to strip a large portion of the history from them."

Her words resonated within my aching heart.

I've sent Kody multiple messages only to be met with silence. Everything from a simple "Hi" to a "Can't we figure out a compromise?" to an "I miss you."

Finally, I went back to my daily habit of wishing him happiness. After all, the love I have for him is enough to let him have what he so desperately deserves, a wife and family of his own.

As for me, "It's better than nothing," I say aloud.

An unfamiliar voice says, "I'd say it's remarkably more beautiful than that. So are you."

I drop the chair with a thump. Leaning on the door is a gorgeous redhead dressed in jeans and a long-sleeve T-shirt. "Your hair's darker than the photos Kody has of you, Greta," I blurt out.

She smiles and the waterworks start again—his smile gracing her face. "God, is the pain never going to end?"

I don't know if she intended to do this when she came in, but soon I'm engulfed in another strong pair of Laurence arms for a hug. They're just not the right ones. We stay like that until I manage to pull back and ask, "Why are you here?"

"Well, I certainly didn't expect to be hugging you. That's for damn sure."

I sniffle. "I bet not."

"At first I thought about coming to punch out the woman who broke Kody's heart, not once but twice." I wince. "But it's so clear to see how unhappy you are as well, Meadow."

"How could I be happy? He's gone. And my explanations weren't the greatest. I've tried to contact him since, but nothing." Walking away from her, I move over to where I can see the landscaping being repaired from where the dumpsters and equipment sat on it for months.

"He offered you everything," Greta reminds me.

I whirl on her. "Don't you think I know that? Don't you understand there's a part of me that wanted nothing more than to capitulate and say yes?"

"Why didn't you?"

"I've lived for too many years because of a man, a marriage. I need to prove I'm strong enough to do it on my own and have a man love me enough to let me. Even if it's just for a little while." And my heart is breaking because I know never will there be another man anywhere who will love me the way Kody did.

Is my pride worth that?

Then I recall the call I had from Elise and Mitch last night. "It has to be."

"What has to be?" Greta's voice startles me.

"I'm sorry. I didn't mean... I was thinking about my children."

"What about them?" Greta comes closer.

"That for the first time in a year, I heard excitement in their voice, for an adventure, and even to see me. God, is it impossible to under-stand I have to put them first? That their happiness supersedes my own?" When she doesn't respond, I fling out, "What would they think, Greta? 'Gee, Mom's been gone three months and here she is in a new home, giving us a stepdad? How cool is this!' No." I give a tight jerk of my head. "It would set them back. Maybe if it was just me, but it's not. Anyway, it doesn't matter, Kody left. I went to talk with him, and he was already gone."

"Did you tell any of this to my brother?"

Anger and pain rise as I recall trying to plead with him to give me a chance to explain. "No." I swallow hard. "He was too busy telling me I shouldn't count on him." Wildly, I realize I can't do this. I can't be here where so much of Kody has been absorbed into the essence of Nature's Song.

I make a mad dash for the door when Greta's words pull me up short. "I need to tell you a story."

I start to object, but she overrides me. "Once, there was this boy. And he grew up hearing all about love. It was both a blessing and a curse, you see, because by knowing what it was, he recognized it instantly but could never escape it."

"Greta." I start to move away, but she reaches over and grabs my wrist.

"The young boy's parents were so in love, they had seven babies to satisfy that love. As a family they grew up together, one and all, though it should be noted there were times the boy often wanted to murder the youngest of the children."

I give a watery laugh as I recall the story of how Sandra recently drove Kody nuts about prom. Greta winks at me. "But the boy knew, as did the others, they were raised with more riches than any others in the land for they were given the wisdom of spotting true love. Now, as most stories go, here's where tragedy strikes. The boy grew into a man and realized he was in love. And so did she, but she already belonged to another. In his heart, she was always his. And he would always be hers, much was the way of his family."

"All I wanted was for him to be happy."

"And he was," Greta assures next. "Every time he saw your face, each time your souls brushed, every time you spoke." Her eyes remain sad even as her lips curve. "But the man has a lot of the boy still in him. He's frustrated because he had to wait. Had he not seen the heart of his love before now, I believe he might not have been so clumsy, so impatient when it was time to expose who he really was to her."

By now, I'm squeezing Greta's hand so tightly, it must be hurting. "Who's that?"

"The greatest man in all the land. One who will worship her forever." Letting my hand go, Greta turns around until she spies the clipboard Kody left on the counter. "Now, let's see what else is on big brother's punch list, shall we?"

"Greta?"

"Hmm?"

"I don't want the greatest man in all the land." Her head snaps my way. My lip trembling, I finish, "I just want Kody. If he can understand why..."

"You said no?"

I nod. Then my heart sinks. "What am I thinking? I lost my shot."

Greta puts the clipboard down with a snap. "Meadow, first things first. We have to finish the house."

"Right. The house. Then I have to get my kids." As much as I want to surrender to the dark, I can't. I have to move on. I have to live.

Otherwise, why did I give it all up? Squaring my shoulders, I say determinedly, "Let's finish. Then it's time for me to go."

Something flashes across Greta's face briefly. "Yes, it is. So, tell me where that chair goes?"

I begin to order Greta around while I go to the garage for more furniture. We work long into the night resurrecting this magnificent house. Because for me, the home part disappeared the night Kody left.

LESS THAN A WEEK LATER, Greta and I are escorting Kristoffer Wilde and Russell through the restored Nature's Song. I'm as empty a shell as when I first arrived in Montana with one exception.

There's a small scrap of honor that we managed to pull it off—me and Kody. We repaired one family's sense of devastation even as we caused one in each other.

Too bad I feel as destroyed inside as Nature's Song was when I first walked in its doors a little over three months ago. Despite my attempts to contact him, I've heard nothing.

It's over and I have to accept that and move on. I know this is going to be worse than having ended my marriage of sixteen years. The part of my heart Mitch still has a part of is entwined with Elise and MJ; Kody owns the piece that was always exclusively his.

And no matter what, it will always be his.

He may have stopped loving me, but every time Kristoffer and Russell exclaim over the quality of the work, the surge of love and pride I feel is enormous. Lingering behind in the room Jed had stayed in, I run my fingers over the doorjamb.

"I knew all those years ago you were destined to do great things, my love. You just gave the Wildes such happiness." I blow my breath out so hard, it stirs my hair. "I just wish you were here."

"I tried," Greta's voice comes from behind me.

I can't manage to turn around. For the rest of my life, I'll know my words weren't enough. Maybe it was me who wasn't, but finally I did the one thing I wanted to do all those years ago. I set Kody free. Finally, I manage, "Maybe it's better this way."

"For who? For you? For him?" Greta's next to me before I manage to find a way to explain my thoughts.

"For him. As long as it's better for him, then nothing else matters." My voice is listless.

"What's next for you, Meadow? Where do you go from here?"

"Back to Juneau."

"For good?"

I shake my head. "This is where I'm meant to be now. I can't go back to who I was before everything happened. I'll spend some time there with the kids. From our calls and the talks with my family, it sounds like they're finally ready."

"So, you'll bring them home—" Greta starts, but I interrupt her.

"I said I'll bring them here. Kody's back in Portland. If I was bringing my children home, I'd be bringing them to him." Before

Greta can say another word, I turn my back on the sparkling water and the memories of lying with Kody on the sun-warmed grass.

I wonder if the kids would like living in town. Surely I can find a place there I can afford. The memories here are killing me more each day.

That's when I notice some activity across the lake. "Oh. I guess someone finally bought the house. I guess I'll have to let Russell know so he can update our website to advise renters." Finally turning my back, I walk out of the room.

But the other home is put out of my mind when I catch up with Russell and Kristoffer in the great room downstairs. Russell is explaining, "...ready for Cal and Sam at any time, isn't that right, Meadow?"

"Yes, but if you could tell Sam the next time he comes I expect to have my children with me? I really don't need MJ trying to emulate him by scaling the side of the house." My mind flits back to the first time I met Calhoun Sullivan's business partner. Mentally, I shudder.

Kristoffer lets out a robust chuckle that seems to echo off the walls. "I'll let his wife know. He has his own brood; he should know better than that."

That drags a small curve of my lips. "Why do I imagine the Akin household to be extremely regimented or extraordinary chaos?"

"Because you have exceptional intuition, perhaps?" Reaching into his jacket, Kristoffer pulls out an envelope. Handing it to me, he takes a step back. "That's for you, Meadow."

Frowning, I turn it over and over. "What's this for, sir?"

Greta comes down the stairs and stands next to me, saying nothing. Kristoffer urges me, "Open it."

I frown but do as I'm asked. Inside is a check that causes my eyes to widen. "What on earth is this for?" I blurt out.

"For doing an exceptional job. It's a bonus, Meadow," Kristoffer explains.

My hand holding the check trembles. I could do so much with this. I could make certain my kids didn't want for anything, invest it. I could take Mitch back to court for full custody of the kids. Maybe I could be free and find a way back to Kody. And yet, "What did I do except agree to hire Laurence Construction?"

Kristoffer frowns, Russell laughs, and Greta grins. God, the sight of her smile makes me ache, but it assures me what I'm supposed to do deep down. Pulling a pen from my pocket, I sign over the check to Greta and hand it to her. "Will you make certain that's divided evenly between members of the crew? They're the ones who made this house sing again." Turning back to Kristoffer, I explain, "It's a lovely gesture, but those men and women deserve it. You already do more than enough for me. Truly, your thanks are enough."

And stepping forward, I hold out my hand.

Kristoffer takes mine. Then he tugs me forward into a tight embrace. "Thank you, Meadow. You will always be welcome in our home. After all," he adds on as I pull back, "a part of you will live on here. That's the beauty of this property."

I nod. I can't form words. It's nice to know a part of me will belong to a home.

Somewhere.

KODY

The weather couldn't be more reflective of my mood. It's rained for the last week straight since I left Bigfork, as if the heavens are able to shed the tears I can't.

She said no.

There was no way for me to stay. I barely remember getting back to the lodge let alone the eight-hour drive back to Portland. After stumbling into my condo and immediately coming face-to-face with a picture of Jed, shame washed over me. It was stupid to drive in that condition; what if I'd had a wreck? After all, that's how we lost him. Grabbing a bottle of whiskey, I muttered, "Sorry, Jed," before dropping onto the couch and adding to the acid burning in my gut from realizing Meadow doesn't feel the same way about me as I do about her.

She said no.

Bleary-eyed the next morning, I called my sister to find out what the schedule was. What I didn't expect was for her to show up less than thirty minutes later with coffee and donuts.

The minute I opened the door, I barked, "I don't want to talk about it."

Greta shoved past me. "I don't give a shit. You walked off the job,

Kody. And so your wants don't matter. I've already fielded calls not only from Meadow but from Russell Covington this morning."

Fuck. I run my hand over my face. "Send Shane back," I began.

"He's working on—"

"Do I own the damn company or not?" I shouted. "For once can someone do what I ask?"

Greta didn't say a word. She stood there as my hurt lay between us. I stormed over to the floor-to-ceiling windows and gripped my neck hard. "I'm sorry. You didn't deserve that."

"What happened, Kody?" she repeated.

I gave voice to the words that had been echoing in my head for almost a day. "She said no."

Greta hisses out a breath. "I know. What did she say no to? Exactly."

"To marriage, to me, to everything. What does it matter?" I rub a hand over my heart because of the pain.

I wonder if it will ever truly go away.

Greta made all the necessary arrangements to finish up Nature's Song, to my surprise deciding to head to Montana to wrap up the punch list herself.

Now, my cell phone is ringing constantly. I miss the serenity of the mountains where calls couldn't get through. I long for the air that's so pure you feel your soul's being cleansed. And, damnit, I want Meadow.

Instead, Greta's calling me back-to-back, which means something's wrong. On her third attempt to reach me, I snap, "What?" as I answer.

"You're a fucking idiot. I don't know what happened, I'm not entirely sure I want to know, but what? Did you run off and lick your wounds?" Greta bites back.

Maybe I should have answered Amelia one of the six times she called; she'd have been more sympathetic. "What's your problem?"

"No, Kody. What's yours? I've worked with Meadow all week, and that woman looks like she's closer to death than she is to living. Then she signed over a six-figure check that I know she could have used to Laurence Construction."

"What the hell did she do something monumentally insane for?" I yell.

"Because, 'What did I do except agree to hire Laurence Construction?' She asked me to divide that check among our crew, Kody. She has no idea you've likely sunk a huge bonus on each member of that crew."

"I swear I'm going to..." Then I freeze when I realize what can I do?

"Exactly. Nothing. You can't do a damn thing. You don't have any rights where she's concerned. You ran, brother. Instead of talking to her, your ego got hurt. Big deal. You know what? The tragedy is, all she keeps saying is that maybe finally you'll be happy. By the way, I deposited the check. Do with it what you want." Greta disconnects the phone in my ear.

"Fuck!" I yell to no one and nothing because that's exactly what I have in my condo. Nothing. I left everything that matters in the shadows of a land carved by a glacier in Montana. "What did I do?" I ask the empty air.

But there's no answer.

My phone rings again. I frown, not recognizing the ring. Swiping it up, I answer, "Kody Laurence."

"Well, don't you sound like you're in a fabulous mood," Maris's laconic drawl sounds in my ear. "I need your address."

"You have my address."

"Where you are in Montana, Tinkertoy. I need to send you something."

"I'm not in Montana. Not anymore."

There's a long pause before, "I'll have the package to you tomorrow morning. Be at home." Then without another word, she disconnects.

Wondering what Maris has to send me that's so important, I shove it out of my mind. Deciding to get some work done, I head into my home office. But I can't get inspired. For months, home has been a hotel room with a stone fireplace, leather chairs, and a deck that showed me infinite possibilities. Now, the cold modern decor I lived in before feels claustrophobic. "At least I can get payroll finished," I mutter. Stalking over to my glass-and-metal desk, I open my payroll software and pull up my business account.

Then I start choking.

The amount Meadow signed over to Laurence Construction is pending in our account. "What was she thinking?" The amount Kristopher Wilde wrote out to her has enough zeros she would have comfortably been able to take care of Elise and MJ.

What did I do except agree to hire Laurence Construction?

"She loved me. She did that too." Then what was it? Why did she turn me down? In my mind, I can see the heartbreak on her face as I walked away.

And for the first time since I walked away, I start thinking instead of reacting.

I'm still sitting in the same place remembering every moment I spent with Meadow when there's a knock the next morning at 9:00 a.m. "Shit. The package." Stiffly struggling to my feet, I stumble to the door.

After signing for the envelope, I tear open the back.

Inside there's a manila envelope with Maris's handwriting. I open that and shake out a sheaf of paper, another envelope, and a photo. I pick up the paper first.

Kody —

I found these when I was going through some of Jed's old things. I thought you should have them.

— Maris

Bracing myself, I flip the photo over, expecting to see Jed's face. Instead, I find a picture of me and Meadow. My back is to the camera as we lie facing each other on the grass—a common occurrence. We're a respectable distance from one another, but there's a look on her face. Holding the picture as close to my face as I can get it to my eyes, I see everything in her face that was there last week when I asked her to marry me: love, fear, and something else I can't quite name. It's terrible to see it captured on film because it means whatever it is has been there for seventeen years, and I still haven't managed to crack through it.

Setting the picture aside, I reach for the letter. It's slightly yellowed, and my throat swells as emotions pass from the aged paper through my fingers.

"Just when I need you the most, huh?" I carefully pull open the back flap, and the burn starts before I read the first word, recognizing his handwriting. Hell, it could be a litany over a baseball game and I'll be thrilled.

My name leaps off the page, and a few words in, I have no doubt Maris read this.

Kody,

Maris is complaining downstairs because I keep playing the same song over and over. I've written this letter so many times and I honestly don't know if I'm going to give it to you. Maybe a hand higher than mine will make the decision when the time is right.

I paid to have the film express developed from the party the other night because I wanted to be sure. And man, I hate being right.

You and Meadow.

I have to admit I'm a little hurt you didn't say anything. We've been friends for two years now. We've had talks about all kinds of shit. Did you think I would have told the others you were in love if you didn't want me to?

But Kody, she's scared. No, let me rephrase that — she's terrified.

I overheard Maris talking to Rainey. Meadow's interested — I'd have to think she was a fool if she wasn't — but she thinks there's no way a guy who goes to school at MIT wants anything permanent with a girl like her. She believes she's meant to live in Alaska for the rest of her life. However crazy that sounds to a guy like you. And she's resigned to holding her feelings back, to suppressing what she's feeling until you go.

It sounds crazy, but when you've lived this life, experienced the tranquility here year after year, it's hard to imagine anything else your life. Nothing short of a bomb is going to blast you from this place.

Or maybe a love so strong you're willing to do anything for it. Trust me, I know. I have the same worries about Maris.

I don't know why I'm writing this. Am I trying to warn you to be cautious about your feelings about Meadow or to go all in and take her with you? Maybe I'm just terrified because I saw the expression on her face last night and I know what it means.

It means she's going to let you go to live your life because she'll do anything to make sure you're happy.

I know that expression because it's the same one I've seen in the mirror each time you guys leave at the end of a summer. It's the knowledge you may never come back, but I pray to God that wherever life takes you, I hope you'll be safe and happy.

It's an expression of love, fear, and agony because nothing hurts so much as wishing nothing could change.

Fuck. Maris just threw the fuse box to my room. Now I have to go beat her ass. By the way, where are you motherfuckers? You all took my car to go somewhere and we need to get the ferry soon to head back to work. I hope you assholes left some gas... oh, hell no. Tell me you guys didn't just come back into my house smelling like crab and not bring me some.

Bastards.

Anyway, I guess I'll finish another draft of this the next time we come up.

The letter is unsigned. I fling it onto the coffee table in front of me before my tears wreck the ink so carefully penned on the school-lined paper. Picking up the photo, Jed's words spark memories long suppressed. "I remember that night. I remember the next day. It was Nick's birthday, and Maris was pissed because we wouldn't stick around one more day."

And Rainey and Meadow came by. I gave her a hug goodbye that brought the same smile from the photo to her face.

And Jed recognized it for what it was.

I'm just about to open my mouth to say something else when my phone rings. Pulling it from my pocket, I answer immediately, "Maris..."

"You were blind then, and if you left her, you're a fool now. I don't care about what happened. She's alive. You both have a chance. Now, fix it." Then she hangs up.

Everything inside me still shaking, I make two phone calls. One to confirm the work on the house I bought in Montana is underway. The other to my sister. Her grouchy "What?" makes me wonder if she was sleeping.

"When are you coming home?" I don't want an audience for when I go back. I want to sit Meadow down and explain I'm not going away. We'll figure out the rest, but she needs to know she can rely on me to not leave. Not that I have a great track record.

"Tomorrow. Meadow's giving me a ride back to Portland before she flies to Juneau. Why?" Suddenly Greta's way too awake and suspicious.

But my mind's whirling. If I call Jennings...yes. I'll have hours on the plane to explain. And if it doesn't work out, if she ends up walking away, I can go to Jed's grave and lie down next to him to die. "Because I'll be getting on that plane."

"Are you kidding, Kody?" Greta screeches. "You can't just charm your way back after the things you said to her."

"Well, it's nice to know you're taking sides with the woman I love. That will make her getting to know the family easier," I drawl sarcastically.

"You haven't seen her. I have. Besides, you're a man." As if it explains everything.

Catching sight of Jed's letter out of the corner of my eye, I realize there were so many things I missed. Meadow's feared our love now twice. No more. "Maybe you're right," I admit.

I roll my eyes as Greta begins applauding on the phone. "Now, can I ask for your help?" And before I call Jennings, I tell my sister my plans.

MEADOW

My stomach lurches from the moment we take off in Kalispell. Jasper greets me like we're old friends, asking me to sit on the right side of the plane. I frown because this will mean my back is to the door, but then with Jasper's explanation of "With Ms. Laurence on board, I need to shift the weight, Meadow." I shrug and merely do as asked.

Greta flutters her lashes flirtatiously. "Call me Greta. I've known Jennings for years."

His low laugh in the gorgeous redhead's direction makes me reevaluate my musings a few months ago. Maybe Jasper's closer in age than I originally thought. "Well, that will give me something to think about." For all of five minutes of the hour or so we'd be in the air.

"What will?" Greta drops into the seat facing mine across the aisle.

God, even after all this time, looking at Kody's sister still causes my heart to ache. As much as I've appreciated her assistance, I need to be alone—even if it's only for a few hours—to lick my wounds before I pick up Elise and MJ. "Nothing. Just a wandering thought."

"Are you excited to see your children?"

"Anxious," I admit.

"Why?"

I spend the rest of the flight explaining to Greta about what happened with Mitch, with the kids, how I had to move to Montana, and what's still occurring with my ex. By the time I'm finished, we've just landed, and as we taxi to the hangar, I'm back to the part of the story she knows about—my saying no to her brother's proposal of marriage. "I love Kody, Greta. I'll always love him."

We're so involved in our conversation, both of our heads jerk as we hear footsteps on the stairs. Presuming it's Jasper, I know it's almost time to say goodbye to Greta. I don't want to lose this last connection to Kody, but I know I have to. The door to the plane opens. Instead of getting off the plane as we hear Jasper unloading her bags, Greta sits there and frowns. "I understand so much more now. Hearing all of that, I can see why you said no. Marriage is a huge leap. You weren't saying no to him, but to the institution itself."

"Exactly. Never in a million years did I have any idea that's where his thoughts were headed. He lived all of this with me."

"Your children would be set back so far."

"In the end, I've made some hard choices for the people I love," I say wearily. "And years from now, I guess I'll look back on the health of my children and be proud. And I'll always be devastated because of Kody."

"You sacrificed it all for your children, didn't you? Including him?"

"What is love but a sacrifice? Then again, years ago, I didn't think I was good enough for your brother."

"Why not? He's a royal pain in the ass." Her chin is in her hands.

My eyes widen before I bellow out a laugh. "God, that felt so good. Take away the fact he's your brother for a moment."

"If I must."

"Even when we were in our twenties, he was the nicest guy I'd ever met. He was so damn smart, he made my head spin, and he wasn't a hardship on the eyes. Quite simply, he was so much more than me."

Greta nods before undoing her seat belt. "I have to say, I'm so glad you see the man before the looks."

"To be honest, I had to. I never would have spoken with him."

Greta laughs and then stands. She holds out her arms.

I do the same. "Would it be too much to ask you to pass along a message to your brother?"

She opens her mouth and then closes it. "Before I answer that, why don't you turn around? Then you can decide."

Prickles raise the hair on the back of my neck. I shake my head.

Greta's eyes are sympathetic. "It's okay, Meadow. I promise."

"What are you afraid of, Flower?" Kody's dark voice washes over me. I hear a thud before Jasper's voice confirms, "Welcome aboard, Kody. Let me finish loading your bags, and then we can be on our way." Jasper's footsteps make a thumping sound down the stairs.

My body begins to shake with tremors so hard, I'm about to topple over. Somehow, I manage to turn around and there he is. He's beautiful.

He's perfect.

"You're an asshole," Greta declares, as she shoves past me. Standing next to her brother, she tilts her face up for his kiss. "Make this right. Meadow's one of us."

"I will. Now, get the hell off the plane. Meadow and I are on a schedule."

"You've always been ungrateful," she grumbles.

"No, that's Sandra." They share identical smiles. "Call Mom? Tell her I'll get in touch in a few days?"

"Will do. I suppose you want me to keep the office going?"

"That is what I pay you for." He runs a finger down her nose before bopping the end.

Her lip curls before she throws herself into his arms. I turn my head away. I wish I had the right to do that, but I lost my chance when I said no.

Before I can sink back in my seat, Greta's rushing back at me for a quick hug, but before I can ask her if she knows why Kody is here, she's off the plane. And now Kody's making his way toward me.

"Hi."

Such a simple word from his beautiful lips. He's said it a thousand times. So, I don't know why this time I turn away to hide my face when I respond, "Hello."

"I hope you don't mind sharing your ride to Juneau." His voice holds nothing but polite inquiry.

With a quick shake of my head, I sit back down and redo my seat belt. *Remember, he's not here for you*, I chastise myself.

Quickly enough, Jasper's announcing to prepare ourselves for take-off. I debate, for a second, announcing I can't do this. I can't be confined to this space with this man for hours. I feel the wheels move and realize it's too late.

We're alone—well, as alone as we can be with Jasper flying the plane. I want to scream *Why? Why does he have to be on the plane with me?* but since Jennings is his best friend, I can't. All I can do is try to ignore his presence as we go back to where we started. Risking being caught, I hazard a glance to find Kody staring out the window. His fingers are tapping against his lips in contemplation. I study every inch of his face. It may be my only chance before we land.

I need to memorize what he looks like right now so I never forget when he's back home with my heart.

Jasper announces we've hit our cruising altitude. Kody shifts in his seat, still not saying a word. And sadly, I realize it's over. He won't even speak to me. Shivering, I reach down in my bag for my sweatshirt and shrug it on. As I'm zipping it up, I think I must be hearing something. Just to make certain, I ask politely, "I'm sorry. Did you say something?"

Kody's jaw works for a moment before his head turns. "I asked you the wrong question all those years ago."

I'm jolted. "What do you mean?" I remember every word of our last confrontation clearly.

And based on his words, it appears Kody does as well. "I asked you if this was what you wanted. What I should have asked you was if you felt the same way about me that I felt about you."

"And that was how?" I ask cautiously.

He settles back. "I'm not sure that it matters. What matters is how we feel about each other right now." His words are deep slashes to my already wounded heart.

"Of course."

"After it's all said and done, we each had to live to get right here."

To a place where we can say goodbye. I feel my soul breaking over and over at his words, but I merely nod. One day I'll look back and know I'll be grateful for loving Kody Laurence, but it's taking every-thing inside me not to shatter in front of him—to not beg him to listen to me. But I won't. I clench my fists tightly beneath the sleeves of my sweatshirt. I'll stand back and open my arms to let him go. After all, the only gift of value I've ever been able to give him has been a life without regrets which is what he would have had if he'd taken the terrified girl out of Juneau as he left to build an empire.

And even though I love him—God, I've always loved him—I won't hold him with pain and brokenness.

"Yes, we did," I push out. "You know I want nothing but the best for you, Kody."

"Good. Then you won't be difficult about this."

"Difficult about what—" But before the question is fully out of my mouth, Kody's unhooking my seat belt and hauling me to my feet. His arms are wrapped around me so tightly, I can barely breathe. Then again, I don't care if I never breathe again as I drown in the scent of his cologne.

Tears I've managed to hold back leak from my eyes against his dress shirt. "Let it out, sweetheart," his voice croons in my ear. "I was a damn bastard. You have to know I'm sorry."

"There's no need. You were right. I can't expect to rely—Kody!" I exclaim as he swoops me up and sits down with me on his lap. "Jasper's going to complain about too much weight on one side of the plane or something."

"I. Was. Wrong. I didn't listen, and I took my hurt out on the person I claimed to love. Sometimes, emotions surge inside me so much I can't get the words out, or if I do, the wrong ones come out. Like those summers I wanted to ask you out. The last night when you told me you were married. When..." He swallows hard. "You said no."

"Will you let me explain?" I ask quietly. When he shakes his head firmly, my heart withers inside my chest. "Why not?"

"Because I know you love me. You tried to explain to me that day, and I wouldn't listen—or more appropriately, I listened to what I wanted to hear. I overheard what you said to Greta, sweetheart. Right now, between that and a letter I received from Jed, I'm feeling pretty fucking ashamed of what I said and did to you." Kody's jaw clenches. "I was an adolescent instead of a man. Your man."

"Kody, you were hurting; I understood."

"I promised myself I'd never leave you. And the first time things got hard, I did just what he did, didn't I?" His voice is tortured.

Now it's my turn to struggle with words. "Kody, I get it. Love by itself isn't enough. I was just trying to explain—" I pause and find his encouraging eyes on me. "All I wanted to do that day was to tell you I need time. I have so much to explain to Elise and MJ. Trust me, I never wanted to let you go."

I can feel the sigh he lets out ruffle my hair. "If I go to my grave knowing that, it's enough."

Tears start to build, but the practical side of my nature kicks in. We're not over all our hurdles. "It's going to be difficult with you in Portland. And well, you're you and I'm just me. I don't have a great track record; I don't know how this ends."

"I could give you a hundred reasons why this will work, but the easiest explanation is you complete me. This past week, I felt like the other half of myself was gone." He pulls my hand to his chest where his heart is beating so fast, I can feel the pounding. "Do you think my heart could shut off so easily? I lost you once; I refuse to lose you a second time. If it takes a month, a year, ten years, I'm not giving up on us again. We'll figure out what this family needs and make it happen."

"This family?" I echo.

"Yes." His voice is resolute. "Whether or not we're ever married, Meadow, we're going to be a family. In fact, I have the ring to prove it." Kody reaches into his shirt pocket.

I begin to protest, and then the words die in my throat because I want the ring in his hand more than I want any other piece of jewelry in my life.

It's a perfect circle of woven grass.

"I know who and what you are, Meadow Borneman. You're a strong woman who is fighting her way back to knowing who she is. You're an exceptional mother who will do anything for her children. And you're the woman I'll never be able to let go. Do you know me? Do you love me?"

And without hesitation, I answer, "With my whole heart. Forever."

After sliding the ring on my finger, Kody kisses me. His kisses start out as soft touches mingled with words of apology, but after weeks apart, the passion flares between us. Long minutes later, Kody curses. "Damn, I forgot about Jasper," he grumbles before sliding his hand out from under my shirt. Lifting me off his lap, he places me in the seat next to him. Taking my hand, he brushes my mussed hair off my face before asking, "How did everything go at Nature's Song?"

And for the first time since he left, I smile when I think about the house we rebuilt together. After all, it's not many couples who can say they got down and dirty at both home and at work and survived.

MEADOW

Despite the perfect landing, my nerves jump into my throat the moment we're wheels down in Juneau. I'm uncertain how the kids are going to react to seeing me despite the improvement to our recent calls. Reaching over, I grab Kody's hand and squeeze it hard. "I'm terrified."

He threads his fingers through mine before raising them to his lips. "Why?"

"They're not perfect, but they're mine. This emotional separation between us has been worse than anything I endured from Mitch."

Brushing my knuckles back and forth across his lips, Kody doesn't immediately say anything. When he does, the words both settle me and churn me in a completely different way. "I know you're scared, but it will be all right. It might take time, but love is always worth waiting for. Aren't we proof of that?"

I suck in a breath. Five minutes after seeing him again, eleven weeks in each other's pockets, seventeen years too late, love is a damn miracle.

Just as I open my mouth to tell him for the millionth time since we reconciled, Jasper announces, "Meadow, Kody, welcome back to Juneau. Local time is 12:42 p.m. The tower just let me know local temperature is a balmy fifty-nine degrees, so I hope you brought coats. We'll be pulling up to the hangar shortly."

And just like that, the moment is lost. But as I bring Kody's hand up to brush against the side of my face, I know deep in my soul it won't be the last one. After all, I have a ring on my finger and a promise in my heart to prove otherwise.

After renting a vehicle, we make it to Brad and Rainey's an hour later. I make no move to jump out when Kody shoves the vehicle into park. "What are you thinking?" he asks.

"That a few months ago, I never could have imagined leaving."

"And now?"

"Now it's complicated. It will always be home, but I love where I am now, who I am now," I correct myself.

"Speaking of where you are now, what would you think about..."

But Kody doesn't get to finish the question. The front door bangs open and Rainey comes flying out. I laugh, even as I unbuckle myself. "Brace. She's going to come for you next."

He brushes a finger down my nose. "Go. You know you need this as much as she does."

Truer words were never spoken. I scramble from the seat and fall into my sister's waiting arms. For long moments, I absorb one of the most treasured feelings in the world—the imperfect yet constant love of family.

Pulling back, I grin before saying absurdly, "Hi. Miss me?"

"Not at all. I just greet everyone..."

But before she can continue with our banter, the front door slams open a second time. I face it, expecting to see Brad's blond handsomeness. Instead, there are two faces I've missed long before I left Juneau the first time. Even coming back that one day didn't give me enough time to study them since I had to put on an act to break through the defenses they were holding so close. "Is it my imagination, or has Elise grown too?" is all I can choke out as I fall back against the truck for support.

"In so many ways," I think I hear Rainey say cryptically, but I'm too focused on my children's quiet descent down the same steps my sister flew down like her life depended on it.

Thirty feet. That's how far apart we are. It's no more than the distance of a few cars, but it might as well be the thousands of miles I just flew from Montana. I catch Kody rounding the back of the truck out of the corner of my eye, ready as always to be there for me.

I look forward to the day when I can return the favor.

Tentatively, I raise my hand not squeezing the life out of Rainey's shoulder and call out, "Hi, kids. You both look..."

I don't get a chance to finish my sentence before Elise takes off at a dead run. My heart stops. When it starts beating again, it's such a magnificent pain, but it feels so good because I'm too busy catching my daughter's lanky frame as it crashes against me. "Mom," she sobs against my shoulder. "Mommy, I'm so sorry. Please forgive me."

"Shh." I stop her before she goes too much further. "There's nothing to forgive, baby. You were scared and hurting."

Within seconds, we're almost taken to the ground by MJ as he collides into us both. His arms stretch as far as they can to wrap around us both. "Mom, are you here to take us home?" His voice cracks on the last word.

My eyes fly up and connect with Kody's. Without words, I know what he's thinking because he said it just a few hours ago before sliding my ring on my finger. *"I know who and what you are, Meadow Borneman. You're a strong woman who is fighting her way back to knowing who she is. You're an exceptional mother who will do anything for her children. And you're the woman I'll never be able to let go. Do you know me?"*

As he slowly makes his way toward us, I nod through my tears. I know exactly who Kody Laurence is.

He's not perfect; he's just a man. And like all men, he'll make mistakes.

But what he is, is mine.

And he wants to be ours.

God, I'm so grateful he didn't give up on loving me. Then and now.

Lifting my arm from MJ's shoulder, I hold my hand out to him. Kody squeezes it as he passes by, instinctively understanding he's a part of this moment even though on the plane we both agreed to take this slowly for the kids' sake. Because no matter where we return to, we've finally figured out where our hearts are meant to land. Right next to each other. But our movements are still noticed by the curious eyes.

"Mom, what's Kody doing here?" Elise asks curiously.

Brushing her hair back, I whisper words that are no less than the truth. "He's here to be with us. Is that okay?"

"I guess," MJ mumbles.

Elise doesn't say a word. Instead, she burrows closer.

My eyes meeting Kody's over both of them begin to fill. Yeah, we're going to figure it out. Together.

"COME ON, MJ. You know I love hot dogs," Elise complains.

"But you've already had two," her brother points out logically.

Rainey rolls her eyes before holding up an uncooked pack. I step in by placing a hand on each of their shoulders. "Why don't you see if Uncle Brad or Kody wants a dog while Aunt Rainey and I cook some more up? Then you both can have some?"

"Great idea, Mom. I'll go ask them now." MJ races for the back door.

Elise lingers behind for just a moment. She opens and closes her mouth before shrugging.

I loop an arm around her shoulders. "Nuh-uh. Something's on your mind, Lise. Come on into the kitchen and talk with Aunt Rainey and me about it." I deliberately suggest a spot where she'll feel comfortable, but she shakes her head.

"Actually, Mom, could we go into the front yard? I really want to talk to just you. Alone."

My stomach is churning up the few chips and dips I've managed to choke down. "Of course, sweetheart. Now?"

"Please. I'm afraid I'll chicken out if I don't."

We head out the front door, and I can see the shadow of the mountains in the distance. I let Elise precede me, deliberately closing the door behind me. She walks over to the center of the grass, plops down, and kicks off her shoes.

I smother the smile that wants to come out. It's amazing how many mannerisms my children have picked up from me. Doing the same, I bump her shoulder. "Okay, Lise. Fire away. What is it?"

Much to my shock, Elise bursts out crying. Quickly, I scramble to my knees. "Baby, no. Tell me. What's wrong?"

"Mommy, I'm sorry. I'm so sorry. I..." Her voice cracks.

"Shh. Whatever it is, we can fix it."

But her next words freeze my body. "I can't fix you and Dad. And it's my fault."

Pulling back slightly, I ask carefully, "What do you mean, Lise?"

"I knew you were lying about why you and Dad split up. I...I saw him with a woman one day. While you were still married. Daddy knew. He said it was something you both accepted."

"So, that's what you meant all those times when you said that Daddy said I was keeping secrets," I surmise aloud, all the while thinking about if I'd look good in prison orange.

She nods. "I told Aunt Alice. She said that likely wasn't true, but I should talk with you about it. After seeing you that day, finding out the real reason behind why you and Daddy divorced, and how happy you look now, I couldn't let it fester anymore."

I cup her cheek. "Honey, if I'm happy today, it's because I finally have my children back. I knew you were hurting. I would take any pain and bear it if that's what you needed."

Eyes swimming with tears, she replies, "I know. A long time ago, you told me to find someone who reminded me of my father."

I wince. "I remember."

"You know what I learned from all of this?"

"What?" I brush her hair back from her face.

"You told me to find someone strong, someone who would fight for me, Mom. I realized I shouldn't be looking for someone like my dad. I should be looking for someone just like you."

After hearing that, I can't bear even the slightest space between us. I yank Elise hard against my heart and sit there rocking her. I whisper words of love over her head. And as she relaxes against me, I sink down to the warm earth, holding her weight.

That's when I feel him.

My head turns slightly to the left. He's far enough away that he hasn't overheard what's been said, but he's been there with me. For me. Loving me.

I mouth, "I love you, Kody."

It's not the first time I've thought it here in Juneau, but it's the first time I've said it. And when he does the same before disappearing around the corner back to the impromptu party, I know my heart's come home.

And I'm glad I can take all of these feelings back with me to Montana.

I think we'll make a good life there, me, Elise, and MJ. Kody hasn't told me yet what his plans are. But as I catch a glimpse of my grass-green ring out of the corner of my eye, I know he will.

It just might take a little time.

EPILOGUE

Kody

It was a lot easier to blend our lives than Meadow originally feared.

The summer after her kids moved to Bigfork, I put a ton of miles on my truck driving back and forth between Portland and Meadow's home. Greta bitched about my taking summer Fridays. "It's a perk of owning the company, sister. Get your grubstake together, buy in, and maybe you can complain more," I challenged her.

In the meanwhile, every weekend I stayed at the lodge while Elise and MJ included me in their exploration of their new home. Meadow and I took them to Polebridge for face-size bear claws. We took Meadow's RAV4 up the Road to the Sun. When MJ complained we weren't riding in my truck, I explained, "I don't have a death wish, kid. I'd like to get all of the passengers home," much to everyone's amusement.

We went to nearby Whitefish and rode the ski lift up the mountain and let the kids take the ride down. And as much as I loved kissing and touching her, building this family foundation with my Meadow became everything to me. My need for her was just building.

Every night I left to head back to the lodge until one day in early August, MJ just asked, "Mom? Why doesn't Kody sleep over?"

Meadow spat her wine across my shirt. I rolled my eyes and said, "Pray I don't get pulled over, Flower," as I mopped it up.

Then Elise piped in. "I agree with MJ. I mean, the guy drives eight hours a week to spend time with us. He's not some catfish or just trying to get into your..."

"Elise!" we'd both yelled. Then we looked at each other and started laughing.

I swallowed the end of my mirth when Meadow leaned over as if she was going to kiss me before telling her children. I held my breath, not certain what she was doing. "Both of you should know, I love Kody."

Their reaction was not what I expected. They both started laughing.

"Are you planning on hiding this year's Christmas presents as well as you hid this?" MJ snorted.

"Yeah, hate to break it to you, Mom, but that's kind of obvi. We really like you too, Kody," Elise was quick to reassure me.

Meadow's mouth touched mine briefly. "How about next weekend, we give it a try?"

And we did. For the next few months, we spent every weekend together. And when Thanksgiving approached and as my house was ready for me to move in, no one was particularly shocked by the question—except Meadow.

"Wait. You're willing to move here from Portland? Permanently?"

I hooked an arm around her waist and pulled her close. "This is where we belong. Together. What did you think I was building the house for?"

She opened and closed her mouth, imitating the fish I imagined MJ and I would have fun catching come spring. "Weekends? Summer?"

"Weak, Flower. I bought that house before we finished Nature's Song and, no. That wasn't the original intent." Before she can speak, I finish softly, "It's a family house—our family's house. The last thing we have to do is let the kids fight out what room they want." Just as I finished that sentence, the front door blew open and in came Elise and MJ.

"Oops." Elise grinned.

"Ugh, gross. They're kissing," MJ complained.

"Not yet. I was trying to convince your mother of something."

Elise unwound her scarf from her neck before hanging it up on the peg next to my coat. MJ just tossed his right on top, without a care in the world. And both actions made my head spin. It wasn't until that moment, I realized what family meant until I caught those little mannerisms that meant the kids accepted me into their mother's life.

But this? This was huge. My body frame locked beneath Meadow's hands. "Kody?" she questioned.

"It's not just you, it's them. I want them every day."

Her hand came up to touch my cheek. "Then ask them," she said simply.

After I found my voice, I choked out my request, adding, "If here is where you're happiest, then that's okay. There's no rush. It's just I love all of you and..."

Before I could finish the sentence, I had three Bornemans in my arms. I clutched them tight, cherishing this gift.

That night, we grabbed dinner out so Elise and MJ could argue over who was getting the bigger bedroom at the new house.

When we moved in two weeks later, we christened the house Treehouse Ridge. It meant come spring, I had some work to do, a promise to keep.

"Good job," I praise MJ as he hammers the nail into the bench seat we're adding to the tree house we completed over the summer.

"Thanks, Kody. I thought my friends would totally razz on me about the curtains Mom hung, but telling them it was to cut down on the glare for when we were gaming helped."

I chuckle. "Mind if I teach you an important life lesson, MJ?"

He puts the finishing nail gun aside. "Nope."

I think back to all the years Meadow and I were friends, the years we spent apart where I felt incomplete, and our tumultuous reunion. "There are times when it's worth it to plant your feet and take a stand about what's right with a woman who means everything to you. In the grand scheme of things, do the curtains bother you?"

"No."

"Do they make your mom happy?"

"Oh yeah," he agrees with feeling.

"Then it's not worth fighting over. Pick your battles, kid."

MJ nods sagely. "I'm glad we're out here working on this, Kody. There's way too much crazy happening in the house."

I laugh because he's not wrong. "Why do you think my dad suddenly determined we needed a lemon cake with huckleberry sauce for dessert tonight? We grew up with seven women in the house. Add in your Mom and Elise and even I'm terrified."

He bumps my hip before he leans over to fill the nail holes with wood putty. Unfortunately, it dislodges the velvet box that I've been hiding on my pocket. "What's that?" MJ nods to the floor.

I panic. Do I tell him? I've already spoken with Meadow's father, Rainey, and the guys. But as my hand closes over the small box, a rush of emotions hits me square in the chest, almost knocking me to the ground.

I don't want to tell him; I want to ask him. After all, we're going to be a family if everyone says yes, right?

Clapping my hand on his shoulder, I say, "Why don't we take a break up in the tree house for a bit? The putty has to dry anyway."

He agrees, and we make our way out of the workshop and across the expansive yard. Across the water, Nature's Song is standing strong and beautiful. Her heart and soul were repaired with hard work and not a few battles.

Then again, anything loving is worth keeping; it's worth years of devotion. I can't wait to spend mine with Meadow, Elise, and the boy waiting patiently for me.

But I frown when I get to the foot of the tree where I built a gated staircase only to find it open. Listening closely, I hear Meadow and Elise.

And Elise is crying.

I break into a run up those turning stairs, pausing only for MJ to catch up. A minute later, we burst through the door to find the two most important women in the world holding each other.

"Elise, what's wrong, honey?" I crouch down next to her. Forgetting about the box in my one hand, I place the other around the back of her neck since her hair is in a crazy mess of rollers that have spikes.

Meadow shoots me a warning glare, but Elise announces, "It's Dad. He just called and"—she air quotes—"'has to work tonight. I understand, don't I?' No, Kody. I don't. I really don't understand. This is my first homecoming in a new town. I have a date. What father wouldn't want to check out my date?" Her voice holds a wealth of hurt and understanding about her father she shouldn't for a freshman in high school.

It wasn't what I planned. My entire family is sitting in the house—Mom, all my sisters, their spouses or significant others. Dad will be returning with a cake soon. Even Sandra flew out from Perdue for the weekend. I was going to wait until it was just the four of us, but I can't stop the words.

"Marry me. All of you. Please."

Elise goes into shock, even with the tears still coursing down her face. MJ shouts, "That's what's in the box! It's a ring!"

And then, I turn my head and there she is—my Meadow.

And I ask again, "Will you marry me, Meadow? Will you share your family with me?"

Elise slowly sits back, letting her mother loose. She holds out her hand for her brother, not saying a word as Meadow stands.

Her words are better than a simple "yes." Instead, as she grabs my hand, she replies simply, "I thought I already had?" Then she smiles at me, and it's the same smile that first grabbed my attention almost twenty years ago. It whispers of hope and dreams.

I was right all along. Meadow was meant to be mine.

"When they lay me down in the ground, this will be the image I remember. You, us, here. Together. Family." My voice is strong as I pry open the box with one hand. I pluck out the ring of faceted emeralds that are woven together in a braid. On top sits the petals of a forget-me-not made from Montana sapphires.

"Oh, Kody." Meadow's hands fly to her mouth.

"Mom, it looks so much like the rings Kody made for you when we'd be lying around the yard over the summer," Elise breathes from behind us.

"It's too much," Meadow's sobbing.

"It's made to last, just like we are, Flower." I get to my feet, pulling her into my arms. After a few moments, I turn slightly and open an arm to her kids, my family. "Just like we are."

Elise and MJ rush at us both.

It's so reminiscent of that day in Juneau where they both hurled themselves at their mother. We worked together to get to a place where Elise and MJ understood whatever life might throw at them, there was one constant.

Love.

And they would always have ours regardless of other people's actions, even their father's.

Long moments later, Meadow lifts her head from my chest. Rising up to her toes, she places her lips against mine. "Meadow Borneman-Laurence. How does that sound?"

"Perfect. Real. Like I might be dreaming."

Her smile blooms, but before the kiss can deepen, Elise shrieks, "Oh, my God. I can't wait to tell Jen tonight," her earlier distress over her father forgotten. "I have to hurry!"

MJ lets out a beleaguered sigh he's perfected. I love hearing it since it reminds me of Brad, who picked it up from Jed. And having even a small part of Jed here right now means everything. "I think I'll see if Grandpa Toby is back with the cake. A man puts in a hard day's work, he needs something to eat," he says in perfect imitation of my father.

Meadow bursts out laughing as MJ takes off running.

When we're alone, Meadow wraps her arms around me and tips her head back. "Thank you."

"For what?"

"For taking a risk on me. For rebuilding someone's dream. You showed me, us, so many definitions of love, Kody."

My head lowers until our lips exchange a kiss that promises everything I yearned for in the shadow of one glacier long ago.

Even though our family landed near a different one. After all, we have plenty of reasons to return to Juneau—especially now that Nick's decided to get his head out of his ass.

Finally.

THE END

ALSO BY TRACEY JERALD

AMARYLLIS SERIES

FREE TO DREAM

FREE TO RUN

FREE TO REJOICE

FREE TO BREATHE

FREE TO BELIEVE

FREE TO LIVE

FREE TO DANCE (COMING SPRING 2021)

GLACIER ADVENTURE SERIES

RETURN BY AIR

RETURN BY LAND

RETURN BY SEA (COMING JANUARY 11, 2021)

STANDALONES

CLOSE MATCH

RIPPLE EFFECT

LADY BOSS PRESS RELEASES

EASY REUNION

CHALLENGED BY YOU

1,001 DARK NIGHT SHORT STORY CHALLENGE

COMING DECEMBER 2020

ACKNOWLEDGMENTS

Since this is my thirteenth book coming out on my thirteenth wedding anniversary, I want to take a moment to wish my beloved Nathan Happy Anniversary. Much like Meadow and Kody, our connection started by a lake with a conversation between two people who recognized an undeniable spark. Also, like them, we had a challenging road to travel. But know I love you more today than the day I said, "I do." And I'll love you forever.

To my Jen, the sister of my heart. I promised you I'd bring you home a lumberjack. Sorry I couldn't sneak one on board. While Kody's not flesh and blood, I did my best. I hope you approve of my choice.

Mom, thank you for giving me the gift of imagination and feeding it over the years. I love you.

To my beloved son, you are the heart and soul of me. I'd do anything, fight anyone, to bring a smile to your face.

My Meows, without all of you, life would be ridiculously mundane. Just imagine the mischief we will get ourselves into when we're able to do more than Zoom!

To Sandra Depukat, from One Love Editing, thank you for pushing me harder. You know I appreciate it even if I don't always remember to say it!

To Holly Malgieri, from Holly's Red Hot Reviews, a.k.a. my twin. You add the final polish to everything! I love you.

To Deborah Bradseth, Tugboat Designs. All I can say is WOW! The cover for Land just BLEW ME AWAY! XOXO

To photographer Wander Aguiar, Andrey Bahia, and model John Dewall, thank you for sharing your talent, your time, and for being so generous and kind.

To Gel, at Tempting Illustrations, your ability to pluck images from my mind astounds me. XOXO

To the fantastic team at Foreword PR, GROUP HUG! My ongoing thanks to every one of you for your time, your dedication, and your heart.

Linda Russell, in a world where there seems to be a cost for everything, nothing can't put a price on what you mean to me. Love, loyalty, and friendship are invaluable. XOXO

To Susan Henn, Amy Rhodes, and Dawn Hurst, the dream team! You all are unique, strong women who go above and beyond every day. Thank you for being who you are to me!

For the members of Tracey's Tribe, my Facebook home away from home, I'm sending each of you your own hugs!

And for all of the readers and bloggers who take the time to enjoy my books, thank you. Every day, I find myself humbled by your support.

ABOUT THE AUTHOR

Tracey Jerald knew she was meant to be a writer when she would re-write the ending of books in her head when she was a young girl growing up in southern Connecticut. It wasn't long before she was typing alternate endings and extended epilogues "just for fun".

After college in Florida, where she obtained a degree in Criminal Justice, Tracey traded the world of law and order for IT. Her work for a world-wide internet startup transferred her to Northern Virginia where she met her husband in what many call their own happily ever after. They have one son.

When she's not busy with her family or writing, Tracey can be found in her home in north Florida drinking coffee, reading, training for a runDisney event, or feeding her addiction to HGTV.

Made in the USA
Columbia, SC
24 November 2020